Reaper's Redemption

Simone Elise

Inkitt

Copyright © 2017 by **Simone Elise.**

All rights reserved. This book or any portion thereof may not be reproduced or used in any manner whatsoever without the express written permission of the publisher except for the use of brief quotations in a book review.

All characters appearing in this work are fictitious. Any resemblance to real persons, living or dead, is purely coincidental.

This book is published by Inkitt. Join now to read and discover free upcoming bestsellers!

Chapter 1

Reaper

It was as if the planet stopped moving. It was as if everything that kept me sane and glued to this earth was gone. Every time I closed my eyes, images of what could be happening to Abby filled me. It was all my fault. I had put her in danger. I had left a loose end. And now? Now I was following the only lead I had. And I wasn't going to take no for an answer.

"I know you, Reaper. I was at your wedding." Jones sucked on a cigar, looking across at me as if he knew me. As if he knew what I was capable of. As if he understood the anger boiling inside me. "I understand what you're after. But I can't give it to you."

"I'm not asking." Had I not made my point clear? I wanted answers. I get the fucking answers. It's not *if* you want to answer me. There was no choice. I'd take what I wanted and right now, I was ready to break bones to get those answers.

"Where does the brotherhood stand on this?"

Where did he think the brotherhood stood? They stood behind me. They didn't dare not.

I looked around the room.

Five men. Wasn't many to take. Brad could take at least two. I could knock the other three out. What did I have on me? Two guns, a knife and two fists. That would be all I needed to get the job done.

"Reaper, where does the brotherhood stand on this?" Jones repeated himself. "Or is this a suicide mission?"

"It's Jed Harrison's daughter." I reached into my vest and pulled my gun from my left holster. "And my wife. So you either answer, or I'll make you answer."

"Threatening another brotherhood. Is that wise, Reaper?" His voice had an edge to it. Some would take that as a warning. Some might back down. But I wasn't just anyone. My nerves were raw. My anger was uncontrollable and right now, the only lead depended on Jones and his muppets of members.

They knew where the drug houses were. They knew where Jake operated. He trafficked ice. I knew that much. But I didn't know how or where. Jones' black brotherhood did the hardcore drugs. Roach had little to do with it because he believed the drug ruined more lives than anything else and only bottom feeders would make a living from it.

He was right about one thing. Jones' crew were bottom feeders. Feeding off the junkies by running protection for Jake.

The tension in the room was thick. Brad, standing behind me, already had his gun pulled. So did Jones' members. They were just waiting for my next move. This move could decide if I found Abby or not. I had to think smart. Even though my mind was racing. Even though I could barely function.

"The decision is yours, Jones. You either go to war against us, or you feed us intel. Either way, you are making an enemy today." This was me keeping calm. We had been at peace with the black brotherhood for years. Was I ready to risk that friendship and bring on bloodshed just for information? Fuck yes.

I wasn't called the Reaper because I was afraid of blood. I saw it as simply as this: it was blood in or blood out. You either stood with Satan's Sons, in it with your blood, willing to put your life on the line, or you didn't.

He kept a steady face, calculating. Risk money or risk lives.

Fuck this. I was over waiting.

I pulled out my gun, clicking the safety off.

"Well, how could we go to war against our brothers? Jake earns us money. But you are family." Jones' crooked grin was met with my gun to his forehead. Like I said, my patience was up. "Now, now, brother. No need for guns. You lower the gun and I'll start talking."

I liked the feeling of having my gun pressed to his forehead. Right in the middle, between his eyes. It was with regret I pulled back, leaving a circular imprint.

"Details." I put my gun back in its holster.

"He runs them up the coast. But all the drugs come through here. We run protection from here to there. But he has houses. He also has a sideline job, you could say."

"That being?"

"I don't think you wanna hear it."

"Do I have to pull my gun again?" I was on edge, ready to bounce.

Jones' eyes flicked to my vest. At my threat, their guns went back up. Brad reacted. But he was shifting his gun from man to man, trying to determine which one would fire first.

"He traffics women." Jones licked his lips. "Younger ones, but he has a connection with the overseas market. It's his side business. Not where he makes the most of his money."

That gut-pulling, heart-wrenching, blood-boiling feeling was suffocating me. But I pushed the possibility to the back of my mind. Jake was smart. He would keep Abby close. He wouldn't be shipping her off.

No, he wanted to torture me and it was going to be slow and painful.

But I would make sure I was the one having the last laugh. I'd be the one putting him in the ground for doing this to my family.

"Next protection run you do, we are joining. I want a list of the houses he is set up in." I reached into my leather vest and pulled out a cigarette, needing one now more than I had ever needed one. My stress levels were high.

I hadn't slept in days. But that was nothing to the pain I felt every day knowing Abby was out there, alone, kidnapped. A disgusting feeling washed through me at the thought of what they could be doing to her, how they would be treating her. She had to know I'd come for her. She had to know that every bone, blood vessel and beat of my heart would drive me to find her.

That I'd never give up.

"What you going to do? Bust down every door?" Jones sniggered. His men joined in.

I looked him dead in the eye, inhaling on my cigarette and exhaling slowly. "That'a fucking promise."

I'd knock down door after door till I found Abby.

***

My Harley roared as I pulled up to the clubhouse. To say we were full was an understatement. Roach had called in all the charters. The town was crawling with bikers. It had gotten to the point that every bed was full, so hotels and motels were now full up with bikers as well. Roach had to pay more because of the risk of possible damage.

Bikers were known for leaving a trail of destruction.

There was barely any room on the lot that wasn't taken up with bikes or vans. However, being a president meant you got a spot. Brad wasn't as lucky and parked out on the road.

I was taking my helmet off when I heard a familiar voice.

"I'm telling you NOW. You come near him again, I'll chop your hand off!" Kim screamed at Drunk Duke, waving a knife at him.

Kicking my kickstand out, I lowered my bike and walked over. Seeing as Kim was meant to be looking after Tyson today, I wanted to know where my son was.

"I just wanted to give him a hug." Drunk Duke was slurring and it was only mid-morning. There was a reason why we called him Drunk Duke. He was never sober. He had been a president for years. His charter was small. Only did petty crimes. When I said Roach had pulled every charter, I wasn't joking. Even a useless one like Drunk Duke's.

"WITH A CIGARETTE! How many times do I have to say it? NO SMOKING AROUND TYSON! You could've burnt him!"

Rounding the corner, I got an answer to my question as to where my son was. He was safe in the stroller next to the table used for food prep. Looked like Kim was chopping up meat for the BBQ.

Her eyes flickered over Duke's shoulder and she spotted me.

"Thank fuck Reaper's back." She said the words and automatically, Duke scooted inside. Didn't know the old man could walk that fast.

"Kim."

"Do you know this whole place is a hazard? Smoking alcoholics everywhere." Kim waved her knife. "I swear every biker has made it their mission to be near Tyson."

"Put down the knife, Kim."

"Oh." She frowned at it, as if she had completely forgotten she was holding it, and then put it down. All while she had one hand on the stroller, rocking it.

"Tyson been OK apart from being attacked by alcoholics?"

She peeked into the stroller. "Yep, slept all day. How was he last night?"

I ran a hand through my hair. I think my lack of sleep was showing. "Awake."

Kim frowned. "Do you want me to take tonight?"

"Nope. My responsibility, Kim." I lowered myself to my knees. Sure enough, he was asleep, his two little arms in the air.

"Abby wouldn't expect this of you."

Just her name was enough to send a sucker punch to my guts. I had made a promise to her that I would be a hands-on dad. And I wasn't about to wipe my hands of that responsibility because I needed sleep. I could keep going on a few hours a night. That was all I needed, physically.

"We have talked about this, Kim. I'm not expecting you to take him on full time."

"Yeah, but," Kim bit her lip and looked at the clubhouse as if double-checking we were alone, "I've been hearing talk."

"What about? Tyson?"

"No, you." She lifted her chin up, ready to defend what she was going to say. "You're taking over from Dad."

I had dreaded having this conversation with Abby, which was why I had put it off. Now I was going to have to step into her father's shoes, without her opinion or approval. I ran a hand through my hair and straightened up. Kim was giving me a look I had seen on her sister's face. Judgment. Abby might not be here to give her opinion or approval, but her twin was. And by the looks of it, she was about to give me a serve.

"Taking over the mother charter, Reaper, when Abby is missing? . Should you really be taking on MORE responsibility?"

"This was planned before Abby went missing. And your father is pushing for it more now because of her being missing."

"It's a lot of pressure, Reaper."

"Are you forgetting, Kim? I'm already a president."

"Of a small charter. This is the mother charter. You will be in charge of the other presidents. Of their members. Not to mention this is the biggest charter in the country. That is a hell of a lot more pressure. AND you are going to be under the police's microscope."

I knew all this. I knew what would happen when I took over from Roach. Overseeing the presidents was just one of the many jobs I'd be taking over. Looking after the mother charter was like putting a target on my back for the police to chase. Taking over from Roach wasn't a simple decision. Every president would vote. Then it would be determined if I was up to the task.

"I know what's involved."

She shook her head, her blonde hair whipping from side to side. "I don't think you do. Because if you did, you wouldn't be letting Dad shove this down your throat."

"I can do this." I was saying it to her but also to myself. I could be the president of the mother charter. I could take care of my son. And I could spend every hour I wasn't asleep looking for Abby. I could do it.

She sighed. "Speaking from experience, I can tell you now. You will be looked on as a father. And the shit doesn't stop."

The one question that was rumbling around inside me surfaced again. And I couldn't stop the words from coming out of my mouth. "What do you think Abby would think?" Kim was her twin. She would have some insight.

Kim chewed her bottom lip, frowning. Then her blue eyes locked with mine with confidence. "She would have given you a similar lecture. But she would want you to do it if it is something you want. She wouldn't stop you."

Was it something I wanted? It was more expected of me. I was Roach's son-in-law. He wanted to hand the club to family. Then, if Roach had his way, I'd hand the club over to Tyson.

Roach was big on family. But you would have to be to be the leader of the brotherhood.

"You should go inside, update Dad with whatever you have been doing. I've got to get this meat on and feed the overbearing men." Kim's attention was back on the food. "Knowing them, they will turn tonight into another party."

"I'll take Tyson."

Just as I went to pick him up, she slapped my hand away. "They are all smoking cigars, playing poker. He isn't going in there."

"You have to cook."

"The girls will help me. You go. Maybe go get some sleep." She gave me a pointed look. "Because, knowing Tyson, you won't be getting any tonight."

She was right. I wouldn't be getting sleep tonight. And it wasn't just because Tyson was giving me broken sleep. It was because my wife wasn't with me. It was because every minute I had my eyes closed, I was tortured with what could be happening to her.

"I should update Roach. I'll be back for him." I pointed at Tyson.

Kim waved her hand. "Don't rush."

I left her cutting up steaks and went inside. She wasn't joking when she said they had been smoking. The air was thick with smoke. They had pulled tables together and created one big one in the middle of the rec room.

Roach stood up as soon as I entered.

"How the fuck did it go?" he barked across the room.

"How did it go for you?" I fired back at him. Seeing as his merry men were all gambling and drinking, I doubted they had done much else today.

"Dead ends all morning." Roach walked around the table and headed for me. "Any luck tracking down Jones?"

"Tracked him down. Threatened him. And he sided with the brotherhood. We are running with them on their protection runs. He is going to feed us their addresses as well."

Roach grinned for the first time in a week. "Finally getting somewhere." Relief flooded his face.

He was right. It was our first real lead. Our first chance of getting Abby back, of finding her. Today marked a week since she was taken. A whole fucking week.

"Now we are getting somewhere with that, it's time us boys sat down." Roach looked me in the eye and I knew exactly what he was talking about.

The vote.

I looked over his shoulder at the many presidents watching us, smoking cigars and drinking. All these men had to support me. Sure, I had a reputation, but it wasn't a good one. I was known for cleaning up the dirt, not for leading men.

"It's got to be done, son." Roach pulled me back. I looked him in the eye.

"Why now? Can't we wait till we find Abby?"

"'Cause I need it to be now." Roach was pushing for this. "I know the timing isn't right but at the same time, it's fucking perfect. You need these men following you." Roach's hand fell on my shoulder, gripping it. "They've followed me for too long."

"You're good at what you do, Roach."

"And now it's time for the mother charter to have a new president. Too darn old to be taking on their problems. I trust you with this club like I'm trusting you to find my daughter." Roach turned and clapped his hands. "PRESIDENTS TO THE BOARDROOM," his voice boomed through the room.

Chairs dragged across the floor and the presidents started to get up.

Whether I became the next mother charter president was about to be determined.

Did I have it in me or not? Would my reputation hold me back? Fuck. My past had haunted me this long. If there was one thing I was good at, it was being the Reaper. I could threaten. I could kill. If someone had to label me, a killer would be the first thing off the tongue. I doubted leader would be one of my named qualities.

***

I watched Roach cut it off with his knife. How long had it been on there? Abby was in her twenties. And it had been on there that long, maybe longer. All eyes in the room were on me as Roach handed me back my leather vest.

Now freshly sewed under my president patch was a patch saying 'Mother Charter'. President of the mother charter.

The votes had been all in my favor. Not one president objected to it or even voiced concerns. Roach had made a speech about how I was the future of this brotherhood. And now, well, now I was staring at the old, but now new, patch on my vest.

"Well, put it on, boy!" Roach whacked me on the back, jolting me forward.

There were cheers as I slipped the vest on. Roach handed me the hammer.

"I think the new president should call this meeting to a close."

My hand gripped the old hammer. And then brought it down, bringing my first ever president meeting to a close.

The men cheered. "Time for a party."

Any excuse for a drink, a smoke and food.

I watched them exit and felt myself being held back. I noticed I wasn't the only one not ready to party. Roach was picking up his leather vest from the table. The black leather shone where the mother charter patch used to be.

"Don't worry, son. You aren't the only one not wanting to party." Roach mightn't have been showing it, but he was aching for Abby as much as I was. Though I doubted that was possible.

"I just need to know she is still breathing," I spoke for the first time about my growing concern over whether Abby was alive or not. While I thought Jake wouldn't kill her, not yet anyway, I knew he would be planning on it ending that way. He wasn't planning on me finding her.

"She is. Otherwise they would have dumped her body at the gate. He is going to torture us with it. The main thing is, Reaper, we find her before he even starts to think about how it is going to end."

Roach was right. We would find Abby before Jake thought about killing her.

I had to hold onto that. She was still alive. Somewhere. And I had a band of men behind me now who would be following my every command.

I would find her.

***

Tyson wasn't sleeping but, for the first time in hours, he wasn't crying. He was fed and changed. I was holding him while pacing the room. The first thing I had done when I got back here was change rooms.

Being in Abby's room without her felt wrong.

So I moved into my old room. I still hadn't set everything up or put anything away. I didn't have cupboards for shit. All I had was a couch, a bed, and a crib and a whole lot of baby shit, which was everywhere.

I laid Tyson down in his crib. He had closed his eyes. I would be lucky if he stayed this way. I pushed the baby crap to the other side of the bed. I lay down. I should sleep.

But I couldn't.

I pulled my phone out from my and dialed a number I had found myself calling more and more.

It rang and, like always, there was no answer and it went to the machine.

"Hey, it's Abby. Leave a message."

Just hearing her voice soothed my fired nerves. But that was short-lived.

Tyson started crying again.

I dragged myself up off the bed and went to his crib. What would Abby do? He was fed. He was changed. I picked him up and started pacing the room.

He was comfortable in my arms and stopped wailing.

Looked like he just wanted to be held. I was admiring how small he was when there was a knock on my door.

"Come in."

It was the early hours of the morning. No member should be wanting me right now.

Kim poked her head in. "Hey." She slipped in, closing the door behind her. "Thought I could take over for a bit."

"Kim, we have already had this conversation."

"Kade." She crossed her arms, giving me a look that I couldn't argue with. "I made a promise to Abby and this is me keeping it. So you get some sleep and I'll look after Tyson." She put her hands out. "Now."

I looked at my son, then back at her. This would be his first night away from me. I didn't like the idea of him sleeping somewhere else.

Kim, as if knowing I didn't want to spend a night away from Tyson, walked over to the couch and, with one swipe of her arm, cleared off one side.

"Come on, give him to me." Kim put her hands out while sitting down.

I walked over to her and gently handed him to her.

He looked bigger in her arms.

"Now go to bed." She waved me away. "Don't worry. We aren't leaving."

I still didn't feel comfortable with this.

She looked up at me hovering. "Don't make me call you by your first name again." She arched her eyebrows.

I put my hands up and walked to the bed.

Lying down on the bed fully clothed, I closed my eyes and waited for sleep to come while Kim hummed in the background.

***

While I might have gotten some sleep, that didn't stop the nightmares. They were all about Abby. It was as if my brain wouldn't shut off and all my worries and concerns were just highlighted in my dreams.

Tyson was asleep in his crib and Kim was curled up on the couch, her head resting on the clothes and baby blankets.

I pulled the blanket off the bed and covered her with it. She stirred, but didn't wake. I didn't know how long she had been up with him.

I walked to the dresser, taking off my vest and putting on my holster. I took the guns and checked that they were loaded before putting them in the holster.

"You should shower."

I turned and saw Kim stretching and yawning.

"Don't have time."

"It's only early."

"I have to organize a group for the run tonight with Jones. And he has already sent me a list of houses to search."

"Do you think Abby is at one of these cookhouses?"

"Don't know. But someone will know where Jake is, or at least someone they report to will." I put my boots on. "Can you look after Tyson today?"

She gave me a look. "Like I would say no to looking after my nephew. Anyway, it's his weekly checkup."

"Fuck. Is that today?"

"Yeah, I thought you would forget." She looked at me smugly. "Abby made the appointment before she was discharged. So I think it's best we keep it."

"I'll come. What time is it?"

"You won't have time."

"I'll make time."

"It's at eleven-thirty." Her eyes dropped to the ground and I knew something was wrong, having seen that look on Abby.

"What's wrong?" I didn't have time to play guessing games or to ask nicely. I had men waiting for me. I had drug houses to search. I had a protection run to invade.

"It's just..." She looked up and for the first time, I saw tears in Kim's eyes. She hadn't cried in front of me before. And I wasn't the right person for her to get emotional in front of.

"What?" I said it softer, trying to be patient.

"Abby was supposed to be getting her checkup today as well. What if she's in pain? What if she needs to see a doctor? What if they're not looking after her?"

Abby's welfare was one of our top concerns. It wouldn't be one of theirs. They wouldn't care if she was in pain from childbirth. They wouldn't be making sure she had pain relief.

Had I had the same concerns as Kim? Every day since she was taken.

"Kim, there is nothing we can do." The only thing I could do was start smashing down doors to drug houses to get someone to cough up where Jake was. I kneeled in front of her, putting a hand on her knee as she wiped away tears with her sleeve. "I'll find Abby."

If there was one thing I was sure of, that was it.

"I know you will. But what if it's not in time? She needs us now." The panic in Kim's voice got stronger. "Tyson needs her now." Kim pointed at him. "I need her."

Did Abby realize how much she was needed? It wasn't just my world slowly crumbling apart. So was Kim's. She had never been away from her twin. And right now she was feeling it.

"Kim, Abby would need you to be strong right now. I need you to be strong right now." Had I been depending on Kim? Yes.

She nodded her head. "You're right. I'll pull myself together." She took a steady breath in. "You should go. Dad came in here looking for you earlier, but said it could wait."

"You'll be OK? Do you want me to get Trigger or something?" I scratched the back of my neck. She needed support. I couldn't give it to her. But Trigger could.

She laughed while wiping away her remaining tears. "No. That's the last thing I want. Like I said, I'll be fine."

"Right. I'll see you at eleven-thirty."

I got up and picked up my phone and wallet from the dresser, put my reaper ring on and then my wedding ring. Time to face another day. Another day without Abby. Eight days. I gripped the door handle and opened it up. I'd kill the men responsible for this. Literally.

***

I spotted Roach at the bar as soon as I came down the stairs. I picked up instantly that something was wrong. The air in the clubhouse was tight, sobering. No one was drinking at the bar and the few members that were around were from the mother charter and they were looking more depressed than usual.

It was early morning and for the first time ever I saw Roach with a whiskey in hand before midday. He normally didn't drink before the afternoon. And if Abby were here, she would be worried. Then she would give him a lecture about drinking on his medication.

"What's up?"

Roach had a manila folder in front of him. He looked up and across at me, his eyes showing he was drunk. How long had he been drinking?

"Came to you this morning." His voice was rough and his eyes glassy. "But thought you would need your sleep after this."

"After what?"

He pushed the manila folder across the bar toward me. "It was left at the gate."

Chapter 2

Reaper

It was as if someone had reached into my chest and pulled out my cold heart. My body slowly shut down as I stared down at the pictures. All of Abby. She was beaten. She was bruised. And her body was lifeless on the ground.

"There is something on the back of that one." Roach gulped down his whiskey and reached for the bottle.

I turned over the photo of Abby lying lifeless on a floor.

You took mine. I'll take yours slowly.

The words were scribbled on the back.

This threw me. Imagining it was one thing, but knowing your worst fears were actually coming true… It sent ice through my veins and made my stomach squeeze so tight I felt like I was going to throw up.

"Did we get them dropping it off on camera?"

"Just a guy in a hoodie. He parked across the street. We ran the plates. They were stolen."

What did I do now? Abby was in trouble and now it was my job to find her and kill the bastard responsible. Someone was going to die slowly, but it wasn't going to be Abby.

"Where is everyone?" I dropped the photos on the bar.

"Sleeping off last night." Roach filled his glass. "Lucky bastards."

"We have addresses to search. Get everyone moving."

Roach laughed, and then looked at me with a soulless expression. "That's not my job anymore, son. That's yours."

"So, what, you wipe your hands of the club altogether?"

"Nope." He swallowed his whiskey and stood up. "I'm going to look for my daughter without the responsibility of men on my back. You're in charge now, son. So if you want them moving, you better start giving orders. And you should decide on a vice president before the day is out."

He had just dumped the club on me so he could go do whatever he wanted? Frustrated and furious at the same time, I marched over to the living room.

"Go wake everyone. I want everyone on their bike ready to go within ten minutes. If they have a problem with that, tell them to leave their patch at the door," I said to the few mother charter members who were clearly upset about Abby. I knew sitting here drinking wouldn't solve the problem. No, we had to get moving.

We had cookhouses to trash through.

They nodded their heads and got up. At least they listened.

"You seen Brad?" I shouted from across the room at Roach.

He turned on his stool. "Garage."

There was only one other man I wanted on my side today and that was Brad.

"You coming to do the raids?" I fired at Roach before leaving.

"Nah, I've got to follow up some other leads."

"Like?" As far as I knew the only lead we had was Jones. It was what I was working on. It was what I was putting all my effort into.

He turned his back to me and lit up a cigar. "If they turn out any good, I'll tell ya."

Frustrated was the one massive word for how I was feeling. "Fine." I pushed the clubhouse door open and walked out onto the lot. If he wanted to play it that way, fine. I was pulling every string I had to try and find Abby. I was doing everything physically possible. But if he thought he could just dump the mother charter on me and expect me to drown under the pressure, he was wrong. I could take the responsibility of being the mother charter president and I could be a father. And I would find Abby.

The garage was open and Brad was under a car.

"Get up, we have doors to knock down." I patted myself down for a cigarette.

"You got the addresses?" Brad slid out from under the car, looking impressed. "Already?"

"Got them early this morning."

"You should have said something." Brad stood up. "You got the boys up yet?"

"Happening as we speak." I sucked on the cigarette and looked over my shoulder to see bodies starting to come out of the clubhouse. Some were stumbling, others shielding their eyes from the burning sun.

"Alright, let's get moving. Doors to bust down and drugos to scare." Brad wiped the grease off his hands onto his pants. "Can't believe Jones came through."

The boys were mounting their bikes as Brad and I walked toward them. I nodded my head. I had hoped Jones would come through. And he had. Now it was my turn to take advantage of it. Abby Harrison being taken was everywhere. I knew we would find someone who had answers. Or someone who had heard something about where Jake was keeping her, even if I had to bust jaws to get answers. If killing one scared the others into talking, then so be it.

Kim

I never wanted to be a mom. I never had that draw to a child. I think it was because my mom died so young. So I didn't have a strong mother feeling. But then there was Tyson. My heart broke for that little boy. I would kill for him. And I had never felt so protective of anything in my life.

When it came to Tyson, my motherhood instincts were brought out. I loved him with all my heart. I didn't know it was possible to love someone as much as I loved him.

So right now, as people stared at me, judging me, I didn't really care. I was at the outpatient department at the hospital, waiting for our names to be called.

It most likely didn't help my case that I was dressed in Satan's Sons gear. A tank top and shorts, both with 'Satan's Sons' written on them.

I was proud of my family. And I didn't hide it.

But people judged this type of lifestyle. Like right now, I was getting dirty looks from other mothers. If Abby were here, she would give them the finger.

They would be coming up with stories about whose child it was. Most likely thinking I was some club whore who got knocked up. People thought it was acceptable to just flat out stare at me.

I knew I wasn't welcome. Heck, the young couple I sat next down to got up and moved.

It was twelve and our appointment was supposed to have been half an hour ago. Talk about running late. I was rocking Tyson, my eyes on his sleeping face, when I felt the air in the room change. People went tense. I followed the direction of their eyes.

Reaper.

He was walking up through the glass passageway and into the waiting room. What did you know? He actually showed up. Late. But better than never.

God, he was built. Broad shoulders, solid build. Tall and dangerous. I shook my head. Abby sure had a taste for danger. He was wearing a t-shirt that showed off the club tattoos up his arms. And the leather vest scared nearly everyone in the room. He walked up to the receptionist's desk.

I should say something. Reaper wasn't known for asking someone something nicely.

The receptionist pointed behind him, to me.

He turned, and the 'Abby' tattoo on his neck stood out more than normal. Maybe it was because I was missing her so much. I put my hand up and waved him over. Now all eyes were on me and I felt it. They didn't dare stare at Reaper, but me, well, they were basically gawking, till Reaper walked over to me.

"I thought I was late."

"You are." I moved the magazines off the seat next to me. "But so are they."

Reaper didn't take a seat. Instead, he kneeled to look in the stroller. "Has he been alright?"

"Yep."

"Did he stay asleep long this morning?"

"Woke around ten. He's had two bottles like a champion." When it came to taking care of Tyson, it was like second nature to me. I didn't know why. I looked up. People were still staring! For fuck's sake! I was a woman with a baby. Get over it. I ground my teeth, glaring at the hospital policy poster.

"OK. Now I know he is alright. What's wrong with you?"

My eyes snapped to Reaper. Why could he read me so well? Was it because he was used to Abby? How did he know something was wrong? Abby and I might be twins, but we surely didn't react the same to everything. But right now he could tell I was frustrated. Or, more importantly, I was pissed off.

"People are staring. They have been staring since I got here and it's pissing me off." I crossed my arms. "Just because they see a club girl with a baby they think I'm some worthless whore."

Reaper's eyes left mine and he looked over his shoulder, standing up. "What the fuck are you looking at?" His voice cut the thick tension in the air. The protection in his voice was clear and also a lingering threat, daring anyone to stand up to him. Everyone's eyes snapped off us, looking in every direction but ours.

I guess when you have a big, scary biker with you, they have manners.

Reaper sat down in the seat next to me, crossing his arms, which caused his muscles to bulge. "You and Abby were never club girls, Kim. Don't let anyone tell you otherwise. Or treat you otherwise. Even Trigger should know that." His voice was softer and I heard it break at the mention of Abby's name.

"I am a club girl."

"No. No, you're not." Reaper's hand landed on my knee, getting my attention. "Club girls are owned by the club. You have never and will never belong to the club. These people are just small-minded."

I looked at Reaper, seeing a completely different side to him. Was this the side Abby fell in love with?

"Thanks." I took in his tattooed hand and fingers. I noticed his knuckles were red and bleeding. Everything about him would scare a sane woman away, but not Abby. "Any luck this morning?" My stomach tightened when I remembered seeing the pictures. Dad had attempted to hide them from me.

"More addresses."

"Do I want to know what you had to do to get those addresses?"

A smirk spread across his face. "No."

I had a strong feeling that those addresses were the result of his bloody knuckles.

He sat up in his seat and turned to me. "Can I ask you something?" His voice was strong like always. When he said something, he got attention. His voice could bring a room full of chaos to order.

"Shoot." I started rocking the stroller back and forth.

"What's your old man up to?"

I rolled my eyes at that. "You don't want to know."

"Come on. You're the only one that has any insight into that old man. And fuck if I know what he is up to."

"You mean dumping the club on you?"

"That and he isn't telling me what he is up to," Reaper sighed, frustrated.

I chewed my bottom lip. Why did it feel like I was betraying Dad if I told Reaper what he was up to? At the same time, Reaper was the mother charter president. If something was happening, he was meant to know.

"He is following up old connections," I finally spat out. "And he has gone off his medication because he thinks it makes his mind cloudy. And right now he needs to be switched on."

"Abby would kill him. What old connections?"

"Old members."

"Why wouldn't he just tell me that?"

"Because these members didn't exactly leave on their terms. Dad forced them out because they were playing both sides. He doesn't like bringing it up because he lost half the charter to it when I was younger. Abby and I always refer to it as the dark days. One day, Dad had a full charter. The next, half were given the boot. Didn't help either that Dad left each one with a bullet wound."

"So he is leaning on ex-members for information? When he personally shot each one of them for betraying the club?"

"Well, he didn't kill one of them. Just wounded them."

Reaper shook his head. "Twisted old man."

"I won't be surprised if he goes wild for a while."

"What do you mean by that?"

"Disappears. He isn't a president anymore. No one's relying on him. He will do anything to find Abby. So if he disappears, don't be surprised." If there was one thing I knew, it was my dad. I knew him nearly as well as I knew my twin.

"Tyson Wilson."

Both our heads snapped in the direction of the doctor. Finally.

***

I didn't know why was I so nervous. But I was. The doctor went over Tyson. It was killing me not knowing if anything was wrong. I was moving my weight from side to side nervously.

Apart from the odd question, the doctor had remained quiet.

I waited patiently.

But it had been twenty minutes and she still showed no sign of telling me if he was OK or not.

I must have been making Reaper nervous because he put a hand on my shoulder, making me stay still.

For some reason, it calmed me, making me stand in one spot.

"OK." The doctor finished doing Tyson's Blooed Glucose Level. And then she smiled at me. "He is doing perfectly. He is one healthy little boy."

I let out a long slow breath, calming down. He was OK. Healthy little boy. I hadn't failed yet. The doctor was putting Tyson back into his jumpsuit when she looked at me.

"How are you, Mrs. Wilson?"

Whiplash. That was what it felt like. As if a whip had just gone straight across my face, whipping my heart and emotions.

I opened my mouth and it went dry. And then I tried to speak again. "I'm not Mrs. Wilson."

She frowned. "But I helped deliver Tyson. I remember you two clearly. You look–"

"I'm her twin," I cut her off. If this was hurting me, only god knew what Reaper was feeling.

"So how is Abby, then? Why didn't she come to the appointment? This appointment was a checkup for her as well." The doctor didn't hide her disapproval.

"She couldn't make it," Reaper snapped rudely. "Can we go now?"

"Yes." The doctor picked up the clipboard. "I don't usually do this, but does Abby need a refill on the pain reliever?"

Again, another whip across my body. The answer was yes. She most likely did need pain relief. But how do you explain that she has been kidnapped?

"She is fine," I lied and picked Tyson up. I had him in the stroller in a blink of an eye and was ready to leave.

"Make sure to make an appointment for a month from now. The girls at reception will help you. Also, tell Abby if she needs anything, just to come in."

I nodded my head and Reaper held the door open for Tyson and me.

I made the appointment at the desk, got a card with a reminder on it and left. Reaper and I walked through the parking lot.

"Where did you park?" Reaper asked.

"Um, just there." I pointed to my car.

Reaper looked at it with disapproval. "We need to update your car."

"I love my car."

"If you are driving Tyson around, you need an update." Reaper leaned against the car as I popped the trunk. "I'll organize it."

"I feel insulted you don't like my car." I picked Tyson up and out of the stroller. Reaper folded the stroller up and put it in the trunk.

Closing the trunk, he looked at me. "Just accept the upgrade, Kim."

I pursed my lips. Well, if I was getting a new car, I wanted a say. I doubted he would let me pick what car I got, but maybe I could push to pick the color. "Can I pick the color?"

He rolled his eyes. "You sound like your sister."

"Did she get to pick the color of her car?"

"No. She didn't."

"But you knew she liked black."

He sighed, running a hand through his hair. "Fine, what color?"

I grinned. "Red. And it better not be a tank like Abby's. Fucked if I'll be able to park a thing like that." I pointed a finger at him.

He took Tyson from me and strapped him in. "I'll make sure you have it by the end of the day." Reaper closed the door.

"That's quick." It was after one and I knew Reaper had more important things than car shopping to do.

"It's just a phone call. Make sure you are around the club to sign for it."

"Reaper?"

"Yep."

"Did you get a solid lead on Abby today?"

I watched his expression drop. The muscles in his face tightened. He pulled his sunglasses down from his head and shielded his eyes.

"I have more than what I had this morning."

I nodded my head and that tight knot in my stomach twisted. Whenever I thought about Abby, that feeling suffocated me. The knot got tighter. And, as more time passed, it was getting more painful.

"I'll see you when I see you." I walked around my car.

"If you have any problems, call me." Reaper headed back toward the hospital to where his bike was parked.

I got in the car and put the key in the ignition. I wondered what Abby was doing right now. I wondered if she was OK. But most of all I wondered if she was still alive. The note said he was going to kill her. Slowly.

We just had to bet on Reaper finding him before he followed through on it

Chapter 3

Roach

I had put my life into the club. I had put that club before my family. I put it before my wife. I was too busy with club business to watch her take her final breaths. I had lived for my club. I would have died for it. But now, now I was seeing things clearly and realizing that the club really was the second thing in my life. What came first was my blood family. My daughters. They held my heart. I lived for them. All this time, I had treated them second to the club. I had struggled to put them first. I had struggled to bring them up while handling the largest charter in the country.

And now? Now, half of my heart was missing. Her room was empty. Her son cried for her. I cried for her. Those pictures were smashing the sense out of me. So, was I desperate? Yes. Was I willing to do anything? Yes. Which had me here, at a bar, on the seedy side of town.

He drank here every Tuesday, as far as I knew. I doubted his habits had changed. I pushed the door open and scanned the booths. I spotted his gray hair and wild beard. We had history and it wasn't good. But I knew he had connections with Jake. I also knew he used to gamble with him.

So, if there was one person who knew where Jake was holed up, it was Billy, my first vice president, and ex-member. I had personally shot him in the leg, causing him to have a limp.

That was back when I saw things as black and white. You either stood with us or against, not on both sides.

"Billy." I came to a stop at his booth.

He was smoking a cigar and drinking before midday. Some people don't change. Though I had been taken to the bottle early lately. But I doubted Billy had a reason like mine. I doubted his daughter was missing.

Shelly was the same age as Abby and Kim. It was one of the things that brought Billy and me closer. Having daughters the same age. Both being single parents, we were close. Which made it even harder when he betrayed the club. Turning his back not just on the club, but on me too.

He looked up from his beer, his eyes widening. He took the cigar from his mouth. "Roach."

I sat down on the other side of the booth. So here I was, about to ask the last man who would want to help me for help.

"What do you want?" Billy was straight to it. He ran a hand down his long gray beard.

"You still in contact with Jake Frankston?"

He chuckled darkly. His beady little eyes flashed to my vest. "You're missing a patch, brother."

"I'm not your brother."

"No. You made that clear when you shot me."

"I told you then. I'll tell you now. You betrayed my trust. I don't forgive that."

"But I see that president patch you were so fond of is gone. Finally found your match, have you?"

"Passed the club on to good hands."

"You must think a lot of him to pass your club on to him."

"He's my son-in-law."

"Ah, yes. The Reaper." Billy nodded his head. "Heard dark stories about that one. Didn't think a serial killer would be the one you finally gave the club up to."

"Men will respect him or fear him. Either way, they will follow him."

Billy took a few gulps of his beer. "Just because he scares the shit out of people doesn't give them a reason to respect him."

"No, but what he's done for this club to earn him that reputation HAS earned their respect."

Billy put his hand up for the bartender to refill his beer. "You thought it through, like everything. But I doubt you came here to get my approval." His beady eyes were on me. "What do you want, Roach?"

"My daughter was kidnapped."

"Heard about that."

"Jake Frankston is behind it. You know where he is. I know that. So, I'm here asking nicely for you to tell me. Otherwise, I'll tell Reaper and you can deal with him. And you know he isn't scared of torture."

He laughed dryly and the bartender replaced his glass with a fresh one. "Reaper enjoys killing, doesn't he?"

"If you mean he isn't afraid of it, then yes. His hands get bloody. And I'm telling you now, he is on a manhunt for answers. So if he even just thinks you know, he will come for you."

"But if I tell you, you will what? Not tell him I was involved?" Billy's fingers ran around the edge of the glass.

"Just tell me where the prick is keeping my daughter."

His expression had been masked the whole way through the conversation. Until now. Now a smirk was on his face. "Remember when I came to you when Shelly got raped?"

I knew this was going to come back and bite me. I nodded my head swiftly.

"And what did you say?"

He was really going to force me to say it again? Fine. "It wasn't a brotherhood problem." I remembered that day crystal fucking clear. I was under a lot of pressure. It was only six months after he left the club. Well, after I forced him out of the club.

"Well, I have an answer for you, Roach. It's not my fucking problem. And your threat of the Reaper coming for me doesn't scare me. He would have to cut off all my limbs before I helped you."

He knew. He fucking knew where she was. "God help you, Billy. Once I get through with this, I'm coming for you."

"Well, Roach, when I see your daughter, which I will, I'll make sure to pass on a hello from you."

Grinding my teeth, I didn't even think about it. I launched across the table at him. His beer went everywhere. He didn't fight back. He just laughed, a sick, filthy laugh.

"NO FIGHTING IN THE BAR!" The bartender pointed a shotgun at us, making me let go of the bastard.

"This isn't over."

"I'll wait for your son-in-law. Because we all know you don't have the balls to get your hands dirty, Roach." Billy sat up, a big smile on his face. He was getting pleasure from this.

How could I ever have been friends with this man? Let alone think he was my brother? I gave him one more look before I walked off, leaving behind the only bastard I knew who had answers. I could tell Reaper. Reaper wouldn't think twice about torturing him to get the information. But I knew Billy. He would hold out. He wouldn't care if he lost his life. He would rather die than help me.

I mounted my bike. Abby was alive and if Billy had seen her, that meant others would have seen her too. Who else did I know who was connected to that side? Suddenly the list of men's names appeared in my head. All had one thing in common. They hated me. Hated the brotherhood.

Their reaction would be like Billy's. But fuck it, I would try them anyway.

***

Kim

I lit up a smoke. Tyson was in his stroller. I took it in. Well, it was red. But he hadn't listened when I said I wanted a small car. Did he do this on purpose? It was a four-wheel drive and there was no way I was going to be able to park it.

"Nice car."

I turned to see Trigger. God, why wasn't he out with the rest of them? No, God wanted to torture me and keep him around.

"Thanks." I looked back at the car, taking my eyes off the guy I was obsessed with, whom I'd loved since I was sixteen. Who also had no interest in me, unless it was for sex. And now that he was getting that somewhere else, he didn't need me.

"You won't be able to park it." I could hear the smirk in his voice.

"I will too." I knew I couldn't. I was going to be taking multiple attempts at parking it. I was going to look like a fool, one of those fuckers who couldn't park their car.

"Did Reaper buy it for you?"

There was something in his voice that made me turn around and look at him. What was the look on his face? Staring at him was like a punch to the stomach and a pull on the heart at the same time. His blonde hair was messed up. He had a five o'clock shadow along his jaw line. He was wearing a tank top, showing off the ink that ran up his arms. Out of all the men in the club, Trigger had the least amount of ink. But he made up for it with muscles. He didn't need the ink to scare people away. Just one look at him and you knew he was trouble. I knew he was trouble. Yet here I was, still obsessed with him.

"Yeah, he did," I said, then sucked on my cigarette.

"You two are getting awfully close." Trigger's words had another meaning behind them and that pissed me off.

"What are you trying to say? That I'm hitting on my sister's husband?" I fired at him. Did he really think I was that desperate? I could have any man I wanted. Why the hell would I go after one that was not only taken, but taken by my sister?

"You are spending time in his room. Looking after his kid. Now he is buying you fucking expensive cars."

"Car," I corrected him.

He crossed his arms and I knew now what the look on his face was. It was jealousy. "I'm just saying what everyone is thinking."

"Well, clearly everyone here is as stupid as you."

He scoffed. "Come on, Kim. You and him are getting close."

"What does it matter?" I threw my cigarette on the ground and stomped on it with a bit more force than needed.

"You said you were over men. Clearly you were just waiting for a certain one to become available."

I laughed and shook my head. "Yeah, that is exactly what it is. I waited till my sister was kidnapped to make a move on her husband."

"You said it, not me."

"God, you're frustrating."

"And you're stupid."

"Why don't you just go back to screwing whores? It's the only thing you are any good at."

"Thanks for the compliment, Kim." He smirked at me. He was getting under my skin and he was enjoying it.

"Fuck off."

I grabbed the stroller and pushed it toward the new car.

"I bet you can't even get that thing out of the lot."

I gritted my teeth and ignored him.

"What, no smart comeback?"

"Fuck off, Trigger."

I opened the back door to the car, expecting to have to go get the car seat out of my old car. But there was a brand new one already strapped in. Reaper really did think of everything.

Trigger leaned against the car. "What do you know? Your boyfriend thought of that ahead of you."

I didn't even think about it. I punched him with all my force on his arm. "Say that again. And I will make sure it's the last thing you will say. Only you would take something nice and make it dirty."

"How was the doctor's today?"

"Like you really care," I scoffed and lifted Tyson out of the stroller.

"I do care."

I narrowed my eyes at him. "What are you playing at?"

I watched his expression change. His eyes flashed with emotion. Finally, he opened his mouth. "Well, if it affects Tyson, it affects you. So I care."

"Why aren't you out looking for Abby?"

He rolled his eyes. "That didn't answer my question."

I strapped Tyson in. He was still asleep, which meant he wasn't going to be sleeping tonight. "You didn't answer mine."

"I asked you first."

"Really, you are going to play that game?"

He arched his eyebrows and nodded his head. "So, how was the doctor's?"

He was doing this on purpose, just to annoy me. I chewed my bottom lip. Should I tell him? I tilted my head, studying him. Why did he care again? Because if it affected Tyson, it affected me. So he cared. Right.

"Tyson passed with flying colors. I haven't failed looking after him yet. They were more concerned about Abby being a no-show."

"Did you explain the situation?"

I laughed and looked at him to see if he was serious. He was. "Only in a movie would Abby being missing make sense. Now I answered your question. Why are you here?"

Considering he was the only guy here, apart from the mechanics, I was interested in knowing why he was still around.

He tilted his head, his expression drying up. "Reaper made me stay."

"Why?" I scoffed. I couldn't think of one good reason for him to be here.

"To look after you. When it comes to you, he is making sure all your needs are met. And for some stupid reason, he thinks I am the best man for the job." His eyes were locked on mine. Jealousy was painted in his eyes, along with anger. Was he mad he was being forced to put up with me? Most likely.

"Well, I'll make sure to tell him you don't want the job." I closed the door and went to walk around him when he grabbed my arm.

"Why would you do that? Do you not want me around?"

I took a steady breath in, trying to focus, but all I could think of was that he was touching me. This grip was firm and warm and it was spreading warmth through my body. Suddenly it was even hotter outside than before.

"When it comes to you, Trigger, I don't know what I want," I finally stuttered out like a complete fool.

I should have pulled my arm from his grasp and then stormed off. But I didn't. I just stood there.

"He thinks you feel safe around me. Is that true?" His hard expression softened. And he was looking at me like I could say whatever I want and he would accept it. But at the same time, it was like he was waiting to hear the right words.

I took a deep breath in. Did I be honest? The longer I looked into his deep blue eyes, the more the truth was just coming into my mind. "Yes, that's true." There, I said it. I was admitting to needing him. He could think what he liked about it. "Not that you care," I added. "Now let go of me. I have to go."

His eyes flickered to my arm and then back on my face. "Where are you going?"

Why did he care? "Supermarket. Tyson needs diapers and we have no food because all these extra charters are eating everything that isn't nailed down."

He let go of my arm, only to take the car keys from my hand. "What are you doing?" I followed him around to the driver's side of the car.

"Driving you."

"I don't need you to. I can drive myself."

He laughed and opened the car door. "No, you can't. You couldn't pull this out of this parking lot even if you wanted to without hitting something."

"Reaper doesn't expect you to babysit me." I crossed my arms.

"No. But he expects you be looked after and his son to be protected. So here I am."

He was acting like he was doing me a favor. I crossed my arms. "Don't you have girls to sleep with?" Since the other charters got here, Trigger had been more focused on the women they brought along than on the fact Abby was missing.

"Only one. And she has made it clear it isn't happening. So I'm good to go, if you are?"

He was referring to me, wasn't he? I turned him down once and he remembered that clearly. How about all the times I did sleep with him? Did he remember them?

I sighed, dropping my arms. Fine, he could drive. At least this way I wouldn't be entertaining the mechanics with my backing out skills.

I climbed into the car. It had that new car smell.

"I wonder how much this set Reaper back," I muttered, taking in all the chrome and the fancy dashboard.

Trigger was backing the car out. "Hundred thousand, most likely."

"He wouldn't seriously spend that much on a car. Especially for me. Abby, now that makes sense."

Trigger glanced at me. "Like I said, he is making sure you are looked after."

I rolled my eyes. "Nothing is going on." I looked out the window. "Anyway, I've sworn off men."

He laughed. "You and men are one and the same, Kim."

"Nope."

"Yes."

"You have always been with a man."

I looked at him. "No, I've always been waiting on you." I was being deadly serious. Ever since I was sixteen, I'd been hooked on a drug I could never get a full dose of. Only now was I putting a stop to it. "And if other men looked my way, you made sure they were less than interested. Between you and my father, other men didn't stand a chance."

Trigger's eyes flashed from the road to me, his expression unreadable, before he looked back at the road.

"And now?" he said, with a bitter tone.

"Like I said, I've sworn off men."

"Except for one."

"I already told you I'm not after Reaper!" How many times did I have to say it? Did I literally have to scream it at him? Where were these people getting these crazy ideas from? As if Reaper would even look at me in that way. The only woman he had ever cared about and looked at was Abby. The same woman he had half the country looking for.

Trigger glanced at me with a smirk. "I was talking about me."

I gulped, meeting his intense eyes. Maybe I had given up on him. But he hadn't given up on me. Yet.

"What makes you think I want anything to do with you, after the way you have been acting?"

He scoffed.

"What, Trigger? You have been screwing your way through the charter girls."

His jaw tightened. And he wasn't taking his eyes off the road. I thought he wasn't going to answer me. Like always, he would shut down.

"Maybe I'm just trying to fill a hole," he gritted out. Then he glanced at me. "I wasn't trying to hurt you."

He could say what he liked. Actions speak louder than words. I leaned forward and turned the radio on. Then I sat back, looking out the window. I couldn't look at him. Did it hurt me that he was with other women? Yes. Tyson had been taking my mind off it. But if I was honest, I wasn't sleeping because all I could picture was Trigger with other women. They were glued to his side at the club. Then he was forever dragging one off to his room. Sometimes he didn't even make it to his bedroom. I had caught him in the kitchen only a few days ago.

Whatever. I was over it. Being so close to him was like suffocating with a plastic bag around my head. My senses were alive and waiting for only one thing: for him to touch me. Why was my body craving him so much, yet my brain was able to understand he was no good for me?

What was Reaper thinking, leaving Trigger with me? I was better off with a prospect. At least then I would be feeling nothing. Instead of this slow torture.

It was my heart against common sense.

***

So, it turned out well that Trigger came, 'cause I needed someone to push the shopping cart. I couldn't push the stroller and a shopping cart. And Tyson was too little to go in their baby seat. Plus I didn't know if they were safe or not.

Trigger was pushing two shopping carts. I had filled one up completely and the second one was nearly full as well. When the men ate, they really ate.

Trigger was in the frozen section getting French fries. I was in the meat department. I had a hand on the stroller and was bending over, looking at the porterhouse steaks, when someone whacked me hard on the ass.

I jumped up, only to find two dipstick college kids gawking at me. I glared. How dare they touch me! They were laughing. I was used to men being pigs. But they always knew the boundaries.

"Come on, sweetheart. You can't put it on display and expect me not to touch," one laughed.

Just breathe, Kim. "How dare you just whack me!"

"You put it out there," the kid had the guts to say.

My grip on the stroller tightened.

"Kim, I couldn't find the crinkle cut fries so I got straight. Will that do?" Trigger came up behind me. I looked over my shoulder.

"Yeah, that's fine."

"What's wrong?" One look, he knew me that well.

"Nothing."

The guys sniggered and then their eyes ran down me like I was a piece of meat and they were dogs.

"Can we go?" I went to bend over and grab the meat, but stopped. "Can you get the meat for me?" I turned to Trigger.

"Why can't you get it?" His eyes narrowed, going right through me.

"'Cause I can't bend over," I hissed. "Please just do it."

He looked at me and then at the college kids. He let go of the shopping carts and headed for them. What the hell was he doing? I hadn't said anything.

"Something funny, man?" Trigger's voice was actually friendly, like he was in on the joke.

"We were just admiring, man." One of the guys put his hands up. "Can't help a guy wanting to touch."

"So you touched her?" Trigger said lightly, like it was no big deal.

"She has one firm ass. Can see how you ended up knocking her up." They laughed.

I was getting the same feeling I had this morning at the outpatients'. As if I was nothing more than a biker whore.

"Right," Trigger said. "I just wanted to check." Then within two seconds, like a blink of an eye, Trigger's fist connected with the guy's jaw and his friend didn't even have time to block Trigger before he punched him too. Both were on the floor, one with a bleeding nose and the other wailing.

Trigger kneeled. "Girls like her are out of your league. And men like me will make sure of it. Have a nice afternoon, boys."

I was literally still gawking at him as he got up and walked toward me. His jaw was clenched and he looked like he was holding onto a lot of anger right now, like they were getting off lightly.

"You can pick up the meat now." Trigger was back at the shopping carts.

I nodded my head, still in shock. I picked up a couple dozen packets of meat and threw them in the shopping cart.

"OK, we can go." I couldn't look him in the eye. I still couldn't believe he'd just done that. The guys were still on the floor as I pushed the stroller around them.

I could feel him following me with the shopping carts. We lined up and I put Tyson at the end of the checkout and went back to the shopping carts. This was the bit I hated about shopping, loading all the stupid things on the belt. I bent over and picked up the diapers. Just as I did, I felt a firm hand whack my ass. My eyes widened and I looked over my shoulder, not believing Trigger had just done that.

He smirked at me. "Now, that's mine to touch."

I shook my head at him, taking in his smartass smirk. He thought I was his to touch? I didn't know how I felt about that. "Just help with the groceries."

"Nah, I get a better view if you do it."

"Trigger."

"Kim."

"Fine, if you aren't going to help, go look after Tyson." I pushed him in the chest. He laughed. At least he would be doing something then and not just checking me out.

When I got home I was burning this outfit. All it had done all day was draw attention to me.

Chapter 4

Kim

I couldn't think of a time I wasn't with her. Even when we fought, we always made up. We could call each other names and could say the most awful things to each other, but we always made up. We always stood together.

I was struggling as I gripped the sink in my bathroom. I needed my sister. I just needed to know if she was OK. I needed to know she was still breathing. I knew she was strong and would fight to the death. She was also smart. They were two of the things I loved about her. Did she know I loved her unconditionally? She trusted me to look after her son. She had put all her faith in me to care for him.

So far I hadn't let her down.

Everyone was doing everything possible to find her. And all I could do was just wait. Wait for news. Wait for them to get back. Then wait to be told what they had found out. So far it was just more leads to other cookhouses.

Jake Frankston kept his location quiet. Reaper had found out that he collected his money from a post office box in town. He got a message when one of the cookhouses dropped off the money then he collected it the next day.

His post office box was currently being watched.

I looked in the mirror at my reflection. I was the spitting image of Abby and people were noticing. Dad was treating me like a ghost. Reaper's eyes always hardened when he looked at me. And most of all, it was a stab in the heart every time I caught a glimpse of my reflection.

I was her twin. I should have some feeling about whether she was OK or not. Running a hand through my blonde hair, I turned my back to my reflection and flicked the lights off. It was after three in the morning and I should have been sleeping. Instead, I was up worrying.

All I did was worry. I worried about Tyson. Abby. Reaper. And then when I wasn't worrying, I was feeling sick to my stomach about a man who couldn't care less for me. He saw me as good for only one thing and when that stopped, so did his attention.

I looked at my made bed. I should try and get some sleep.

Or I could go down to the bar and drink.

Maybe after a few I could find some peace.

I slipped on a black t-shirt dress and opened my door. One good thing about living in a clubhouse was there was always an open bar.

I was walking down the hall, when I stopped at Reaper's door, listening. Nothing. Tyson must be asleep.

Finally.

The little thing slept so much during the day I was positive he would be awake all night. I kept on walking. Past Dad's room. Past Trigger's room and straight down the stairs till I was walking into the bar.

No one.

Great.

At least no one would witness me drinking my worries away.

I walked around the bar, grabbing a bottle of vodka, orange juice from the fridge and a glass.

Walking back around, I pulled out a stool. The bar lights were still on and the living room lights too. So the place was still lit up. Like always. These rooms never slept or closed down for the night.

I had been sober since Abby was taken, just in case I was on call for Tyson. But tonight I was drinking and I was going to drink hard. I could handle being hung over and looking after Tyson. For one day anyway.

I poured myself a drink, my fingers wrapping around the glass.

"You shouldn't be drinking."

Out of all the people to be up at this time of night, of course it would be him. I glared down at my glass. I didn't look up. I didn't acknowledge him.

"Ignoring me, huh? Well, that's new."

I took a sip from my glass. God, it tasted good, so refreshing. I was about to take another sip when it was ripped from my hand, spilling all over the bar.

"TRIGGER!"

"You really think you should be getting off your face right now?" He held the glass in the air.

"I was having a drink! ONE!"

"You never stop at one. You and I both know that." He was looking at me as if I was a disappointment. Well, he could think what he liked. I didn't care. "You are the sole caretaker of a newborn, Kim, and you want to get off your face at three in the morning. I thought you were better than that."

Did I need a lecture? No. Did I want one? No. Did I know I was doing the wrong thing? Yeah, maybe. But I couldn't sleep and I needed sleep.

"Just give me the glass back." I reached for it, but he was quicker.

"No."

"Fine, I'll get another one." I got up off the stool, only to have his hand on my shoulder force me to sit back down.

"What's wrong?"

"Why are you even up?" I glared at him. No one else was up. Reaper had made sure everyone was worn out today. He was riding them hard and wanted results. If anyone dared to even think about getting wasted, he was down their throats. He was planning an even bigger day tomorrow, which I guess was today now.

"Trigger?" a low female voice said.

I looked over his shoulder, noticing a half-dressed girl standing at the bottom of the staircase. Well, that answered my question. She barely looked to be in her twenties, maybe late teens.

I glared up at him. I was stupid to think he really cared. He was only up because he was getting laid. "You should go," I said, and took the glass from his hand. "I'm fine." Was I fine? No. I was so far away from fine it wasn't funny. If anything, I was screwed up. Seriously.

I swore I saw regret in his face. But then if I admitted to seeing that, that would be admitting he had feelings. Which he didn't. What was he waiting for? Why was he hanging around? I turned to look up at him.

"You can go." I didn't want him around anyway. I didn't need his disapproval. I didn't need to be lectured.

"Yeah. No, I can't." He turned around. "Just go to bed, Debs."

"But we haven't—"

"I said, go to bed. Any bed. Apart from mine."

"Trigger, just go with her," I groaned. All I wanted to do was get hammered to the point that I could sleep. I didn't need him around. I didn't need anything from him.

I watched the girl disappear up the stairs. I was refilling my glass. Considering I only got a sip from my last one, I made this one stronger. Shaking my head, I couldn't think of one reason why he would turn down a girl willing to go to bed with him. This was Trigger after all. Women always came first.

I was swallowing a mouthful of vodka and orange juice when his hands wrapped around my waist.

"What the hell are you doing?" I went stiff from his touch. My automatic reaction was to get out of his grip. So I started to wriggle. My hands went to his and I attempted to unlock them. But while I was doing that, he lifted me up off the stool. "Let me GO!" I pushed down on his arms.

Only to be thrown over his shoulder, like I weighed nothing at all.

"If you don't put me down, I'll start screaming." It wasn't a threat. I seriously would.

"Do you want to wake Tyson?" His voice had an edge to it.

Of course I didn't. He walked us up the stairs. Even if I couldn't scream, I wouldn't just be a dead doll on his shoulder. So I started punching his back and wriggling. "Put me down Trigger! I'm not yours to pick up. Or to touch!"

I wasn't anyone's. He scoffed, but didn't put me down. All I wanted was to have a quiet drink. Alone. Was that asking for too much?

"Put. Me. Down," I gritted out each word while punching his back with all my force. I couldn't see what he was doing, but we stopped at a door. I only had a clear view of the floor.

I heard the door open and then heard it close. He finally put me down. Slowly. Making sure his hands ran up my sides. As soon as my feet touched the ground, I was out of his grasp.

His room. Why were we in his room? I looked around the too familiar room. The clothes on the couch. The bathroom I used to keep clean. The photos on the bedside tables. And then there was that bed. How many hours had I spent in it?

"What am I doing here, Trigger?" I wasn't having sex with him. I might have had a sip of liquor, but I wasn't drunk and I also wasn't stupid.

His face softened and he gave me a look I rarely saw on his face: concern.

"You need sleep, Kim." He took a step toward me and I took one back, backing into the wall.

"And what makes you think I'd sleep here? With you?" This was the last place I'd dare close my eyes.

"Kim." He took another step toward me and I shot a hand out.

"Don't come near me."

"You need sleep. Take your dress off."

My mouth fell open. "You don't honestly expect me to sleep here where you have been banging your way through every whore possible."

He had his hands on his hips and was looking at me patiently, like he was waiting for a little child to behave. "Dress, Kim." His words were calm and steady. The way he was looking at me, it twisted something inside me.

Like he knew me better than I knew myself. Like he knew what my body needed and he was here willing to give it. He did know me. Too well. I gripped the bottom of my dress and pulled it off over my head. I should have felt embarrassed being in my underwear in front of him. But I wasn't. He had seen me completely naked many times.

But it'd been a while and there was no chance he was getting anywhere tonight. Not with me, anyway.

He caught my dress. He had a smirk on his face and I didn't know why. While I was glaring at him, he kicked his boots off, took off his leather vest and t-shirt. How many times had I run my hand over those tight muscles? How I loved to touch them and kiss them. Trigger had the body of a god and he worked hard to keep it. Always in the gym.

"In bed." He gestured his head toward his bed. When I didn't jump to it he added, "Don't make me make you."

He would, too. I frowned, and then sighed. It wasn't worth a fight. I walked around to the side of the bed.

"There's no point anyway. I won't sleep. I can't sleep." I threw the blankets back and lay down.

"Why can't you sleep?"

I chewed my bottom lip, not wanting to answer. The bed dipped as he climbed in, lying next to me. He grabbed the blankets and pulled them over me.

"Kim, look at me. Why can't you sleep?"

He thought he had a magic spell over me. He was wrong. I wasn't about to open up to him. Not after how he'd hurt me. Not after I watched him drag woman after woman away with him. I scoffed. Most likely to this bed, too.

I rolled onto my side and stared at the wall. He didn't deserve answers. And he was no priest so I wasn't confessing.

I felt his hand on my hip and he gently pulled me closer to him. My back was against his chest. I should get up. I should leave. I shouldn't be here. But darn it, it felt so comfortable and right. Just being against him. I was back to being my sixteen-year-old self, who just loved to be touched by him.

Gently he slipped his arm under my head and I naturally curled back in to him. I was going to hate myself in the morning.

"I know you don't trust me. But I will earn your trust back. I promise." His words were just below a whisper. As if I wasn't meant to hear them. He then planted a soft kiss on my shoulder and pulled me in even closer toward him, making sure there was no gap.

Why did I feel so comfortable? So content? Being in his arms just calmed me. As if the storm I had been battling for days was gone. And now I could rest. My worries about Tyson. About Abby. About Dad. About Reaper. All gone. And my mind was quiet as I lay between his arms, listening to him breathing in and out, his hot breath against my neck.

My eyelids got heavy and the last thing I remember was him kissing the back of my head as if I were something special to him.

***

Reaper

It was early. I was in the bar, Tyson was in his stroller and I was going over the list of addresses we were going to crash today. It didn't help that club business was backing up either. While finding Abby was at the top of my list, the club still needed attention. Members needed to be pulled into line. Guns needed to be delivered. Then there were our businesses which owed us rent that I hadn't sent anyone to collect.

"You wanted to see me?"

I looked up. Brad. Right. I was trying to track him down last night. "Yeah, take a seat." I pushed out a stool.

Tyson slept like a champ last night, giving me a few hours peace. But my mind was racing with what needed to be done on top of finding Abby. I had been trying to get hold of Brad last night to ask him something. But he was nowhere to be found.

"What's up?" Brad glanced in the stroller and then at the stool. "Are those the addresses we are hitting today?" His eyes were on my map as he took a seat on the stool.

"Yeah, they are, but that's not why I wanted to see you."

"What? Have I pissed off the mother charter president already?" He smirked at me.

"Something like that." I lit up a cigarette. "You know I only want men I can trust beside me, right?"

He looked at me defensively. "You know I'm behind you one hundred percent. I'm more dedicated to finding Abby than any of the other men. Hell, I was out all night crawling around bars looking for leads."

"That's where you were." Well, that answered why I couldn't find him last night. "I can't have you off running leads by yourself."

"Why the fuck not?" he scoffed, looking at me with disapproval. "If finding Abby means I don't go by the rules, then so be it." His temper was flaring, his fingers rounding into a tightly clenched fist. Brad's temper was nearly as bad as mine. Nearly. "You got a problem with how I work?"

For the first time since Abby left, I found myself smiling. Fuck it. I hadn't had a reason to smile since she was taken. But right now, as Brad but right now I was smiling.

"What the fuck you smiling about?"

"You," I smirked and leaned over the bar, grabbing two shot glasses and a bottle of whiskey. I hadn't had a drop of liquor since Abby was taken. But one shot wasn't going to put me off my game. Fuck it, I could get blasted and still be sharp. But I wouldn't take the risk.

"What you getting the whiskey for?" Brad's voice rose, as if I had gone completely mad.

"'Cause we are having a toast."

"Did we find Abby?" The hope in his voice shattered my smile, and instead, I found myself frowning again.

"No."

"Then I don't see a reason to be fucking toasting anything."

I pushed the shot glass toward him. "Like I said, I have something to ask you." I took the cigarette out of my mouth and put it in the ashtray.

"More like tell me off. Fuck it, Reaper. When have you been about rules?"

"Never."

"Exactly."

"But I have to change that. I have to set an example, and so do you," I watched him roll his eyes, ready to give me another serve, "if you are going to be my vice president."

The expression dropped off his face and he just stared blankly at me. The anger from before was gone. I think he was in shock.

"But I'm not next in line. Fuck that. I'm nowhere near the fucking line. I haven't served enough time to be a mother chapter vice president. You need someone with experience by your side, like Trigger. Fuck, he has heaps. He should still be up for it."

"Don't want Trigger. I want you. Plus, he wanted to give up the patch to begin with. He was Roach's VP. Not mine. I want someone I can trust my charter and family with. And that's you."

I had never trusted a guy more than I trusted Brad. He took care of Abby when I was on the road. He went to every one of Tyson's ultrasounds. He managed to keep my charter in check while managing my family. I thought a lot of him. And right now, I was ready to pay him back for all his hard work.

"So, you up to it?" I said, pushing the shot glass toward him. "But fuck the rules, we can make them up as we go." I wasn't used to having such a large volume of men behind me. I was going into this half-blind, so having a man I trusted by my side was going to make the difference between me sinking or floating.

"I've never been a role model."

I scoffed, "'Cause I make such a fucking good one."

"Yeah but you're the Reaper. Men were born to follow you. They either admire you or fear you."

"They also won't question my decisions. So when I say I want you as my VP, if anyone had a problem with it, they wouldn't be saying much. My charter. My rules."

"You're serious about this, aren't you?"

I looked him in the eye. "Deadly. So are we going to drink to this or not?"

Brad's fingers wrapped around the shot glass and a smile spread across his lips. "Fucking oath."

"To... raising hell." I raised my shot glass.

"To raising hell."

"What has you two drinking so early?" Trigger came down the stairs, looking fresh from a shower. What had him up early? He normally didn't surface till mid-afternoon. And when he did, he was in a foul mood with a hangover.

"Just gave Brad the vice president patch," I said while looking at him more closely. Why the fuck did he seem so happy?

"Pay raise, brother. It's fun and games. You'll do alright." He whacked Brad on the back and then kneeled to look at Tyson. "Didn't hear this one crying last night."

"Yeah, he slept. For a few hours anyway."

"You heading out soon?"

"Yeah, I'll give the boys till eight. Then Brad gets the pleasure of getting them up."

"Great," Brad muttered. "Do you know how much stuff I get thrown at me when I go to wake them up? Bones pulled his gun yesterday."

Trigger laughed. "Boys just aren't used to early mornings."

"Neither are you." I looked at him, curious. "Why are you up?"

"Kim's sleeping so I thought I'd take Tyson for the morning," he said to me as if it wasn't a big deal. He even shrugged his shoulders, as if what he just said was totally normal and not completely out of the blue.

"You? Look after Tyson? Do you even know how?" Brad was just as shocked as me. He was asking the same questions I was thinking.

Trigger rolled his eyes. "I'm not stupid."

He might have thought he was up for the challenge but I had one question first. "How do you know Kim's asleep?"

Kim normally got up right about now. Every morning since Abby was taken she was up by eight and taking over from me. It wasn't like her to change routine. Trigger was never volunteering for babysitting either.

Sure, I had him on lockdown, watching out for Kim. But that was different from caring for Tyson. I wasn't one of those dads who would just dump their kid on anyone. Kim, I knew I could trust with his safety. I also knew I could trust Trigger to make sure both weren't harmed. Kim felt safe around him, so he was the best pick to watch her.

"Does it matter?" Trigger said with a defensive look in his eyes. As if he was hiding something.

"It does to me."

"I'm just making sure she is sleeping and not running herself into the ground. You wanted me to look after her, so there I am." Trigger said the words, but the actions behind his words weren't crystal cut. He wasn't doing this for me. He was doing this for Kim. He also wasn't just looking after her for me. He was doing it because, deep down in that twisted soul of his, he loved her. Even if he wouldn't admit it.

I stared at him. Abby and Tyson were the two most important things in my life. My life revolved around them breathing. Did I trust Trigger with Tyson? He had proven this week he could keep Kim and Tyson safe. Kim still hadn't given a lecture bout leaving him with her yet. I had thought for sure she would be knocking my door down as soon as she found out.

"Fine." I pointed a finger at him. "But if one thing happens to him, I swear, Trigger—"

"You will chop off my balls or something. I get it Reaper. Nothing will happen to him. We will watch some crap-ass kids' shows. I'll give him his morning bottle. And if he starts crying, I'll walk him and rock him. So you can stop stressing."

"Well, as long as you're prepared for a slow death if something happens to him, I don't see why not." I got up off the stool. "Kim OK?" I was asking him because it seemed like he knew more about her than he was letting on.

"Fine. Just needs sleep." Trigger looked at Brad, then back at me. "I think you two should start your day."

"Go wake up the boys, Brad." I folded the map and put it in my back pocket. "Rent to collect, guns to deliver and cookhouses to search. We will have to split up today to get it all done."

Trigger gripped the stroller. "While you boys do that, Tyson and I are going to watch television."

"I think I prefer his day to ours," Brad grumbled before heading off.

"Life as a vice president isn't easy," Trigger shouted after him. Brad turned around and gave him the finger.

"So you and Kim sorted things out then?" I followed him as he pushed Tyson through the bar to the living rooms.

"If you mean by her not wanting to stab me to death, then yeah, we have sorted things out."

"I meant it when I said you are not to lead her on."

We came to a stop in one of the living rooms and Trigger took a seat on the couch in front of a television.

"And as I told you, mind your own business."

"My charter. My sister-in-law. My business. You fuck around with her, you answer to me. Simple as that, Trigger."

He was grinding his teeth as he turned on the TV. "You know, it's a bit weird you being so protective of Abby's twin. Kim isn't stupid. She knows what she gets herself into. Unless the problem is more about you feeling something for someone you shouldn't." Trigger was dancing on a very thin line. I would have had him off that couch and against the wall, smashing in his jaw… if Tyson hadn't been in the way.

"You implying I have a thing for Kim?"

He shrugged his shoulders. "Makes sense. She is Abby's twin after all."

"She and Abby are nothing alike. Don't let my calmness fool you. I will have you breathing through a tube if you ever mention this fucking shit again."

His eyes met mine. While I was boiling with rage, he was deadly calm. "Just making sure we are on the same page, Reaper, and you aren't falling in love with another Harrison."

No one could replace Abby. Not her twin. Not anyone. The love I felt for that woman was undying and beyond words. I would go to hell and back to make sure she was back where she belonged, with me. In the meantime, I was going to make sure everyone else she loved was safe. That included her father and her sister and her son.

If he was trying to piss me off, he had succeeded. "You might have competition here for Kim. But it isn't from me. And remember where you are in the food chain, Trigger. You aren't the golden boy anymore. And I'm not scared of reminding you of that."

"Yeah, you and your temper, Reaper. You're notorious for it." Trigger turned on the TV. "But you aren't the only one protective of Kim." He looked me in the eye. "Just making sure you are protecting because she's family and not because you are falling in love with her."

"I've only ever loved one woman. And I'm planning on loving her for the rest of my life. If you were a real man, Trigger, you would stop flirting around and nail Kim down before someone else does." I kneeled and pulled Tyson from his stroller. Men were starting to surface now, grumpy and hungry. "I have to go. Tell Kim to call me if she needs me." I handed Tyson to Trigger. "Take care of my son."

"He's family. I protect family with my life. You know that." He took Tyson. "Now, what are we going to watch, Tyson?"

Colorful, loud and annoying kids' shows. Torture, if you ask me. I headed back to the bar. The boys were already reaching for the liquor bottles. The girls weren't up yet and there was no food prepared. I should organize things so that doesn't happen again tomorrow. The boys were grumpy enough, let alone without food.

"We will get food on the way," I said to them as they piled into the room. I supposed a café would be open in town. I doubted their morning crowd would like a bunch of bikers showing up. But they would like the money I'd throw down for food. Knowing Tyson was settled for the day and I now had a vice president, I could move on to my list of things to do. First thing was food, and then splitting the boys up. Today I was planning on raiding every cookhouse we had on the map.

Then there was the post office we were camped out at. We would turn up something. Some lead. Something or anything that would lead me to Abby.

***

Kim

The sun coming in through the curtains woke me up. I blinked a few times. At first, I didn't know where I was till I recalled the night before. Well, this morning. Right. Trigger's room. I sat up. He was nowhere to be seen.

I lit up my phone that was sitting on the bedside table. And my eyes sprung wide open when I saw it was after one in the afternoon. Holy hell! I scattered, picking up my dress and threading my arms through it. I didn't have any missed calls from Reaper, which meant he was still here looking after Tyson. I usually took over from him at like seven in the morning!

Oh my god! I had held him up all morning. He had more important things to be doing than looking after Tyson all day. I could do that. It was the only thing I was any good at. Why didn't he call? Why the hell didn't someone wake me the fuck up?!

I grabbed my phone and opened the door. I couldn't believe I'd slept for so long. I doubted any of the girls had organized the boys' breakfast and now it was after lunch. Considering it was me who organized the meals, it would be fair to say I was about to walk down to a bunch of hungry and grumpy bikers. I was prepared for the worst. Right down to the Reaper being in a foul mood. But, after taking the stairs two at a time, I entered an empty bar.

OK. Where the hell was everyone?

Why wasn't I walking into chaos right now?

I heard the sound of the TV and followed it. Rounding the corner, I saw something I had never expected to see in my lifetime.

Trigger with Tyson. Trigger was holding Tyson with one arm and they both were watching something on television. I went unnoticed till Trigger glanced away from the TV for a second.

I was just standing here, staring in complete awe. Words weren't coming to me.

"You're up. You hungry? Thought we could go out for lunch." Trigger turned the TV off and got up.

"You... me...Tyson...," I stuttered, unable to form words.

"They are the three people in the room, Kim." His voice had a mocking tone to it.

"No." I shook my head. "What are you doing with Tyson?"

"Looking after him."

My mouth hung open. I was still processing. "Why the hell didn't you wake me up?"

"You needed sleep." His eyes narrowed slightly as he looked at me. "Did you even have a shower before coming down here?"

My hair would be a mess, and I was sure I still looked half asleep, but I was wide awake. "Of course not! Reaper counts on me looking after Tyson. The routine is I take over from him at seven. You should have woken me up!"

"As you can see, we managed fine without you this morning. Believe it or not, Kim, the world doesn't fall apart if you sleep in. And you needed it, too."

"Did the boys get breakfast this morning? Does Reaper even know you are taking care of Tyson? 'Cause I doubt he was jumping for joy about the idea."

"Yeah, Reaper has no idea. I just took Tyson when he wasn't watching." Trigger rolled his eyes at me, walking around me. "You ready for lunch?"

"Don't even think you are getting out of this that easy. Why the hell did you volunteer to look after Tyson? In fact, why the hell did you get up this morning before me?" I gasped. "YOU TURNED MY ALARM OFF!" That was the reason I was always up at seven. Or before. Alarms. Why did it take me this long to remember that?

Trigger walked past me, holding Tyson. "You grab the stroller, Kim."

"What did Reaper say when he couldn't find me this morning?"

"Just grab the stroller, Kim."

"Did you tell him I slept with you last night?"

Trigger turned and looked at me. "I'm not telling anyone my business. What happens between you and me stays between you and me. Simple."

"So you're ashamed."

"Fuck, you're annoying. Grab the stroller. I'm hungry."

I wouldn't let this happen. Nope. Not now. Not ever. I was not letting Trigger play with my heart again.

"I want to make something crystal fucking clear to you, Trigger." I took a step closer to him, poking a finger into his chest. "You and I aren't anything. Not friends. Not lovers. When it comes to you and me, we are nothing. Got that? So next time you see me drinking at three in the morning, leave me the fuck alone and don't get involved with Reaper's and my plans. You might be acting sweet now but I know you. I know you better than you know yourself. Come tonight, you will be with another girl and I won't be heartbroken. Because I'm over you. Now give me Tyson. And you get the fucking stroller." I took Tyson and walked around him. I had to hold my ground. If I didn't, I would become the crushed girl with the broken heart again. I wouldn't go back to that. Not for him. Not for anyone.

Men used and abused.

I wasn't stupid. I'd learned my lesson.

Trigger equaled heartbreak. So when tonight came and I saw him laughing and drinking with another girl, as if she was something special, I wouldn't be tearing up about it and I wouldn't be wanting to rip the girl's hair out.

Trigger wasn't getting in. Not again. My heart was sealed when it came to him.

***

The boys were partying. Hard. They were actually celebrating. We finally got a solid lead on Abby. It took Reaper's fists to get it out of the guy, but we knew now she was staying at Jake's house. She was alive. And he had people coming to the house for pick-ups and drop-offs.

So there was going to be one person out there somewhere who knew the address of Jake's house.

Reaper also found out Jake's house was on the outskirts of town. So Abby hadn't been taken that far. The chances of finding her alive were higher now than ever.

"You alright?"

I turned around to see Reaper. "Tyson's with Dad." I turned my back on him and started to flip over the meat. It was after eleven at night and the men were looking for midnight snacks. So meat was on the menu. I had already cooked half of it and it had basically been taken off the BBQ as soon as it was cooked.

"I didn't ask if Tyson was OK." I felt him walk toward me till he was standing next to me. "I asked if you were."

I reached for my cider and took a gulp of it. "I'm fine."

"You haven't said much tonight."

"Nothing to say." I kept my eyes on the meat.

"Trigger giving you a hard time?"

I scoffed. After my outburst, he didn't speak to me again. Which made for an awkward lunch and an even more awkward day, since he still insisted on hanging around. As soon as Reaper rode through the gates, though, Trigger was back to being himself and nowhere near to be seen.

When I didn't respond, Reaper pressed me for more detail. "Kim?"

"Does he have to be the one to watch me? Can't you get someone else to do it?" I gritted my teeth. I really didn't need anyone to watch me to begin with.

"You feel comfortable around him."

"No. No, I don't. In fact," I turned to look up at him, "I would prefer anyone else watching me. Why can't Dad do it?"

Reaper scoffed and crossed his arms. "He is too busy doing whatever it is he is doing."

"What about Brad?"

"I need my VP."

"Well, don't you need Trigger? Surely he is good for something else other than just stalking the crap out of me."

"I trust Trigger with you. And if he is with you, he isn't pissing me off."

I scowled at him. "So I get to be pissed off instead?"

He smirked at me. "Come on, you two will make up."

"There is nothing to make up over. He is... him." That was the trouble to begin with. I turned back to the meat, having burnt some of the steaks. I flipped them quickly.

"He loves you."

I looked up, seeing him across the lot with a girl under one arm and beer in his hand. Just as I expected, he was laughing and having a gay old time.

"Yeah, of course he does. Because that's what love looks like." I pointed the tongs at them, then started to pick up the meat and dump it onto plates. "Here, do something useful and put these plates on the table. I'm going to bed."

I handed Reaper the meat and he frowned, looking at me, like he was going to say something. But instead, he nodded his head and walked off with the plates.

I wiped my hands on a dishtowel, turned the BBQ off and turned around, walking straight into a hard chest.

I gasped as a cold beer spilled all over my chest. It was cold. It was wet. And it was completely unwanted.

"Oh shit, I'm sorry," a guy I had never seen before started to apologize. Clearly not thinking about it, he reached out and attempted to dry my wet shirt with the sleeve of his sweatshirt.

I slapped his hands off my breasts. It didn't help I was wearing a white t-shirt and no bra underneath.

He noticed.

"Shit, sorry."

I scoffed and started to walk around him. Having a see-through top on around so many men wasn't going to go down well. I stepped to the left and he met my step, smirking down at me.

"But I'm not sorry about the view though."

"PIG!" I couldn't believe he just said that. Yes, my top was see-through. Thanks to him!

I wanted to wipe the smirk off his face with my fist.

"Here, hold this." He handed me what was left of his beer.

It was an automatic response to take it. So here I was, holding his beer, with my top see-through. I watched him take off his leather vest and then his sweatshirt.

Revealing him in a t-shirt. He handed me his sweatshirt.

"Here, take it."

"I was going to bed anyway, so don't worry about it."

"Yeah, but if you go to bed, that means I can't buy you a beer to say I'm sorry."

"Considering we don't charge for beer, I'd be interested to know where you were buying this beer from."

"Come on, let me make it up to you." He glanced over my shoulder. "And if I were you, I'd put the sweatshirt on. Before the men start circling."

He had a point. It was bad enough being clothed around them. I took the sweatshirt from his hand and slipped it on. It was huge on me, going down to my knees.

"Now that you are covered, how about that drink?" He gave me a charming smile I didn't think many women had said no to. He was charming. He was tall. He was handsome. Yep. Not many women would say no to him.

Even in this light, I could pick out his chiseled facial features, his strong jaw line, the tattoo that ran up one side of his neck, the way his blue eyes were twitching with desire. His hair was half shaved on the sides and longer on top. He was good looking and as he slipped his vest back on, I noticed one patch on his vest. President.

I knew most of the presidents. But I didn't know him. Why hadn't I seen him around before today? Seeing as I was feeding most of them, and was brought up meeting most of them throughout my life. But he was a complete stranger.

"Why don't I know you?" I tilted my head, still studying him.

"The more important question is, why don't I know you?" He smirked back at me. "So you on for that drink?"

I glanced over my shoulder. Trigger was still with that girl. Why did I let it bother me? "Yeah, why not?" I finally said, running a hand through my hair.

I was still glaring over my shoulder at Trigger when the guy came back with two beers. He gestured with his head for me to follow him. And I did. I was expecting us to just blend into the crowd of bikers. Instead, he peeled us off to a corner and an empty picnic table. He handed me a beer then stopped in front of me.

His hand went to my stomach and I was about to scream when his hand went into the pocket of the sweatshirt.

"Just need my smokes, sweetheart. Don't stress." He pulled them out of the pocket. And I took a steady breath in. Why did that make my blood spike?

There were still a hundred or so bikers and their friends in the lot. But I felt like we were separate from them.

He sat down at the picnic table and cracked open a beer. "So, what's your name?" He lit up a cigarette.

"What's your name?" I fired back at him. "And you still haven't explained why I haven't seen you around here."

"You don't like answering questions yourself." He blew out a mouthful of smoke and smirked at me again. "Trent, and the reason, sweetheart, is I just rode in this afternoon. Reaper called my charter in last week but it's a long ride to get here."

"So you've been on the road for the last week?"

"Yep. So what's your name?"

I chewed my bottom lip. Why did it seem like a big deal if I told him? I was so used to people just knowing who I was. I never had to introduce myself to anyone. I took a deep breath in. "Kim."

"So, you hooked up with any man here?" He handed me the cigarette.

I took it from him, slowly putting it to my lips and sucking on it lightly. He was testing the waters, making sure he wasn't stepping on anyone's property. Not that I belonged to anyone to begin with.

"If I was, do you really think I'd be over here talking to you?" I handed him the cigarette back. "Trent. That's not a biker name."

"Don't have one of those."

"A president without a biker name. Interesting."

"So what's a girl like you doing at a party like this?" He tilted his head, trying to read my reaction.

"I live here."

"So you're a club girl?"

I laughed, nearly choking on my beer. "You saying I look like one?"

I felt like his eyes were going through me. "No, you don't. Which is why things aren't adding up." He put his beer down and counted on his fingers. "You live here. But you said you don't have a guy. You don't look like a club girl. Yet something is telling me, despite all this, you are loyal to the club."

"What has you saying that?" Him picking up that I was loyal to the club threw me. He barely knew me.

"Your shirt." The smirk was back on his face. "I got a good look."

"Right." I blushed. My Satan's Sons top. Well, at least he noticed the logo and not just my breasts. "Glad to see you looked so closely."

"What can I say? I liked the view." He laughed, and it lit up his whole face, causing me to laugh too.

"You and any other man," I added.

"Yeah, you are right there." He took a large gulp of his beer. "So, do you know the girl who went missing?"

That sobered me the fuck up. The smile that was on my face dropped and I found myself finishing my beer instead of answering. Abby wasn't missing. She was kidnapped.

Trent arched an eyebrow. "Did I hit a sore point?"

I put my empty beer on the table. "Something like that."

"So you knew her?"

"Know her," I corrected him. "And yes. I'm her twin. And she isn't missing. She was taken." It was the first time I had admitted I was Abby's twin. Usually people saw us together and just knew. All through school, throughout our life, people just knew. There was a difference between her being missing and being taken. It wasn't like she ran away.

His charming smile dried up. "That explains why you live here then."

I nodded my head.

"So you're Roach's daughter?"

"Yep." If he had even been mildly interested, he wouldn't be now. I came with strings. Big and strong ones. Heck, being Reaper's sister-in-law added to my reputation. I was about to get up and head inside when he spoke, stopping me.

"So what's your favorite color?"

I frowned. "What?"

"What's your favorite color?" His sober expression from before was gone. That charming smile was back on his face.

"Emerald blue, I guess." I looked at him in complete amazement. What a random question. Just after finding out I was Roach's daughter and the sister of the girl taken, he wanted to know my favorite color?

"Emerald blue." He nodded his head. "So what do you do with yourself? Do you work?" Trent finished his beer. "Should have gotten more of these."

"At the moment?"

He nodded his head.

"I look after Tyson."

"That's Reaper's son, right?"

"Yes. My nephew." I wasn't embarrassed about looking after Tyson. As far as I cared, he was the only man in my life. Saying you look after a newborn would scare a lot of men away. But not Trent. He just looked at me more intently.

"He is lucky to have you," Trent said with a smile. "So you're close with Reaper?"

"He is my brother-in-law. And I do care for his kid all day. So yes."

"Good, 'cause I might need you to pull some strings so he doesn't kill me."

"Why would Reaper want to kill you?" I couldn't think of one reason for Trent to be on Reaper's bad side.

"Took me a while to get here." Trent ran a hand through his hair. "He expected me here last week."

"Trust me when I say this, he has had other things on his mind."

"So one missing charter might have gone unnoticed?"

I laughed and shook my head. "No. No way. Reaper will know. He knows all."

"Scary fucking dude."

"He isn't that bad." When it came to Reaper he had two sides. And not a lot of people got to see the softer side of him. But then again, I knew his reputation. Everyone did. "Well, thanks for the drink."

"Next one I'll pay for." He stood up. "Let me walk you to your room."

"You don't have to. I know this place better than you." We started to walk toward the crowd together.

"Yeah, but with all the drunks around I'd feel more comfortable knowing you got there without being harassed."

"I'm used to it. Most guys know I pack a mean right hook." Most guys stayed away because I was Roach's daughter. I was off limits. The only biker who had dared go there was Trigger and that hadn't turned out so well.

"Well, I hit harder." He winked at me. "Plus this way I know where to go when I want to find you."

"I'm easy to find." We were in the crowd now. I didn't go stiff when I felt his hand on my lower back. Instead, it sent waves and bubbles of excitement through me. That a man would actually be seen with me was one thing, but the fact he was willing to touch me and not be scared of what might come his way said a lot to me.

He looked tough. Like he could take a few good punches and then come out the other end swinging.

"Kim? I thought you were going to bed?" Reaper spotted me and stopped us as soon as we walked into the clubhouse. His eyes hardened when he looked at me. "Tell me you are wearing fucking shorts."

Oh. Oops. I lifted the sweatshirt up, showing my shorts. "Yep. Shorts on."

"Trent." Reaper's eyes darted off me and onto him. "Expected you last week." This was the side of Reaper everyone knew, the terrifying and scary side. Most men would crumble, but Trent smiled.

"Took longer, brother," Trent shrugged it off. "Would have called but knew you had more important things to deal with."

I could tell by Reaper's body language he was about to serve Trent a new one. So I cut in.

"Trent was just walking me to bed. So I'll see you in the morning. Seven, yeah?" I redirected the conversation.

Reaper's eyes went from Trent to me. His eyes glanced at the hand Trent had on my back. Reaper was chewing on words, and I was sure he was going to rant at Trent regardless. But he nodded his head.

"Seven. But if you sleep in, don't stress. I'm not planning on leaving till eight." Reaper said the words to me but he was glaring at Trent.

"I'll be up early. Have the girls organize breakfast for you all before you leave. Night, Reaper." I gripped Trent's hand and pulled him away.

I could literally feel Reaper's eyes on us as we walked through the thick crowd.

"Nice save," he whispered in my ear and I smiled.

"You can thank me later." I was saying that when we walked past Trigger and his blonde for the night. His eyes were on fire as they locked with mine for a split second. Pity for him. I didn't care. I wasn't even jealous of the woman under his arm.

I had set my limits on him and only him for years. And tonight I realized there were other guys out there. I glanced down at my hand, which was linked with Trent's. He knew I came with strings. Yet here he was holding my hand.

***

Abby

Strength. At times you feel like you have zero, that you're weak. You think you know what your limits are. Strength was something I had a lot of right now. I wouldn't let him beat me. I had to be strong. For my family. I knew what it was like to grow up without a mother. I knew the pain at every birthday and vacation. I wouldn't let that happen to Tyson. And I wouldn't let Reaper be a widow. Not when we just started our life together. I was going to be there for my son's birthdays and I was going to be there for my wedding anniversaries.

Before this happened, I thought I knew how strong I was.

That was before now. Now I knew what strength was. And I had a hell of a lot of it.

I looked in the mirror and saw a sickly reflection. He was wearing me thin. But I wasn't breaking. No, he couldn't break me even if he wanted to. I wouldn't let him. I was strong. I was going to survive this. And after I had, I was going to make sure Jake Frankston had a slow death, hopefully at the hands of Reaper.

I was locked in a master bedroom. The room was free from anything that I could use to hurt him. He had made sure of that. I was in the en-suite bathroom when I heard the door being unlocked. Considering it had been two days since anyone had checked on me or given me food, I was interested to know he wanted.

The real bitch of the situation was Jake wasn't ugly. He could have whatever woman he wanted. But he only wanted one woman and Reaper had killed her. I knew I was in this situation because of Reaper. I knew I could die at Jake's hands as well. But I also knew he wanted me for something. Otherwise he would have shot me in the car.

Jake's hand pushed open the bathroom door. He stood in the doorway, tall and demonlike. He didn't look drunk. Normally, when he was drunk, he would beat me. Last time he used his fists till they were bleeding. Did it hurt? Yes. But I was strong. I had to be to get through this.

"Food." Jake looked me up and down. "Downstairs, now."

"I'm not hungry." My stomach was growling for food. But I wasn't going to let him have the pleasure.

"Haven't eaten in two days. Did you really think I would let you starve to death?" His tone mocked me.

"I think when I'm going to die, you will make sure it is hands on," I fired back at him, knowing how a sick and twisted man like him works. He was going to make sure it was bloody and painful. Dying slowly didn't seem like an option.

He tilted his head. "You're right. Now, come eat. I have guests."

"Maybe one of them will have a problem with you kidnapping a girl with the intent to kill her."

He laughed. "No, they will just ask if they can watch."

I crossed my arms, glaring at him. "Like I said, I'm not hungry."

"You either eat or I'll force the food down your throat."

I would like to see him try. There was one thing he knew about me. I was stubborn. But having food forced into my face wouldn't be pleasant.

"Fine, I'll eat." I uncrossed my arms and he held the door open for me as I walked out. I hadn't been outside of this room. So I didn't know what I was in for. Why was he all of a sudden letting me out of the room?

I paused at the door. I was so used to seeing it locked that seeing it slightly ajar made me want to bolt. I was fast. I could make it to the front door before him. Sure, there were stairs and I didn't know where I was running to, but I could do it. Now was an opportunity.

"The house has central locking. You couldn't get out a window or door if you wanted to. Without a code of course," Jake's voice said behind me, as if he was reading my thoughts.

I was forced to turn around and look at him. "Well then, you lead the way. Seeing that I don't know where to go." I stepped out of his way.

"Smart girl." He patted me on the head as he walked past. With great regret, I followed him. The room I was locked in was styled with expensive taste. And one look outside the room told me the rest of the house was the same. Jake had expensive taste. I followed him down a flight of wooden spiral stairs that overlooked an open living and dining room and kitchen.

At the table, there were two men. One young, in his early twenties. The other was older, gray hair and a long gray beard. They were both watching me.

"This is Abby. She will be cooking us dinner." Jake stopped at the bottom of the stairs, grabbing my hand. "I know you are used to cooking. Considering I hate cooking, I thought you would be up for the task."

Maybe there was some way to give him food poisoning. "Sure." I gave him a fake smile.

I snatched my hand from his and made a beeline for the kitchen. It was large and had an expensive marble top. Jake obviously made a lot of money selling his dirty drugs. I walked to the fridge, opening the double doors. To my surprise, it was fully stocked. For someone who didn't like to cook, he sure did have a lot of food that need preparing.

Men liked meat. That was one thing I knew about them. Cooking for the club always involved meat. So I was guessing these men would be the same.

I pulled out the meat and headed for the stove. Seeing as I didn't know where anything was in this kitchen, it was going to be a nightmare. I dumped the meat on the bench and my eyes flicked to the knives.

If there was only Jake, I would stand a chance. I looked up. The three of them were at the table, gambling and playing cards. I had to think smart. Going at him with a knife wasn't going to work. I turned the knob to the stove on.

Now to find a saucepan.

I had to be strong and smart.

***

I cooked them food. They ate and I actually ate something as well. I was full for the first time in days. I would prefer physical torture over what they were doing to me. Starvation was the worst. Being hit was one thing, but at least then you could deal with the pain.

"So, Abby, you ready to play a game?" Jake pushed his plate away from him and reached behind him, pulling out a gun.

I swallowed hard. What if this was it? My last meal. My regrets were endless. Would Tyson know how much I loved him? Would Reaper ever recover from losing me? Would Dad be OK? Would Kim cope without me?

"I never told you how my wife died, did I?" Jake kept talking.

I shook my head.

"Painless. One bullet between the eyes." Jake looked me in the eye, a twisted expression on his face. Some would call it pain. But I knew this man wasn't capable of pain.

He took the bullets out of the gun. It was an old revolver. Then he put one bullet back in, spinning the barrel.

"I believe in fate. So let's see if you will be as lucky as my wife, or I have my wish for a slower death." He slid the gun across the table to me.

"What do you want me to do?" I didn't understand. He was giving me a loaded gun. Well, it had one bullet in it.

"Simple, sweetheart. Put it to your temple and pull the fucking trigger." Jake's words sent ice through my veins. When I didn't pick it up, he yelled, "NOW."

My hands were sweaty as I picked it up. So this was it?

"Jake, you sure you want it to happen this way?" the old man spoke, seeing how upset I was getting.

"BILLY, SHUT THE FUCK UP!" Jake shouted at him. "Abby. Gun to the temple now."

My hand was shaking as I picked up the old gun. I closed my eyes, taking a deep breath. If this was going to happen, there was nothing I could do. I put the gun to my temple. And I prayed to god to look after my husband and son. Give Kade the strength to be a father. I knew he could do it. He just had to have faith in himself.

I let one long breath out.

Then I pulled the trigger.

Chapter 5

Kim

Tyson wasn't settling. To say he was unsettled was an understatement. He was wailing and I didn't know what to do.

"Where's Reaper?" I asked Dad, who, for some unknown reason, was actually still in the clubhouse, while every other man had cleared out as soon as the wailing started. Did it bother Dad? Nope. He was drinking his coffee and reading the paper as if it was the most peaceful place to be.

Then again, everyone else could be avoiding the place cause of last night...

"In the gym." Dad looked up from his coffee. "Where else would he be?"

Of course he would be there. Reaper was a living, breathing machine at the moment. He had given up drinking and drugs and was training more than twice a day. I knew why he was doing it. He wanted to be in the best possible shape when he found the bastards who took Abby.

He was taking it seriously, too. When he wasn't following leads or being with Tyson he was in the gym.

I got Tyson out of the stroller and headed for the gym. Maybe Reaper could settle him.

I was walking past Abby's bedroom when I stopped. Maybe Tyson needed his mom?

I opened the door. The room was dead. Reaper had moved everything into his old room. I walked in with the wailing baby.

Walking into the closet, I flicked on the lights. It hit me hard. Abby should be here. It smelt like her. It was suffocating.

I pulled down one of her sweatshirts off a hanger and walked back into the bedroom. Laying it down, I placed Tyson in the middle of it and wrapped it around him, picking him up.

Then I turned off the lights and left the shell of the room that used to be full of life.

Tyson stopped sobbing. I went to the end of the hall to Reaper's room and walked in. I placed him in the crib. Maybe he would sleep.

I hoped to god it would work. It had been two straight hours of wailing. I didn't know what was wrong with him but he was working up a temperature from it all. I gave him something for that. But I doubted it would work. Then, for the first time in hours, Tyson was quiet.

Full on. Silent.

I sighed and fell back on Reaper's bed. It was the middle of the day and now that Tyson was silent, my thoughts decided to kick into overdrive. About what happened last night...

Why did I feel all giddy inside? Like a teenager who had just been kissed for the first time. I remember my first kiss but still, that had nothing on what I was feeling right now. I had sweaty palms, my thoughts were racing, but at the same time, my mind was cloudy. All this because of attention from one man?

Trent.

Kind of sweet.

No, he was more than sweet.

All he did was walk me to my room. But the way he treated me was like I was something special. As if I shouldn't have to put up with the drunken sleazes as I walked to bed.

I was so fixed on his kindness I jumped when my door swung open.

My good mood went sour right away.

"What the hell are you doing? Coming in here like you own the joint?" I crossed my arms and did my best to be serious when my

head was in the clouds, thinking about what it was like to be with a guy who didn't treat you like you would always be there.

"What were you doing with Trent?" *Trigger was drunk. Angry. Intoxicated. What was new?*

The only thing he was missing was the girl under his arm.

"Not really any of your business. The only person I owe answers to is Reaper and I already gave them."

"Why you wearing his top?"

"Why aren't you with the blonde?"

"Fuck it, KIM! Don't play games with me!"

"Says YOU! You consider me a game. You are hot and cold. Like I said yesterday, you and I are nothing." *I was trying to keep calm, but that went out the window the moment his eyes narrowed at me. As if I had said the one thing to piss him off.*

"You like this guy, huh?"

I scoffed. "I barely know him! We talked, that's it."

Trigger looked at me with a look he had never given me before. Possession. I saw it in his eyes. As if someone had just touched something that was his and now he was pissed: beyond words, totally fuming, pissed.

He took an unsteady step toward me, pointing a finger. "If that was 'just talking,' well I'll make sure there is no more talking."

I opened my mouth to start yelling at him, but he spun round and stormed off before I could. He better not be doing what I thought he was about to do.

I groaned. Fucking hell, Trigger.

I quickly followed in his wake. I started to run to catch him. But he was on a mission. I got to the stairs at the same time he was at the bottom. Basically jumping the last few, I was pushing my way through the crowd when I heard him.

"Hey, Trent!" *Trigger's voice stood out from the laughter and conversations that were going on. You could hear the anger.*

Oh god, someone stop his big fat mouth! He was drunk, so I knew reason was gone.

"What?"

I just pushed past Bones in time to see Trigger's fist connect with Trent's jaw. I gasped. The cracking sound that followed did not sound healthy. No, screw that, it was disgusting. It likely caused the kind of pain one would be knocked out from.

I was expecting Trent to pass out. But he didn't. I think what happened next was worse. Trent took a couple of unsteady steps backward. Then, as soon as he regained his balance, he charged at Trigger.

Both of them were going at it. Somehow, fists that missed hit nearby men and then a brawl started out in the bar area. Every man was going at it. But all I could focus on was the cause of brawl. Fucking Trigger.

I was being pushed about as men went at it. All drunk. All pissed off from the long day. And now they had a reason to fight, thanks to fucking Trigger.

Where was Dad?

Where was Reaper?

They should be breaking this up.

Without thinking about it, I pushed through the fighting men and headed for the cause of this spitfire.

"Trigger, stop it!" I grabbed his back, trying my best to separate them. But they turned. So now I was behind Trent. I pulled on Trent's arm. "STOP IT!"

No one was listening, especially not Trigger and Trent, who were fighting blindly.

A gunshot went off, causing everyone to panic and freeze, except Trigger and Trent, who were still going at it. Trigger's right hook went flying at Trent again, and this time Trent was quicker and moved out of the way, unluckily for me. I was right in the firing line.

Tears filled my eyes. Blood filled my mouth. I flung my hand over my mouth.

Trigger's eyes went wide when he realized what he had done. But before he could open his mouth, Reaper was there.

"What happened?" Reaper had somehow spotted me in the crowd. I had tears running down my cheeks and blood creeping out the side of my mouth. I noticed he had his gun out. Looked like he

was the one to break it up. His eyes darted between Trent and Trigger who were both puffing and looking furious. "Who the fuck hit Kim?"

I spat out a mouth full of blood and wiped my tears. "It doesn't matter." There was no point in Reaper getting involved. Trent had already done a good job at messing Trigger up.

I wiped the side of my mouth and stepped forward. Tears were still running down my cheeks. As soon as I wiped them away, they were back. The pain was crippling and went through my whole body.

"Kim I didn't mean to–"

"You know what, Lucas, just stay away from me. Don't look at me. Don't speak to me. As far as I'm concerned, you are dead." I had never called Trigger by his real name. I had never once disrespected him. "You're a jerk."

With that said, I pushed past him, leaving him speechless. I had made it to the stairs when Reaper stopped me.

"You want me to handle it?" He was saying that like I hadn't done just that. I had handled it. I was done with Trigger. He had always emotionally hurt me, but this time it was physical.

"I did. Night, Reaper."

"Put ice on it," he shouted at my back as I walked away. I just wanted to disappear.

My fingers ran over my swollen, cut lip. A bruise had formed around it. It was an ugly brown color. Not even makeup would cover it.

"You alright?"

I sprung up off Reaper's bed. Shit, how long had I been in here for? I glanced at Tyson, who was sound asleep.

I looked back at Reaper. He was sweaty and shirtless, puffing. He was pushing his body to the limit. And it was showing. He was even bigger now, if that was possible.

"Yeah, I'm fine. Just getting Tyson to sleep." I ran a hand through my hair and straightened myself up. "Sorry, um, for crashing your room."

Reaper's eyes went from Tyson to me. "You didn't put ice on it, did you?"

I pursed my lips. "No."

He scoffed and went to his dresser, putting his rings back on. "You sore?"

"I'll be fine."

"Trigger been near you?"

"I think he is attached to living too much."

"So I take it he was the one to hit you?" Reaper was fishing for me to come clean. I might hate Trigger right now. That didn't mean I wanted him in trouble with Reaper.

Then I found myself saying what I was thinking. "Doesn't matter." And it really didn't. Trigger would be sleeping off his hangover with most of the other members. And I was moving on. At least that was what I was telling myself.

Chapter 6

Reaper

The breeze was burning my skin alive, the sun beaming down at over 100 degrees. The guard dogs were panting in the shade. I was topless, with my holsters on and the shorts I was wearing were weighed down from the extra two guns I was carrying, plus all the keys. The metal pole I was leaning against was burning my arm, so I straightened up. I could feel the eyes on me. So why would any sane person be out in this weather, when inside was nice and air-conditioned?

Because there was a tow truck backing into our driveway.

Usually, this wouldn't matter at a garage. But it mattered today because of what was on the back of it.

Abby's car. What was left of it. The police had finally released it. Why they had it for so fucking long was beyond me. They didn't find one fingerprint.

Seeing it sent a sucker punch to my guts, making me nauseous and dizzy at the same time. The what-ifs hit me again. What if I had ridden with her? What if I hadn't left her? I would have been there. I would have stopped this all from happening.

Instead, I let my wife drive alone with my newborn son, knowing I had a man on the hunt for me.

When it came down to it, it was all my fault. Now I was paying the price.

"I'll help them get it off." Brad stomped on a cigarette and walked over to them.

Nodding my head, I was about to do the same when Kim walked out, with black fucking hair.

Nearly every single man was out watching the show, so Kim was darting through them with Tyson on her hip. I knew right away she would be avoiding me.

I grabbed my shirt off the table and weaved through the crowd. She was putting Tyson in his car seat when I got to her.

One glance from her and I could see the dread on her face.

Like I expected, she was avoiding me.

"Kim."

"Reaper."

"Want to explain the hair?"

She slammed the door shut and ignored me. Opening the driver side door, she was about to slam that shut too, but my hand caught it in time.

Her eyes narrowed and I was ready for the spray she was about to give me. The black hair shaping her face was slightly shorter and I knew the hate in her eyes wasn't directed at me. She had been in a foul mood ever since getting punched by Trigger.

"I'm going to the drug store. So either get in or get lost."

My gut was telling me for some reason not to let her go by herself. Considering she had basically scared Trigger into staying away from her, she had no one following her. I glanced in the passenger side window. Tyson was wiggling.

Yeah, fuck it. I wasn't letting her go anywhere by herself, no matter how much she hated having a tag on her.

"Looks like I'm going to the drug store too." I closed her door and walked around, putting my shirt on.

She could be as furious as she wanted. It didn't bother me and it didn't scare me like it did the others. I swear I had never seen so many grown-ass men avoid one woman. Considering she was in charge of their every need, they all seemed happy with the burnt food, late money and lack of club girls. Even the girls had disappeared.

Yep. It was fair to say Kim's attitude was costing the club.

So it was my job to pull her back in line.

As I climbed into her car, she didn't wait for me to buckle in as she took off.

Yeah, I had no fucking idea how I was meant to pull her back into line. After all, she didn't belong to the club. She didn't have to stay. She didn't have to do what she did for the club. Hell, her father had washed his hands of the club, basically, leaving me to deal with more shit. So how was I supposed to get her to calm the hell down?

***

Kim

I rocked the stroller out in front of the pharmacy. Reaper was paying for the scripts and I had all the drugs stuffed under the stroller. Running errands for the club didn't bother me. What bothered me was Trigger.

The fact he was avoiding me annoyed me. So did the fact he had moved on from me so easily. Heck, he never was on me. I was so busy cursing silent swear words about Trigger I hadn't noticed an older woman cooing over Tyson.

"He is adorable," she said, straightening up and addressing me.

"Thanks." I was used to getting comments about Tyson. He had Abby's eyes and Kade's dark hair, making the most adorable baby ever. I was a very proud aunty.

"I always knew Kade would have a stunning child."

I nodded my head. Then it hit me. What the fuck? Did I hear her correctly? Frowning, I looked back at the woman I had given no attention to before.

"Excuse me?" I said, still not sure I heard what she said.

She looked me in the eye. "I said, I always knew Kade would have a stunning child. Look at Tyson. He is the spitting image of him. Apart from the eyes. They're from his mother."

Yep. I had heard her correctly. "You know Reaper?" I didn't know this lady. She wasn't an old lady I knew. She was a stranger, a complete stranger. Yet she knew Kade and Abby.

She was using his first name too. Like she had permission.

"How do you know Reaper? Sorry, it's just I've never seen you before. And I normally know everyone around the club."

She opened her mouth but before she could speak, Reaper was at my side.

"What the fuck are you doing here?" He was cold. He was mean and very rude. I hadn't seen him treat a woman like that before. His tone was enough to send any sane person running. But this woman just looked at him with a smile.

"Kade, we came to help." She moved from the stroller to him.

"Well, you can fuck off. And while you're at it, tell him the same." Reaper took the stroller from me. "Walk, Kim. Now."

"But–"

"Kim, now."

I frowned, looking at the woman. She had to be in her fifties, maybe early sixties.

"NOW, KIM!" Reaper yelled, causing me to jump.

Right, move.

I started to walk away from her, but Reaper stopped, turning back to her.

"Stay away from Kim and Tyson. I'll find out if you come near them." His tone sent ice through my veins. I would have hated to know how she was feeling right this second.

Before I could say anything, Reaper gripped my arm and pulled me along beside him, not stopping till we hit the parking lot.

"Just what I fucking needed," he muttered under his breath, not expecting me to hear him.

"Who was she?"

"No one."

"Didn't seem like no one."

"Drop it, Kim."

We came to a stop next to my car. I put a hand on my hip, wondering whether I should go for the kill and find out, or if I should leave it.

He unclipped Tyson out of the stroller and looked at me.

"Fuck me. Not that look."

"I haven't said anything," I defended myself. Just because he could read my twin so well didn't mean he could read me so well. "But if I asked, would you tell me who that was?"

He grunted. "Unlock the car, Kim."

"You haven't answered my question."

"No. No, I wouldn't tell you who that is. Now unlock the car."

I pressed the button and the car unlocked. He might think that by doing that I was taking his no as an answer. But I wasn't. Nope. We had a long car ride back and I was going to annoy the hell out of him till he gave me answers.

"You can drive." I tossed him the car keys after he buckled Tyson in and closed the door. "I have to focus on something."

"If that is getting answers from me, Kim, it isn't going to happen."

"You say that now. But I don't give up on a fight. I'm not one to tap out when it gets bloody." I walked around the car and climbed in.

I heard Reaper groan before I got in the car. He knew I wasn't going to give up. If he was smart and if Abby had taught him anything, he would give in.

***

We pulled into the lot. Like normal, it was crawling with bikers and their families. God, it was hot today, I thought, as soon as I stepped out of the air-conditioned car.

Reaper had Tyson out.

Reaper hadn't budged with his whole 'not telling me,' even though I'd used every trick in the book.

I was glaring at his broad back as we walked to the clubhouse. Abby really hadn't trained him well. He should cave just by getting 'the look.' Instead, he was as cold as ever.

Reaper walked into the clubhouse and I expected him to hand me Tyson. Instead, he spotted someone in the club and charged across the room.

I had to break into a run to catch him.

"REAPER, what are you doing?" I yelled at his back.

"WHAT THE FUCK ARE YOU DOING HERE!" he screamed at someone.

I reached his side and a smirk spread across my lips. Maybe I would get my answer. The woman we had seen earlier was sitting at a table next to Dad and a man I had never seen before.

"I invited them." Dad looked up at Reaper with a look I knew too well. It was the look he would give Abby and me when he wanted us to get lost, when he had done something that he knew would upset us.

One glance at Reaper and I knew shit was about to get messy.

"Reaper. Tyson." I grabbed his arm. "And calm the hell down." I made him remember he was carrying a newborn. Why was he fuming? Like he was about to knock my dad out, and then the woman and man. He looked like a charging bull. "Who are these people?"

Dad was smirking. Reaper handed me Tyson and, with a face of disgust, he looked at the two strangers.

"They're my parents."

Chapter 7

Abby

Jake's sick game of Russian roulette was just the beginning of my torments. I thought starvation was bad. That was nothing to loading a bullet into a chamber and spinning it. Jake's little game followed every meal.

I knew my days were numbered.

One day that bullet would go off, shooting through my brain and ending my life.

"Abby?"

My eyes creased tightly. Why was he here so early?

I knew it was early because I had watched the sun rise only a few minutes ago. I wasn't sleeping. Couldn't sleep. Not here. Sometimes I would pass out from exhaustion. I was expecting that to happen because it had been days since I slept.

The door swung open and I stayed seated on the couch, looking out the window.

"You are up early."

I ignored him.

"I have a proposal for you."

I scoffed. I doubted very much he was letting me go.

"I'm going to leave this door unlocked from now on. You have free range of the house and that way I won't be forgetting your meals."

I turned to face him, taking my eyes off the bright sunrise.

"But then we might miss your favorite game," I said sarcastically.

I watched his lips twitch up. "Don't worry. I'll make sure we still play."

I rolled my eyes and looked back out the window. I wondered if Kade was seeing this sunrise. It was beautiful.

"You can't get out anyway, so you might as well have free use of the house."

"What, aren't you scared I'll find your stash and kill you?" I said, still looking out the window. I was sick today. Physically. Not because he had hit me. He hadn't hit me for days. No, I was in pain from Tyson. I was bleeding as well. I didn't know if that was normal. But it was making me lightheaded.

He laughed. "Don't keep guns in the house. Unless they are holstered to me."

He was forgetting about his favorite gun. The one he would give me and force me to put to my temple.

"Whatever." I knew there was a slim chance I would ever get out of here alive. Why was he giving me free range of the house?

"Come on, I'll give you a tour." Jake was actually being nice. Why? What did he want? I turned to face him again, taking my eyes off that beautiful sunrise. What had he done? I narrowed my eyes at him.

He arched his eyebrows. "You coming or what?"

My head turned to look at the chest of drawers that was across the room. I had spent hours looking at the photos on it. They were the only entertaining thing in the room.

"Was that your wife?" I said, nodding my head to the photo of him and a woman with black hair.

His eyes flashed to the photo and I saw the grief on his face.

"Yes," he spat out.

"What was her name?" I asked. I had so many questions about this woman. Her life was going to cost me mine. It was only natural.

"Rebecca."

"She was beautiful," I stated the obvious. "Did she agree to your type of life?"

He laughed, causing me to look at him. He walked into the room. "No, she was against it."

"Hard to live the life you live without support."

"She supported me. Just didn't agree to the drugs and, well, the women."

"So you are one of those men." I rolled my eyes, starting to understand his character a bit more.

"No. I never cheated on her. Didn't look at another woman from the age of eighteen. We fell in love in high school and never separated."

"High school sweethearts. Cute."

"She was a schoolteacher."

I frowned. This wasn't adding up. Dad had said she was a bottom feeder. I expected a hardened criminal with baggage. Not a schoolteacher.

"High school or primary?"

"Primary."

That made it worse. It meant she was good with kids. A beautiful schoolteacher. She wasn't sounding like the woman who'd deserved to be killed.

"Now do you want a tour of the house or not?" Jake changed the subject. He stood tall and dominant in the room.

"Sure." I went to get up, but my head started to spin. I reached out for the couch to catch myself but it was too late. My mind went white.

***

"Extreme blood loss."

"Is that normal?"

"No."

"Well, what do you do?"

"Nothing we can do. Maybe an infusion if it doesn't ease. But she should be seen by a specialist. I'm just a GP."

I opened my eyes to find Jake hovering to my left, standing with a man I assumed was a doctor by the bag he was carrying. He was checking my pulse.

"Abby, hello." He smiled down at me.

He must be on Jake's payroll. "Hi."

"How long ago did you give birth?"

I attempted to count the days in my head but they were a blur now. "I don't know." God, how long had it been since I seen Kade? How long ago did I have Tyson? I knew it was over a week, maybe two.

"Sixteen days," Jake answered for me, crossing his arms. "Why didn't you tell me you were sick?"

"I didn't think you would care." I was honest. If he wasn't forcing a gun to my head, he was beating me. Sure, he hadn't touched me in the past two days but I didn't know why. I didn't know what had changed.

"I'm not a monster." He shook his head. "Where are her pills?"

"Iron and painkillers should be all she needs. But again, if it doesn't ease, I would suggest she see a specialist."

He was actually going to give me painkillers? What had changed?

"Right. Thanks, Jeff. You know your way out," Jake said nicely. Jeff left, leaving me alone with Jake.

"You feeling like you can walk?"

I sat up on the bed. How did I get here? "Hold on a minute. How did I get on the bed?"

"I carried you."

"You touched me?"

"Yes."

One question ran through my mind. "Why?" Why didn't he just leave me on the floor and lock me in here?

"Because you were sick," he said slowly, as if I was stupid.

"But you shouldn't care about that. Hell, why didn't you just leave me there to bleed out? At least then you could claim I died of natural causes."

An expression captured his face and I couldn't pinpoint what it was. Regret? Grief? I tilted my head, studying him.

"I have a woman who does my shopping. She comes today. Write a list and I'll make sure she gets you what you want."

Did he have a split personality?

"I don't want anything." I didn't expect anything from him. Nor did I want anything.

"Right?" He arched his eyebrows at me. "Because I can think of a list of shit you need, like clothes for one."

"No point changing when I'm going to die anyway." I sat upright on the bed. But he was right. I did need feminine products, considering I was bleeding.

"Come on, you can write a list downstairs." He gestured for me to follow him. He sat my pills on the dresser beside the bed.

I followed him downstairs, surprised to see the house clean. The table wasn't covered in beer bottles and cards.

"This is the main living room. Guess you know that. The formal sitting room is through there." He pointed his arm toward a room beside large, arched double doors. We came to a stop in the kitchen. It was all open living, walking through the dining room into the kitchen. "Pen and paper." He picked them up from the kitchen island and put them in front of me. "She only comes once a week so don't forget anything."

I stared down at the notepad and pen as he walked around me and went to leave.

"Wait, do you want me to do the grocery list as well?" I turned and said to him. I was usually in charge of cooking his meals.

"Nah, that's pre-done." He stopped and I could hear a phone vibrating. He patted his pockets down.

"OK." I turned back to the notepad and picked up the pen. I guess I could spend his money. So I started the list.

***

There was something about Billy that reminded me of Dad. Maybe it was his short responses and the fact he grunted more than spoke. When he did speak, it was short answers, and he ate like he hadn't seen food in his life.

I took my eyes off the poker game and went back to the pork I was cooking. My supplies arrived this afternoon. I admit it was nice to be in a fresh change of clothes that wasn't covered in blood from the beatings.

I caught a reflection of myself in the mirrored splashback. God, I looked terrible. I had bruising under my eye and down my jaw, and a cut lip. But that was nothing to the bruises that covered my body.

I killed the heat on the stove and dished up the meat and veggies onto three plates.

Billy, Andrew and Jake.

Billy and Andrew were always here, either playing poker or doing drugs. I took the plates to the table and then got knives and forks.

"Dinner is ready," I said to them.

Jake looked up from the game. "Dinner, boys."

They got up and I sank down at the opposite end of the table with a glass of water.

"Not eating, Abby?"

I looked up from my glass of water at Jake.

"Not hungry."

I was thirsty for something stronger than water but I didn't dare touch his liquor.

"Well, do something useful and get me a beer." He started to cut up his meat and I got back up.

I was like his housewife and, as I snuck a glance at him, I swear he was enjoying it.

I grabbed a beer and took off the cap and put it in front of him. I went to walk away but his arm snaked out and grabbed me by the waist, pulling me down to his lap.

"Thirsty, are we?" His hot breath ran up my neck.

Reaper was the only man I wanted touching me. My eyes flashed to my wedding ring. Why hadn't he found me yet?

I nodded my head.

"Here, have something stronger than water." He picked up the beer and handed it to me. Was he serious? I looked at him, frowning. By the calm expression on his face, I saw he was serious.

My fingers wrapped around the cold beer and took it from him.

"Good girl." He smiled at me, a sick kind of smile, like I was *his* girl. I was Reaper's. "Isn't she beautiful, boys?" He reached up and gripped my chin, making me look at him, his face inches from mine. "Don't know how Reaper ended up with someone as gorgeous and captivating as you." He let go of my chin and went back to cutting up his meat while I sat on his lap and drank his beer.

God help me.

I felt a buzzing on my thigh.

"Hop up, would you, sweetheart." He moved his arm and I was off him like he was burning me, taking the beer with me.

Jake looked down at his phone. "Got to go to the post office box. Apparently it is backed up." Jake took a mouthful of food and got up, looking at me. "Thanks for dinner, sweetheart."

Sick, I felt sick every time he called me a sweet name. Every time he looked at me like that, like I was his.

I didn't know what Reaper was doing. I didn't know if he was coming. But I hoped to god he was because I knew one day that look would turn into something more, and I hoped I was dead before that happened.

***

Reaper

I lit up a cigarette and sat back in one of the living room couches. Kim had brought in another crib and I had dragged it into the rec room with me. It was one of the rare times the club was quiet. The boys were out collecting money. We'd raided the last of the cookhouses today.

I found one guy who seemed to be in charge. I flexed my knuckles, looking at them. They were still bleeding. I should really put ice on them. The only information I got from him was only two men knew Jake's address. But he didn't know their names.

I sucked on my cigarette and watched my son sleep peacefully.

My mind was consumed with one question. How the fuck was Abby? Something was telling me she needed me more now than ever and I couldn't get to her. Every path I took was a dead end.

It was beyond frustrating.

The situation was causing my temper to be uncontrollable. I thought I had gotten most of it out on that guy this morning. But I was still tense with rage. I wanted Jake. I wanted my hands around his throat. I had pictured how I was going to kill him so many times. Every night a new way of doing it came to me.

My phone started to ring and I cursed. Fuck, if that woke Tyson, I swore whoever ringing would be a dead man.

"Hello?" I barked into the phone.

"A black four by four just pulled up at the post office box. We're waiting to see who gets out." Jace, who had been sharing shifts with a few other members, gave me the news I had been waiting for.

I got up, knocking over my beer, which was on the floor, and quickly walked through the living room and dining room.

"KIM!" I yelled taking the phone away from my mouth. "KIM!!" I shouted walking through the bar.

"Yeah, he just got out, Reaper. It's him. What do you want us to do?"

Fuck, where was Kim?

I couldn't just leave Tyson.

"Hold on a sec. Someone else just pulled up."

I didn't give a fuck. He was there. That was all that mattered.

"KIM! FUCK IT, ANYONE!"

Of all times for the clubhouse to be empty, this just had to be one of them. Fuck it. What did I do?

"Looks like it is someone who works there. He just unlocked the door and they are going in," Jace said.

"ANYONE!" I yelled.

Then I heard a door slam.

"What the hell, Reaper!" Kim ran down the stairs.

Thank Christ.

"Watch Tyson. He is in the rec room." I patted myself down for the keys to my bike while still on the phone.

"Where are you going?" Kim yelled at me but I was already running for the door.

It, of course, happened to happen on one of the days there were no members around. Fuck it. I shouldn't have sent them all out.

"What are they doing?" I said mounting my bike.

"They're in the post office."

"Don't lose them. I'm coming." I hung up and put my phone in my pocket. Starting my bike, I took off. I'm coming, Abby. I'm fucking coming. And when I got my hands around that man's neck, I was going to make sure he had a slow death. I was going to enjoy every second of it.

The man took my wife, the mother of my kid. I was going to make sure his death was painful and long.

Chapter 8

Jake

"How much?" I asked Andrew as he threw the last of the cash into one of the four black duffel bags. I pulled the cigarette from my mouth, wondering just how much I had made this take. It was our busy season and we had been pumping out double the amount of ice.

"Anywhere between two to four mill." Andrew zipped up the last duffel bag. "Not bad."

"Yeah, now just to pay who is owed and then this money can set up the next run." I handed Grant the money we owed him for storing it. "Let's get out of here. I have a pretty blonde at home who will be waiting for me." A smirk graced my lips. The fact she belonged to Reaper just made it more enjoyable and that bit sweeter.

"How long you going to keep it breathing?" Andrew grumbled. "Biker trash."

"She might be that, but she is also stunning." Even with the bruises I had inflicted on her and her cut lip, there was only one word to describe Abby and that was beautiful, drop-dead gorgeous. I still didn't know how a woman like her could end up with a serial killer. But I guess all women like a taste of something dark.

But, when it came to Reaper, that man just wasn't human.

Why would a sweet girl like Abby go for that? It was really her undoing because being with him was going to cause her an early death. Pity, really.

"She is," Andrew admitted, giving me a sly smile. I had noticed the way he looked at her when he thought I wasn't watching. "Let's go, then. So you can get back to your play toy."

"Grant, as always, it's been a pleasure." I shook his hand and followed Andrew out. He stopped, looking across the road. Stupid fool! I walked straight into him, causing me to drop two duffel bags.

"Fuck it, Andrew! What is your problem?" I cursed and pushed him in the back.

"See that van. It was here when we pulled up." Andrew pointed across the road, dropping his duffel bags and pulling out his gun. And then I heard it. The Harley pipes coming around the corner.

"FUCK IT!" I pulled my gun out of the waist of my jeans. But the men in the van were already out and firing bullets from across the road. We took cover behind the post office.

"We need to get to the car." Andrew pulled another gun out of his leg holster. "I'll cover you. They're reloading."

"Hear that," I said, a twisted smile gracing my lips. "The Reaper is here."

Andrew shook his head at me. "Only you would get excited about being chased by a serial killer."

"Alright, let's do this." I got up and looked at the money that had been abandoned on the sidewalk. "Fuck it. No way we are getting that cash."

"Fuck the money," Andrew shouted. "Hurry up and get ready to run."

That was setup money. That money was needed. I wasn't leaving it behind.

"JAKE, WHERE THE FUCK ARE YOU GOING?"

I rounded the corner and headed for the cash, one gun raised. Andrew was quick to follow. They were still reloading. Andrew reached the back end of the car and took shelter there and started firing bullets at them while I got the cash.

Then I saw him coming around the front of the car. I raised my gun but it was too late. I felt the bullet go through the arm holding onto the bag. Fuck it. Dropping the bag, my gun, I grasped my arm. That was a cheap shot.

"WHERE THE FUCK IS SHE, JAKE?"

I laughed and went to pick up the gun I had dropped. Knowing the crazy fool, he wouldn't be wearing a vest. It was within my grasp when he tackled me.

My head hit the pavement as his fist connected with my jaw, over and over. I couldn't help the laughter that came out. One hand was wrapped around my neck as he held me in place while his fist let out some of the frustration I was sure he was feeling.

I coughed up some blood and smiled at him. "Funny part is, Reaper, if you kill me, you will never know."

The look in his eyes told me he was only thinking of ways of getting the information out of me. And I was somewhat interested in what he had come up with. "Don't you know that losing your wife is more painful than any physical torment you could come up with?" I gripped his arm and pulled my face close to his. "But I guess you are going to find that one out," I hissed across at him and laughed.

The man had taken my everything and now I was going to take his.

When I got out of his grasp, that was. He could beat me till I was dead. It still wouldn't give him Abby back.

His grip around my neck tightened. Maybe it wasn't a good idea to openly threaten his only weakness while he had a hand around my throat. My hands went to pry his off, but his grip just tightened. He dragged me off the pavement and stood me up, hammering me back into the post office brick wall.

I pried at his hand. But the bastard just squeezed tighter.

The oxygen was gone and I gasped, trying to get air. My legs and arms were going numb as he held me in the air against the brick wall. My brain ached and I gasped and gasped. But nothing was coming. Surely he wouldn't let my death be this painless?

But the look in his eyes told me that reason was gone. He didn't care that I was holding the key to whether he got his wife back or not. He wouldn't know that only two other people knew where Abby was. As far as he knew, I was the ONLY person who knew where she was. But he didn't care. He just wanted me dead. And right now he was slowly doing that, getting his wish.

I was sure I was on my last breath when I saw Andrew over his shoulder. Reaper slumped to the side, dropping to the ground. And I started coughing.

Andrew grabbed me by the arm and fired bullets at the van while stuffing me in the back seat of the car.

"Did you kill him?" My voice came out raspy and dry as soon as he climbed into the car. I gulped down air but it wasn't helping.

"NO! He is the fucking president of the mother charter of Satan's Son. I'm not being responsible for his death." Andrew sped off, leaving the money behind. I looked out the back window, seeing the bags lying there.

That money was needed.

Fuck it.

We were halfway up the street when I heard the sound of those Harley pipes.

"Well, if you had, he wouldn't be fucking following us now, would he?" I shouted from the back seat, kicking the driver's seat in frustration.

Andrew picked up the shotgun from the passenger side and handed it to me.

"You want him dead, you do it."

"You need to grow a pair," I shouted back at him. Why were men so scared of one man? You might think he wasn't human by things he had done, but he still bled.

Hanging out the window, I saw he was right behind us, tailgating.

I saw him pull out the shotgun that was strapped to his tank. But in this case, I was quicker. I shot at his tires. I watched his bike flip and come to a skidding halt in the middle of the road.

I climbed back into the cabin. "You know, I hope he survives that because I'm not done with him yet." I dropped the shotgun beside me and turned my attention to my arm. Cheap fucking shot. He should have gone for the headshot. But if I knew Reaper, he didn't want me to die that easily.

Now all that money was gone, and worse, now in the hands of Satan's Sons. My grasp tightened around my arm. That money was fucking needed. I couldn't wipe off that amount of cash.

This was all her fault. She was the reason I was now four million down, had a bullet in my arm and a handprint around my throat.

Her fault.

"Head us home, Andrew. I've got something I need to handle."

"What about your arm?"

"This is more important." Someone was going to be held responsible for me losing all that cash. And that someone was sitting in my house.

Chapter 9

Abby

"Billy, do you want dessert?" I held a knife over the apple pie I had made. He had finished off his meal and what was left of Jake's.

"What is it?" he grunted.

"Apple pie."

"Homemade or bought?"

"Homemade."

"Bring it over." He moved his empty plate from in front of him to the side.

I walked it over. "It's a family recipe." I sat it in front of him. Walking around the table, I took a seat across from him.

"I know. Your mom used to make it." He started gulping it down.

My eyes widened. How the hell did he know that? No one knew that, apart from family– Kim, Dad and I.

"How did you know that?" I asked. I hadn't spoken about my mother to him or Jake. And I certainly hadn't gone into detail about how my mom would make this apple pie every Sunday. It was the one meal in the week Dad would make sure he was home for.

Billy took his eyes off the pie and looked across at me. "You don't remember me, do you?"

I narrowed my eyes at him, looking into those green eyes of his. They were familiar. I had looked into them before. More importantly, I had looked up to them. "You didn't always have a beard," I said, leaning forward. "Do you have a pinup girl tattooed on your upper arm?"

He laughed. "Took you a while to remember." Then he went back to eating my apple pie.

"You were Dad's vice president."

"I was."

"You are part of the dark days."

He scoffed. "Is that what you call it?"

"That's what Kim and I call it. You were all there one day and gone the next. You went from family dinners to not being around."

"Well, that's what happens when you shoot half your members."

My eyes narrowed. "You shouldn't have betrayed the club. Then you wouldn't be walking with a limp."

"Black and white, like your father," he said, between taking bites of the pie.

Then something clicked in my brain, and I was clicking my fingers in front of him. "You are Shelly's dad."

He looked up at me, interested. Bet he wasn't expecting me to remember that. I was only little when he was around. But Shelly and I grew up together when we were younger.

"I went to her wedding, a long time back. I had left the Satan's Sons then. Wasn't talking to Dad. I actually joined another gang. But I always knew she would find someone amazing. Daniel is that. Didn't see her going for someone clean cut though." I shrugged my shoulders. "A banker. Who would have thought?"

Billy was still staring at me. Like he wasn't expecting me to know so much about his daughter.

"How is Charlie? I only saw him once when he was a baby. It's been years now." I reached for my second beer. I gulped some down and remembered something else. "You spend every Sunday with him right?"

Billy cleared his throat. "Didn't know you and Shelly were still in touch."

"She came to my wedding." I tilted my head. "One of the few people I actually called and asked to come. It was mainly a charter party. Wasn't really about me."

"Didn't know she went."

I arched my eyebrows. "Might have something to do with you always firing bullets when anyone mentions something to do with Satan's Sons."

He shook his head. "Don't know what you are talking about."

I laughed. "Right."

"She mightn't have mentioned it because of who you were marrying." He put down his spoon. "The Reaper. Only an insane woman would commit to that man."

"He isn't that bad."

Billy scoffed. "You don't know half the shit he has done or is capable of. A girl with her head in the sky."

"I know my husband." I felt offended that he would imply I was just some stupid girl who didn't know what her husband got up to, that I didn't know who I was committing to spending the rest of my life with. "I know what he is capable of, which is why I know he will come for me. Whether I am dead or not. He will either come for me alive or for my body. Either way, he will come."

I knew Reaper wouldn't rest till he knew where I was. Even if it was just to come for my body. He would come and make sure I was laid to rest. I knew at the very least my son would know where I was buried.

"You are right about two things." Billy moved in his seat, leaning forward. "Reaper has never cared who lives or dies. But he cares about your life. So, yes, he will come. But I think by then, you are right again, it will be too late."

Billy was only confirming what I already knew. I sat back in my chair. Just then the door burst open and in walked a furious Jake. I looked at the door, which was ajar. If I could get there I could get out.

I sat up.

"YOU!"

I knew that look and I knew what followed that look. I skidded up to my feet and ran around the table. But Billy stood up and blocked me from bolting upstairs. Bastard.

I screamed as he gripped my hair, throwing me back against the table. The taste of blood filled my mouth as his fist continued to connect with my face. He pulled me up only to throw me back among the plates. My head ached from the impact.

"YOUR bastard of a HUSBAND took MY money!"

My hand reached above me and I gripped a knife. I knew I wouldn't be able to kill him. I sent the knife with all my force and hate for him into his hand that was wrapped around my neck.

He cursed and let go of me and I struggled for breath. "GOOD!" I spat a mouthful of blood at him. "And I hope he doesn't stop taking things from you. First your wife and next your livelihood!"

I knew Reaper and I knew he wouldn't stop. He was relentless.

"You little bitch!" He pulled the knife from his hand and pulled his gun on me.

"Go on, I fucking dare you!" I knew it was coming. I welcomed death with open arms. It was better than this. The not knowing. The beating. The obeying his every command. Screw him. Screw him wanting my death to be slow.

His hand wrapped around my neck and he started to drag me up the stairs, my feet stumbling to keep up.

"You and your husband can have matching bullet wounds," he hissed in my ear. I screamed as the bullet went through my arm. He pushed me forward, slamming the door behind me. I collapsed, my body hitting the carpeted floor.

I cursed and cursed, and wrapped my hand around my shoulder. I scrambled up, leaning against the door. I looked at my shoulder, the blood oozing out. Shit.

"You going to leave her to bleed out?" Billy's voice floated in under the door. Why did I note concern in his voice?

"No," Jake's voice followed. "Call the doc. Tell him we have two bullet wounds and a stab wound. Can't believe the bitch had the guts to stab me."

I listened as their footsteps went down the stairs.

Fuck him.

But if he meant that Reaper and I could have matching bullet wounds... Did that mean...? My eyes went wide. No. No way. Reaper never got shot. He did the shooting.

My head leaned against the door.

I should have stabbed him harder.

I needed to know. I needed to know if Reaper had been shot. Was it in the shoulder? He never wore a vest. My stomach dropped. Suddenly I was feeling sick and not because of the bullet wound. I needed to find out what happened. But how would I find out? I had to talk to Kade.

***

Reaper

"So, the bike isn't that bad."

I looked across at Brad. Was he fucking serious right now? I didn't care if it was scrap metal.

"I fucking had him. I had my hand around his neck. How the hell did he get away?" I was pissed off with myself. "Fuck, KIM!" I cursed at her.

"Well, if you would sit still! God, have another drink or something," Kim yelled at me while sewing up my shoulder.

The table was covered in bloody bandages, my vest and my blood-stained t-shirt. Pity. I actually liked that shirt.

"Did you see what direction they headed in?" Brad repeated himself.

I dragged my eyes off Kim's hand to glare at him. "Up fucking Albert Street. That's all I saw." How many times did I have repeat the fact I had no fucking idea where he went and I blew the only fucking lead we had on them?

"Should have killed him."

I looked up at the head of the table. Roach. His opinion of the situation hadn't gone unheard. But where was he when shit was going down? That's right. He'd fucked off, chasing old members.

"One bullet to the head, Reaper. Never seen you miss. So you explain why you got him in the arm and not the head?" Roach threw his beer down. "Fucking lost my daughter. Because of YOU! I told you. I told all of you from the beginning that Abby would be the cost of your mistakes and look now."

"WANT ME TO SAY YOU WERE RIGHT, OLD MAN? IS THAT WHAT YOU ARE GETTING AT?"

"REAPER, SIT DOWN!" Kim yanked on my arm, trying to get me back in my seat.

"I FUCKING TOLD YOU TO STAY AWAY FROM HER!" Roach flipped the table we were at, causing Kim to scream and everyone's beer to be spilled. "OVER AND OVER. I TOLD YOU. STILL YOU WOULDN'T LISTEN."

This again. I ran a hand through my hair. My patience was wearing thin. I was so close to giving him the fight he wanted. But he was waiting for me to hit first. And so far, I had ignored every time he said I told you so. How many times had he said I wasn't worth anything? That this was completely my fault? I knew all that. And I was doing everything fucking possible to fix it.

He had even gone as far as getting my parents here. I still hadn't dealt with that.

"Thanks, DAD!" Kim yelled and went to her knees, picking shit up.

Roach was a bull, wanting to charge. But I wasn't letting him win.

"You should get lost, old man, before you get yourself hurt." I was deadly calm. He wanted me raging at him. He wanted me to give him a fight. But if Abby found out that I had decked her father when he was off his medication and stressed, she would kill me.

"Fucking coward, Reaper. That's what you are. Letting a woman pay for your mistakes." He pointed a finger at me. The other members backed away as he stormed past me.

He was disrespecting me. And when he wasn't doing that, he was bringing up shit I knew all too well. I still didn't understand why

Abby agreed to marry me. And I still didn't know what the fuck I'd done right to deserve her giving me a son.

"Reaper, sit back down." Kim rubbed her temples "And can SOMEBODY flip the table back! Seriously, all you men just standing there!" I didn't know what had her on edge.

Brad, Cameron and a few of the other members flipped the table back.

"Thank you!" she said and started putting her shit back on it. "I swear Dad's temper is getting worse every day. Now, Reaper, sit back down so I can finish sewing your shoulder. Because you will be useless to everyone if that gets infected."

She had a point. As much as I didn't want to sit still right now.

"I'll look at your leg after this." Kim focused her attention on my shoulder, she and that needle she liked sticking in my skin.

I glanced down at the gravel rash that had ripped through my jeans. It ached like a bitch and had taken the first layer of my tattoos off.

"We need to start thinking of a plan B." Brad dragged a chair back to the table and put my bottle of liquor back in front of me. "Because our current plan isn't working."

"It was going to work if I hadn't fucked it up."

"There was no winning in that situation. Well, unless you count the cash." Brad smirked and leaned forward. "Three and a half mill isn't bad."

"What do you mean no winning? I shouldn't have fucking dropped when I got shot. Then this would all be fine and Abby would be back."

"Yeah, because he was just going to give you that information now, wasn't he, Reaper?" Kim snapped at me. "Seriously, if you had shot him in the head, we would never know where Abby is. Yeah, the whole him getting away sucks, but if we found him once, we can find him again."

She was confident.

I looked her in the eye. "Before or after Abby's dead." I didn't know if he was in a rush to kill her, but I knew he sure as hell would be taking today out on her. No way he would lose that amount of cash willingly.

I glanced toward the bar, which was covered in cash at the moment from the guys counting it.

"Like I said, we need to come up with a new plan," Brad said, like it was that fucking simple.

We had a plan and I fucked it. Me. I fucked it.

***

Come on, Tyson. Sleep, little man. Tyson was wailing. It was nearly eleven and he had woken up about seven. Kim said he had woken up as soon as I left this afternoon and didn't go back down till after five. He'd had barely any sleep today.

Kim had turned the empty corner of my room into a kitchen. She even had a sink plumbed in and joinery. I was thankful for it now as I boiled Tyson a bottle.

"Come on, Tyson, we have talked about this. You like sleep. It's when you grow." I held him in one arm as he wailed. Filling up the bottle and checking the temperature, I headed back to the couch, giving him the bottle. His little hands grasped for it. I held it in place. He was only tiny but already he was trying to do things on his own.

His eyes were wide as he drank. He had Abby's eyes. I wished she could see them. God, I needed her. I pulled out my phone and dialed her number.

"Hey, it's Abby. Leave a message."

I closed my eyes, hung up and dialed again.

Her voice had a sweetness to it. She sounded happy. I pulled the phone away from my ear and went to the videos. I only had a few pictures of her. I was always too busy to take pictures. I regretted that now.

But I did have two videos of her. One when she was pregnant with Matthew and another one I took the night of our wedding.

"Kade, are you filming?" Abby sat up in bed. "I mean it. You better not be filming."

"Come on, sweetheart, don't be camera shy."

"What if someone sees this?" She gave me a challenging smirk. "You won't be so proud then of your stupid little camera."

My hand went forward, ripping the blanket off her.

"Hey!"

"Come on, I'm going on the road tomorrow. At least give me something to look at."

"Don't go, then."

"Have to. Already had this argument, babe. Remember, you lost"

She pouted and gave me a look that told me she wasn't ready to cave in. "Fine. Stop filming me!"

"Not till you strip."

She shook her head, laughing. "No way am I letting you film that. What if someone else sees this? You really need to think ahead."

"Who would dare touch my phone?"

"Me."

"Well you aren't going to watch yourself, are you?"

She kneeled in the middle of the bed. An expression I had only ever seen her give me captured her face. "Fine. I'll strip for you."

A number I didn't know paused the video as my phone rang. I ignored it. Whoever was calling could get fucked. I had had a long-ass day. If I didn't know the number, then they weren't important. Usually, as a president, you always answer your fucking phone. But tonight, I was taking time off.

Tyson was slowly falling asleep while drinking his bottle. I got up. I took the bottle from him and lowered him into the crib. He had been sleeping with one of Abby's sweatshirts. For some reason, he always curled into it.

Like now, his arm reached out for it. Instead of having a teddy bear, he had a sweatshirt.

***

Abby

The doctor sewed up my shoulder. Why Jake would shoot someone and then get them medical attention was beyond me. I really wanted it over with, but I was still strong, even though my body was taking a hard hit at the moment.

Sure, where I wasn't bruised I was bleeding and I looked like someone had colored me in with purple and yellow marker. But I was still breathing. Which meant he hadn't broken me.

I wasn't going to let him break me.

He couldn't break me.

They left when the doctor was sewing me up in the formal sitting room. The bullet hadn't gone right through, so I experienced extreme pain as he dug it out.

I wasn't just giving up.

Which was why I was going through every kitchen drawer at the moment to see if I could find something with an address on it.

I slammed the last drawer shut. Fucking nothing.

I was here alone. I didn't know how long for. I was surprised he had left me in the house having free range.

I did stab him. I expected to be locked up for that.

I took the stairs two at a time, even with a sore shoulder I was going to take this opportunity. and walked up the hall, pushing doors open. Bedroom. Bedroom. Bedroom. My room. Study.

STUDY!

I quickly went to the desk. Nothing. Nothing. Empty. One locked drawer. I lowered to my knees in front of it. There could be an address in there.

I looked at the keyhole. No way I was picking that. I was good, but not that good. Jake was lazy and I knew the key would be in here somewhere.

I ran my hand over the surface of the desk. No holes. I went through the paperwork. It was all bank accounts, with a post office as the address.

Just when I was about to give up, I noticed the green velvet that covered the top of the table. I picked it up at the corner and bingo.

The first smile I had had since being taken took over my face as I snatched up that small key.

I pushed it in the key hole, unlocking the drawer.

I went through the contents of the door. Passport, money, a gun with no bullets and a phone. My eyes lit up when I saw the phone.

I unlocked it. No PIN. God was on my side.

I had never been so thankful to see an old iPhone. If only it was a new one then I would be able to locate where I am. I clicked on the map app, but nothing happened. I cursed. It looked like it had been forgotten about. I was surprised it even turned on.

I looked out the window that overlooked the driveway. No one was back. Reaper. I could call him. The realization hit me. I was seconds away from talking to him. It was after midnight. Would he be up? What if I woke Tyson?

Fuck it. Just call. My fingers ran across the screen and then his number was there. All I had to do was dial.

Chapter 10

Abby

He didn't answer. He always answered. I didn't remember him ever missing a phone call. He would answer in the dead of the night. Sometimes he would be on the phone in the night and I wouldn't even realize.

A president always answered his phone.

Maybe something was wrong. My eyes widened. Maybe he was hurt. Maybe he was in the hospital. God, what had Jake done? I gripped the phone tightly and stared out the window. No one was back yet. I still had time. I dialed again. I listened to the ringing and then nothing. No answering machine. Nothing.

Fuck it. Who else's number did I know? Dad's, I always got the four and seven mixed up.

Kim.

I knew Kim's.

My fingers dashed across the phone and I pressed dial. Please answer. I didn't know when I would get this opportunity again. I moved the curtains and looked down at the driveway. Still nothing.

"Trent?"

She answered. She sounded half asleep, but she answered. I closed my eyes in relief. "Kim?" Who the hell was Trent?

"ABBY!"

"Yeah, it's me."

"Oh my god. OH MY GOD. Are you OK? Did you escape? Where are you?" She was wide awake now.

"No. I wish. And I don't know. Some mansion that has central locking and bulletproof glass. How's Tyson? How's Kade? Did he get shot? How bad? Is he in the hospital?" Now that I had a chance to get answers to my questions, I couldn't stop them from all tumbling out at once.

"He is fine. They both are. Do you want to talk to him? Why didn't you call him?"

"I did. He didn't answer." I looked down the driveway. "Look, I don't have long."

"I'll get him. I'm running. Just hold on a sec." I heard her trip, most likely over something in her bedroom because it was always untidy. I swear that girl loved living in a mess.

I could hear her running and the opening of doors.

"OK. I'm heading up the stairs. I swear it will only be a second longer," she spoke hurriedly into the phone.

The phone was muffled.

"REAPER, UNLOCK THE DOOR!"

I could hear banging. Kim was going to wake up the whole clubhouse. Was she even thinking about Tyson?

"WHAT, KIM? I just got Tyson to sleep!"

That voice. Oh my god, that voice. It settled my nerves. It gave me the willpower to keep fighting. God, I wished things were different. Just hearing it was like being welcomed home. He was fine. He was breathing. Tyson was sleeping. He mightn't be now, after Kim's attack on the door and the shouting.

"It's Abby."

"What are you talking about?" Reaper sounded frustrated, like he was raw on nerves. I knew that tone. He wasn't coping. He was more Reaper than Kade. Regardless, he was still the man I loved.

"NO, on the PHONE!"

"What do you mean?" He sounded completely confused and tired. Actually, he sounded exhausted. Like he was dealing with too much and it was taking a toll. That was my fault. My eyes squinted shut. I knew this was a stressful situation and I was expecting a lot of him.

"ABBY IS ON THE PHONE! God, are you stupid? Here. Talk to her."

"What the fuck are you going on about, Kim?" Kade sounded furious.

"TAKE THE PHONE, REAPER!"

"Fine!" A muffled sound followed. "HELLO?" he basically barked into the phone. He was rude. He was harsh. He was my Reaper.

I cleared my throat. A part of me never expected to hear his voice again. What should I say? I guess start with the basics before he hung up. "Hi, Kade."

"Abby?" The shock in his voice made me smile. Like he actually expected Kim to be playing a joke on him or that she had finally lost her marbles. It only took a couple of seconds for that shock to go, though, and the realization to kick in that he was actually talking to me. "Where the hell are you? I'm coming. You hear me? I'm coming–"

"Kade, stop! I don't know where I am," I groaned. "I've searched for an address but I have no idea and all I see are trees and a driveway. But don't worry about me. How is Tyson?"

"What do you mean, don't worry about you? Do you honestly expect me not to be worried?"

"Kade, answer my fucking question. How's Tyson?" My son. I wanted to know how he was. The son I gave birth to and was ripped away from.

"He is..." Kade stopped talking. "Do you want to see him?"

Yes! Oh my god, yes! "Yes."

"Hold on a sec."

I looked down the driveway. Still no one there. I guess the worst that could happen was he came home, caught me and killed me. But knowing my luck, he would just beat me.

The phone vibrated and I pulled it away from my ear. Putting it on loudspeaker, I opened the message. He had grown. I smiled. He was healthy. Sleeping peacefully. Wait a sec. "Is that my..." I zoomed in. It was. "That's my Bliss n Eso sweatshirt."

"Yeah, he is attracted to it." I could hear the smile in Kade's voice.

"Well, at least he will have a good taste in music," I laughed. "All those toys I bought him and he sleeps with my sweatshirt." I shook my head, thinking of all those soft teddies Brad and I bought him.

"I'm hoping he still gets my taste in music."

"And what's wrong with him listening to rap music?"

"Just don't want him to be completely like his mother."

"I think he is going to be just like his father. And if you have anything to do with it, he will be taking over your charter. How are the boys?"

Kade went quiet. What wasn't he telling me? "Kade?"

He sighed. "I took over from your father."

"What? Of the mother charter?"

"Yes."

I swallowed hard. No wonder he was stressed. "So you're the president of the mother charter?"

"Yes."

I didn't say anything. I was trying to wrap my head around it. He hated responsibilities and this, this was bigger than Tyson and me. He could leave me. He could abandon Tyson. But once you are a mother charter president, you are that for life. Even if Dad had stepped down, he would still be looked upon as a wise figure. Normally mother charter presidents don't step down. They are that till they die. Usually young. Usually bloody. Dad would be the first to live through the handover to another president.

"Abby, if you're angry, just let me explain it." It sounded like he had had this conversation within himself a million times and was expecting me to be angry about it.

He was taking my silence as anger? It wasn't that. It was shock and something else. "I'm not mad."

"Disappointed? I swear, Abby, I'm doing everything possible to find you. It's not getting in the way of what is important. Which is you. I promise you nothing is coming before you–"

"Kade, stop!" I cut him off. Why would I be disappointed? There was only one feeling consuming me as I thought about him taking over from Dad. "I'm proud of you, Kade. You always hated responsibility and you have stood up and done this. I'm proud." All those years, all he did was avoid responsibility. His fear of it always came between us.

"You are?"

I smiled. I wished I'd been there to help him make the decision. But when it came to it, he didn't need me to help him take responsibility. "Yes, very proud."

I could hear him let out a long breath.

"It's still not as important as you." He was reassuring me, but there was no need. I knew he would be there for Tyson, and the whole mother charter would be there for my son. It was how I was brought up, and if it was good enough for me, I knew it would be alright for Tyson.

"I'm going to send you something but you can't watch it unless something happens to me. OK?" My plan from earlier resurfaced. Here was my chance to have the goodbye I wanted. "I have to go."

"Don't. I need you, Abby. Tyson needs you. Don't go."

He was pleading with me. Like I had a choice. "I have to, Kade. Promise you won't watch the video unless something happens to me."

"I'll never watch it 'cause nothing is going to happen to you. Hear me, Abby. You aren't dying."

He was still in denial. Whether I lived or died was out of our hands now. It was in Jake's. And I saw that tint in his eye. He wanted to kill me. He was looking forward to it. But that didn't mean I was going to give in. He hadn't broken me yet.

"Bye, Kade."

"I'm not giving up on you."

"I know." I sat down in the office chair. "You will end up with me in the end."

"Don't talk like that, Abby." I could hear the anger in his voice at me. He wasn't ready for me to accept it. Didn't he see that was what was important? Me coming to terms with it. "I will come for you."

"Like I said, I know. I love you, Kade." If this was our goodbye, it wasn't bad. Reaper would never know the details of what Jake did to me. And that was for the best because I didn't want him to live with that. "Oh wait, you got shot today!"

"How the hell did you know that?"

"In the shoulder?"

"Did he tell you?" Kade's voice darkened.

I scoffed. "No. Let's just say we have matching bullet wounds."

"HE SHOT YOU!" I pulled the phone from my ear away from Kade's yelling.

"Ouch, my ear!"

"He shot you? Where?"

"In the shoulder." I looked at my bandaged shoulder. "It hurt like a bitch, but getting the bullet out was worse."

Kade was dead silent. He didn't say anything. "I'm going to kill him." He was stating it, like it was going to happen. I knew deep down Reaper would get the upper hand. I just knew it would be too late for me.

"Bye, Kade." I didn't want to hear him pleading with me again. I couldn't take it. I couldn't take hearing him beg me to stay on the phone. So I took it from my ear and hung up before he could say another word.

I wiped the tears off my cheeks and got up. Looking down at the calm driveway, I saw I still had time. I had come to terms with what was going to happen. Like a man put on death row, you knew it was going to happen, that the day was coming.

But if I did it my way, I would get to say my goodbyes and end my life on my terms.

I took a few sharp breaths and wiped the remaining tears away. Time to pull on the amount of strength I had left and do this.

I had a plan and now it was time to follow it.

Jake hadn't broken me.

I was just going to take the power from him.

Chapter 11

Reaper

I never fucking promised her, but I did tell her I would never watch it. It had been four days since I spoke to Abby. And for four fucking days, I'd been staring at my phone, tempted to watch the video. It sat in my messages, teasing me.

But I hadn't watched it.

I blew out a mouthful of smoke. I needed her. The need was so powerful it was affecting my decisions. I wasn't able to think clearly. All my focus was on her, finding her. Some way. Somehow. Getting her back.

I lay on the bed, staring at the white ceiling. It was dark. It was after one in the morning and I was still awake.

Tyson had gone down without any troubles tonight, which was a shame because I would rather have been up with him than lying here with my thoughts.

Fuck it.

I sat up and reached for my phone. I was watching it. There could be something in it that could help me find her.

That was my reasoning as I went through my messages to get to it. But the real reason was I needed to hear her voice. I needed to see her.

My finger hovered over the play button. Was I breaking my word to her? Yes, most likely. Still, I was going to do it. I pressed play, turning up the volume.

It was dark. I only saw blackness and then the lights came on. There she was. My purpose. The woman I loved. The mother to my son. She was there. What had that bastard done to her? I could see her bandaged shoulder. The cut lip. The bruise running from her chin, and, as she looked at something to her left, I saw it went across her cheek.

She looked back at the camera and I saw her black eye. And shit, she looked tired. Had she been sleeping? Clearly fucking not.

"Kade." She smiled. "First off, I don't want you to be upset or angry with yourself. I know you and I know you would have done everything possible. So no need for tears, regrets or what-ifs."

She stopped, squaring her shoulders and sitting straight up. "Now there are a few things I want you to know now that I'm gone. You have to be strong for Tyson. I don't want him growing up with a ghost for a father. You hear me? That isn't acceptable. Pull your shit together and be the man I know you are."

She got up from sitting and moved to a window, looking out it, then back at the camera. "In my room. The chest of drawers. The bottom drawer comes out. Underneath it is..." She pitched her eyes shut and took a few breaths. "There is something there for Tyson and you. I made it when I was pregnant. In case something happened to me again, like it did when I had Matthew. Also, my will is there. I had that drawn up when you were on the road. It basically just gives you back everything you have given me." A grin spread across her face and then dropped as she remembered something. "And making sure you were the soul caretaker of Tyson. Not that I knew Tyson's name then. But it had to be done in case Dad did something stupid." She rolled her eyes. "He told me he was going to take my baby from you if something happened to me again. So I made a will. So if he is giving you a hard time right now, tell him to fuck off. You have my permission." That smile I loved of hers appeared on her face again.

"I know you will find Jake and you will kill him. I have faith in you. But at the same time, Kade, if you never track him down, don't beat yourself up about it. I'm sure fate will take care of him in the end."

She paused looking out the window and then back at the camera. "Anyway, Jake mightn't get his wish to kill me. There is this game we play." She frowned and sighed. "It's sick and twisted and I never want you to know the details. Anyway, I think there is a way I can turn it in my favor."

She stopped talking and a look I had never wanted to see appeared on my Abby's face. It was the one I had seen on men's faces when they accepted that I was going to end their life.

"You heard that correctly, Kade. I'm choosing to end my life. There are two ways to do it and either way I will get it done. Please don't be mad with me." She was pleading with me. "I'm just not letting Jake do it. This isn't your fault and I want you to know that. I love you and I would do everything the same way again." The sadness and acceptance of her death disappeared from her face and she smiled. "Maybe not Hell Bound though. I might give joining the gang a miss second time around. But you, you I wouldn't change."

My heart tightened. No fucking way. I was frozen to the spot, too shocked to pause the video. So it kept playing.

She gave me a confident grin. "I know you will make a great mother charter president. You might even put my dad to shame. In fact, I'm hoping you do. You got this. The members, the other presidents, they will all follow your lead and I know you will be a great example."

She rubbed a hand across her eye and sighed, looking back at the camera. "Now is the subject I didn't want to bring up, but have to because I know you."

She gave a look that she usually would give me before telling me off. "You can't be a widower. Hear me say that? You don't get that option. You opened up your heart to me so I KNOW you can do it again. I want Tyson to have a mother figure. I struggled not having my mom and I don't want him to be grieving over what could have been. So find yourself another woman, Kade." She arched her eyebrows. "I am ordering you to. There will be a girl out there for you. She will see what I saw in you. If not, just hook up with a club girl. Just don't let Tyson not have a mom. And most of all, I don't want you alone for the rest of your life because of this."

I watched the tears well up in her eyes. "With that said, there is only one more thing to say. Which is goodbye." She cursed and wiped a tear off her cheek. "I told myself I wouldn't cry." She let out a frustrated sigh. "Well, if this is it, all there is and nothing more, I want you to know I'm happy with how things turned out. I wouldn't change it. So don't you dare wish you could."

She let out a long breath and looked straight into the camera. She opened and closed her hand. "Please listen to everything I've said and don't ever let Tyson see this." She stopped waving and bit her bottom lip, tears running down her cheeks. "Bye, Kade."

The video stopped.

FOUR FUCKING DAYS! I wiped the tears off my cheeks and threw the phone on the bed and grabbed my jeans.

No fucking way was I letting it end like that. FOUR DAYS! FOUR DAYS I HAD WASTED! The thought that she might have already done it consumed me, taking the breath from my lungs.

I pulled on my jeans. Put on my rings, stuffed my wallet in my pocket and got my bike keys.

Opening the door, I picked up my pace to Kim's room. FOUR FUCKING DAYS! I banged on her door.

"Kim?" I opened up her door and flicked on the lights.

"What the hell, Reaper?" She shielded her eyes from the lights.

"I need you to go to my room and look after Tyson."

"What, now?" She sat up in bed and looked at the clock next to her bedside. "It's ten past two in the morning. Where are you going? Why aren't you asleep?"

"Can you do it or not?"

"I'm getting up." She threw the blankets back, grumbled something about me being like a patient in the insane asylum and grabbed her clothes.

"I don't have my phone. If you need me, call Brad." I left her while she headed for my room. And I headed up the hall and round the corner till I was at Brad's door.

I banged on it. Impatient, I opened it up and wasn't surprised to find him with a girl.

"What the fuck is going on?" the girl yelled.

I didn't really give two shits about waking her up.

"Brad, I need you up and ready to go," I basically yelled over the whining bitch. She was still going on and trying to get the blanket from Brad to cover herself.

"What, now?" Brad squinted at me. "It's late, bro."

"I need you on your bike. I've got a message I need to get out."

"What? That you are a crazy person, going around waking people up at..." he looked at his phone, "two in the morning?"

"No. It's about Abby."

Brad's annoyed expression dropped. "Fine. Getting up," he said before throwing the blankets back and picking up his pants.

"I'll meet you in the bar. Just give me a minute. I need to get someone else."

He waved for me to get lost and I headed up the hall. Taking the stairs two at a time, my eyes were on the end door.

He thought he could judge and wipe his hands of this? He was wrong. Thought I wouldn't make much of a father. Questioned everything I fucking did. Well, he wasn't the mother charter president anymore. I was.

I twisted his doorknob. It was locked.

One swift kick to the door and it splintered, letting me in.

"WHAT THE FUCK!"

Roach sat bolt upright in bed.

"YOU, old man. I'm done with your shit." I flicked the lights on and pointed a finger at him. The control I normally had over my temper was gone. I wasn't furious. I was beyond it.

"Who do you think you are? Bursting in here!" Roach scrambled to the edge of the bed, getting up and heading for me.

My fist connected with his jaw as soon as he was within range. While I was on the road, taking care of this threats, he had been busy threatening Abby that he would take my kid from me.

I knew he didn't think much of me right now. I knew he blamed me for all this. It was my fault and I was wearing that.

He stayed on the floor, spitting out blood.

"That's for putting Abby through shit while I was gone."

"What the fuck are you talking about, Reaper?"

"You threatened to take Tyson from me if something happened to her."

He looked up at me with amazement. "How the hell did you know that? Have you spoken with Abby?" He went to get up. I couldn't stop myself or my temper from sending a quick kick to his stomach. He collapsed on the ground.

I kneeled down beside him. "You're a member. I'm the president. You follow my command, old man. And right now I need your ass on your bike, getting a message out for me. Understand?"

"I'm no shit kicker!" He went for me, but I stood up.

"You do what I say. And right now." I grabbed him by the neck as he lunged for me again, pushing him up against his bedroom wall. He struggled, but gave in when my grip got tighter. My jaw clenched as I hissed, "Your daughter is thinking of committing suicide. And you're going to help me stop it."

***

Kim

I flicked on the television and scrolled through the channels till I was on Sprout and put Tyson in the crib in front of it. For some reason, he would always nap around eleven watching Elmo. I walked out of the living room and into the bar. That's when I froze, seeing someone who was very unwelcome.

"What the fuck are you doing here?"

Kaylee turned on a stool and dared to smiled at me. "Hi, Kim. Heard Abby was missing? Shame really."

"Don't worry. I'm still here to keep her threat alive." I glared at her as she slipped off the barstool.

"Is that Tyson? Guess I should meet him."

I stepped in her way. "Go near him and I'll personally rip your hair out." I guarded the entry to the living room. "He is Abby's son and it is Abby's man you are after."

"Funny," she stepped into my face, "'cause I don't see Abby around to claim either."

I don't remember the last time it was I punched someone. But my fist was already clenched just seeing her. So as soon as the words left her lips, my fist connected with her nose.

She dropped to the floor easily. I pounced. All my built-up rage about what was happening to Abby came out. I just kept punching. Her hands were blocking direct access to her face. But I was still getting a few good shots in.

The clubhouse door burst open and I knew my time with her was limited.

"KIM, WHAT THE HELL?"

Reaper. He shouldn't be here. Not near her. I felt his arms wrap around me as he pulled me off her.

"Put me down!" I yelled and pushed at his stupid, large tattooed arms while kicking. "I'm not finished with her!"

"What the hell are you thinking, Kim?" Reaper put me down and pushed me into the living room. "You can't just deck girls!"

I fumed and pointed a finger behind him. "Is she the reason you left last night? Leaving me with Tyson?" I wanted answers. Suddenly his late night last night made sense. He ran off to be with her. I wanted to kill him, but first, her.

Reaper didn't have his vest on. But had his holster on, with a gun on each side. He wasn't expecting me to move as quickly as I did. I grabbed a gun and darted around him.

"KIM!" Reaper spun around after me. But again I was quicker.

Brad was helping Kaylee up. She might have had a bloody nose but I wasn't finished with her.

I pointed and I shot. Pity I missed her head and got the liquor bottles in the bar behind her. Abby had always been a better shot than me.

She squealed and went to hide behind Brad.

I went for a second shot. Reaper's hand wrapped around the top half of the gun and ripped it from my hand.

"KIM!"

He was furious. But I was breathing fire at this point. "I WANT HER DEAD!" I yelled. "You're the Reaper. Reap!"

I was his wife's sister. I had some pull. If I wanted someone dead, he should at least consider it! I glared at her frightened face as she clung to Brad. I should have taken some shooting lessons from Abby. Fuck me for never listening to her.

Reaper stepped into my view, blocking my view of Kaylee. He was more like a tank than ever, towering over me. He looked nearly as pissed off as I felt. I was breathing heavily but he was glaring at me, like I was the one in the wrong.

"Brad, get Kaylee a first aid kit," Reaper said over his shoulder.

I scoffed. "You have to be kidding me!" I threw my hands in the air and stormed off. I was not standing there getting a lecture from him. He had taken her side. And I saw the smirk she gave me as she walked off to the kitchen with Brad.

She was fucking playing the victim and Reaper was buying into it.

"I had one fucking long-ass night, Kim, and I come back to this shit." Reaper followed me, yelling. Always yelling.

"I don't care how your night was," I snapped over my shoulder and walked to Tyson, who was still awake. I flung around, my hand hitting his chest. God, why was he so close?

"Reel your shit in, Kim. I can't have you shooting girls!" he fired down at me. He was expecting me to be pulled back into this invisible line he had drawn for me. He was always expecting me to 'be in line.'

Well, I was out of line. Fuck the line. Fuck his rules. If he wasn't going to handle the threat, I would.

"Did you sleep with her?" I yelled up at his furious face.

"No! I haven't even been here!"

"So she just so happened to appear today? And you had NO idea she was coming?"

"Believe it or not, Kim, yes."

"Bullshit," I coughed. I pushed a hand into his rock hard abs. "You never deserved Abby."

I had pissed him off by shooting at Kaylee and now I had just pushed him over the edge.

He whacked my hand off him. "I'm not cheating on Abby."

"Oh really! How about when you're drunk at a club party? Maybe Kaylee will look appealing then. When your wife isn't here to stop you." I was angry. I was angry at him. I was angry at Kaylee. I was pissed off at Abby for not being here. She wouldn't have missed Kaylee's head.

Reaper pushed me backward. "I don't know if you noticed, but I'm not drinking or partying and I won't be cheating on Abby."

A bitter smile crept across my face. "You're right. I guess it won't be cheating once she is dead." He wasn't expecting me to say that. He was expecting me to back down. I shouldered past him. "I'm going out. You look after Tyson."

I picked up my bag and keys from the bar and headed outside. He didn't follow me and he didn't say anything.

Good, because I only had mean things to say to him right now.

Chapter 12

Reaper

It was after dinner. Kim had reappeared but wouldn't speak to me. I didn't understand her hormones. I swear Abby and her twin were going to be the death of me. The party following dinner was in full swing downstairs. But Tyson and I were more interested in something upstairs.

I cracked open Abby's bedroom door. It smelt like her.

I closed the door after me. The noise from downstairs was muffled. I laid Tyson in the middle of her bed and headed for the dresser.

Bottom drawer, she had said.

I pulled it out. She must have used it as a junk drawer. It was filled with old phones and chargers and all kinds of shit.

Then I saw what she was talking about. I picked up the cash and threw it aside. Picking up a manila file, I flicked it open.

Eight words sent a sucker punch to my guts.

Last Will and Testament of Abigail Rose Wilson.

I read it, though it was exactly as she'd said it was. She had left everything to me with a special mention of the care of Tyson. But he was referred to as our living child. And in case I was not willing to or able to provide care for Tyson, care of him was to go to Kim.

She had her funeral details written down, her headstone picked, what was to be written on it. She had even bought a plot, right next to Matthew's. I was feeling sick. This was all too much. Why had she put so much thought into this? She had planned this down to the last detail. So I didn't have to do anything. It was paid for. It was ordered. It just needed to be confirmed.

Fuck it. I was going to be sick.

I just made it to her toilet before I emptied my stomach of dinner. Meat was the worst to spew up.

I flushed the toilet and washed my hands, ignoring my reflection in the mirror.

Tyson was still in the middle of the bed. I sighed, running a hand through my hair and looking at the abandoned paperwork.

Fuck it.

I picked it up and put it on the bed.

That's when I noticed what else was in there. I had been so focused on the will I hadn't paid attention to what else was in there.

I pulled out a scrapbook and a phone. It had a sticky note on it. I picked if off. It was in Abby's handwriting.

"Turn on. Our Anniversary."

I held the button in and the iPhone turned on.

It had a PIN.

Our anniversary? Was she talking our wedding? I typed that in. Nope, it wasn't that. Then it hit me. 0312. The day I took her from that club party. It was also the PIN to our bank account.

I had told her that was our anniversary.

It unlocked the phone.

She'd told me I was romantic for that. I remembered her reaction when I told her. It was when I gave her her first car. Well, her first car from me.

No messages. No contacts. No apps. I pressed the photos. Bam. It was filled.

I'd look at that later. I picked up the book and paperwork and shoved the phone in my pocket.

"Come on, Tyson. Time for your dinner." I picked him up. He had started blowing spit bubbles. It felt like every day he was doing something different, something new.

I was closing the bedroom door when Kaylee walked straight into me.

I held Tyson away from me, taking the blow on my body.

"Shit. Sorry, Reaper! I didn't see you," she quickly started apologizing. "You have your hands full. Do you want a hand?"

I wasn't keen on handing her Abby's will or Tyson.

"I'm good." I looked at her swollen lip and bruised eye. "How you feeling?"

"I'm OK. Take more than a few punches to kill me."

"Yeah, well, if Kim could shoot straight, you wouldn't be saying that." I started to walk up the hallway. And to my surprise, she followed me.

"So, is this Tyson?"

"Yeah."

"He is adorable," she gushed.

"That he is." I stopped at my door and she hovered. "You alright, Kaylee?" I arched my eyebrows as I asked her. She was rocking on her feet and looked scared.

"Sure."

"You're lying. What's wrong?"

"Well, Kim was supposed to get me somewhere to stay and I kind of can't go downstairs and hook up with one of the men with her around."

Kim causing fucking trouble. Well, I was the president. This was a problem. How did I fix it?

"Can I come in here with you and Tyson? Not to sleep, but just to hide for a bit? Till Kim goes away at least?" She was nervous.

"Sure." Would I regret this? I unlocked the door and swung it open, letting her walk in.

"Thanks, Reaper."

I closed the door behind her. "No worries." I opened my bedside drawer and put in Abby's will and my scrapbook.

"Here, let me take Tyson." She held her hands out.

Why did it feel like I was about to make a big decision? I slowly handed her Tyson.

She took him with open arms.

Chapter 13

Reaper

What was Abby doing? Fuck, I had to get to her before she did something stupid. What did she mean by a game they played? She said it was sick and twisted. But she didn't tell me what. And my mind hadn't stopped running with possibilities. How could a game cause her to end her life?

Tyson giggled, causing me to looked over my shoulder. They were sitting on the couch. Kaylee was flicking through channels.

"What's his favorite show?"

I turned, taking my eyes off the boiling kettle. Her eyes darted from me to the television screen.

"Elmo puts him to sleep. He gets cranky if you put Thomas on. But he likes Bob," I riddled off the knowledge I had learned from Tyson and the late night hours I had spent watching television with him.

"What time does he normally go to sleep?"

"Nine."

"Well that means Bob then, 'cause we still have two hours," she said, sitting him on her chest and turning him to look at the television screen. She highlighted Netflix and the cartoon started playing.

Fuck that theme song. It got stuck in your head, going over and over. I swear I knew more about construction than I ever wanted to know. The kettle boiled. Right. Bottle.

I mixed the formula, added cold water and checked the temperature.

"You're good at that."

I looked up. Why was she looking at me like that? "Thanks."

"Never thought you would make a good father."

I walked over with the bottle. Nobody thought I would make a good father. I sure as hell never wanted the responsibility. But Abby saw something in me I didn't even know was there. She knew somehow. Abby knew I would make a good father. And I guess I wasn't doing a terrible job. But I had failed as a husband and that wiped the small smile from my face.

"Here, I'll do it." Kaylee took the bottle from me. "You should go downstairs or something." Kaylee gave Tyson his bottle and turned her attention back to the television. "I'm sure the boys are just starting the party."

"I'm not leaving Tyson."

"Then join us." She took her legs off the ottoman and moved down the couch.

There was a knock on my door and then it opened. "Reaper, can we talk?" Kim walked in, sounding upset. I watched her grip on the door handle tighten when she saw Kaylee. "You got to be kidding me." Her eyes narrowed and I wasn't surprised when the look of disbelief turned into fury.

"Can you organize Kaylee a room?" I knew what she was thinking but it wasn't like that.

"Why? When she has yours?" Kim spat and pointed an arm at Kaylee. "Because you're the mother charter president I have to keep what I think of you to myself. But I'm warning you, keep her away from me." She spun around, slamming the door.

"She has some serious issues," Kaylee said, and turned back to television, not looking the least bit scared. She should be. Kim was a loose cannon when it came to her temper.

"Yeah, and I have to deal with them. Can you watch him for a minute?" I asked, heading for my door.

"Sure. No worries."

I opened the door and saw her walking down the passage.

"KIM!"

I picked up my pace.

"Fucking stop, would you!"

She came to a grinding halt and spun around. "You have some nerve, Reaper."

"It isn't what it looks like."

She scoffed, shaking her head. "I tried to see what Abby saw in you and you know what? I thought I saw the real you. But clearly I was wrong because this is the type of guy you are."

"Kim, stop." Why the fuck wasn't she listening to me?

"You want to know something?" She stepped forward. I knew that look. "I won't let Tyson be brought up by some two-bit tramp. You hear me, Reaper. If Abby dies, I'm coming for Tyson. I know she has a will and I know it states if you are FIT to care for him. I wonder who the courts will side with? A man with a lengthy criminal history and known criminal activity or a straight-cut citizen. You and she can rot in hell, but you won't be taking my nephew with you."

She spun around and took off. Normally, as a president, you deal with threats every day. I knew threats against me would increase, being the mother charter president. But Kim had dealt me a low blow. Taking Tyson from me. Like fuck would I let that happen.

He and Abby meant everything to me. Why the fuck did people think they could take my family from me? Kim was just pissed off and protecting her sister's son. I knew that. That was what was stopping me from tearing down those stairs and going after her.

If Kaylee was the problem, I'd sort it out. Didn't anyone realize Abby wasn't replaceable? Even Abby thought she was replaceable. Fuck, she was wrong. So wrong. If something happened to her... screw that. It wasn't going to happen. I'd get to her in time.

I opened my bedroom door.

Kaylee wasn't on the couch. No, she was lying on my bed.

"Where's Tyson?" I scanned the room.

"He nodded off. He is in his crib." She sat up on her elbows. "You look tired. Maybe you should come to bed."

She was fucking with me, right? I just stared at her. Nope. She was serious. She was right, I was tired. I didn't sleep last night and it was showing.

"Yeah, I will." I moved toward her. A satisfied smile spread across her lips.

"You know Abby knew this would happen. That's why she hated me so much." She shrugged her shoulders. "Every president has a mistress."

"Is that so?" I stood in front of her. She was lying on her side. It only occurred to me now, but what had Kaylee said to get Kim so upset?

"Yep. I can handle her sister. And it's not like I have Abby to worry about." Kaylee lay back, looking like a woman who had gotten everything she wanted. "Anyway, you won't let anything happen to me."

I grabbed her wrist. She smiled. Then my grip tightened and, with one pull, she was off the bed. She was on Abby's side of the bed. But that was only her first mistake.

"REAPER! That hurts!"

"What did you say to Kim?"

"The truth! Now I'm all for rough play but you're hurting me." She pushed against me, but I only pulled her closer.

"Look at my neck." I had to keep my temper in check. I couldn't lay into her. She was a girl. Though I doubt Abby would mind. "Is that your name?"

"No."

"What does it say?"

She pursed her lips. "Abby."

"That's right. I'm Abby's. So stay the fuck away from me and our son. I suggest you find a new charter."

"But I came here for you!"

"I don't fucking know why."

"Because you need a woman. Who is caring for Tyson? Think about it, Kade. You need me."

"Don't call me that."

"Fine, Reaper. Either way, you need me. Abby isn't coming back. You should know that by now."

Abby. My Abby. Was she still breathing? Had she done it? Was I too late? Why was everyone talking like she was dead already? Didn't they know I wasn't going to let that happen?

"You're leaving." It wasn't a question or maybe. It was happening. If Abby ever found out Kaylee was here doing this crap, I wouldn't be able to stop her from killing her. My wife was actually good with a gun. I had experienced that when she shot me and watched her take a headshot without a flinch. She was a target shooter. She didn't spray bullets, hoping to get lucky. She aimed for the kill spot and she didn't miss. She only needed a gun and one bullet.

"Stop dragging me!" Kaylee tried to pull her arm free, but it was useless. She tripped down the stairs behind me, falling into my back. But I kept moving, The crowd parted.

"BRAD!" I shouted across the room. I bet he was regretting ever taking that vice president patch about now.

"Yeah, Prez?" He put his pool cue down and strolled toward me, his eyes on Kaylee, then back on me. "What you doing with the girl?"

"I need you to get her on a train, a bus, fuck, a flight. Just get her out of here."

"What, to another charter?"

"No, she's done serving the club."

"I AM NOT!"

I pulled her back as she fought me off, a pointless attempt on her behalf. "You are because I say you are." I threw her at Brad. "Fuck her off. I don't care how you do it."

"Righto, Prez." Brad gripped Kaylee by the shoulders as she attempted to bolt. "Consider it done."

"Thanks." I turned, ignoring Kaylee as she threw a tantrum in the middle of the bar. She was childish. Now I had to find Kim before she did something stupid. I knew Abby and she could be reckless when she was upset. I had a strong feeling Kim was the same.

***

Kim

I twisted her doorknob. It was unlocked. Thank Christ for that. It saved me picking the lock. I put my picking tool back in my boot and I flicked on the lights. My stomach dropped.

Someone had already been here. I looked at the drawer. It had been overturned. Who would know about Abby's hiding place? Reaper didn't even know, as far as I knew.

But clearly he did now.

Bastard.

Had she kept her will there?

Darn, I wished I had paid more attention to her when she came to me about it when she was pregnant. God, she was so doomsday. But she did give me a copy... I cursed. Why didn't I remember that earlier? I'd been waiting and waiting for people to fuck off from the hallway to come in here.

I poked my head out. No one. Good. I darted up the hallway, heading for my room. I glared at Reaper's door before I walked the next few rooms up and opened my door.

No way was I letting another woman bring up Abby's son. No way in hell. My fingers dashed across the PIN code for the safe. Opening it up. I moved my passport, cash and finally found what I was looking for.

I pulled the letter that was paper clipped to it off. This I hadn't forgotten about. Abby's letter to Reaper.

She said if something happened to her I was to give it to him. Something had happened to her. Still I hadn't done it.

But I knew I had to.

Because something had changed. I didn't know what. I didn't know how I knew but something had changed. I guess you could call it a twin thing. But my blood was running cold. I was tearing up nearly every minute I was with Tyson.

All this time, I had been confident we would get her back. But now I knew. I knew something else was going on. Abby had done something or was going to do something. Either way, I was getting the feeling I would be seeing my sister soon. She just wouldn't be alive.

There was a knock on my door and it opened. I spun around, putting my hand with the letter behind my back.

***

Reaper

I knocked on her door and opened it. "Kim?"

She was standing next to her open safe. Her eyes narrowed when she realized it was me. Guess I deserved the dirty look she was giving me.

"What the hell are you doing here? Did I not make myself clear?" Kim clicked her tongue, eyeing me like I didn't deserve a second of her time. God, I hadn't seen this side of her in a while. It reminded me of when she was younger and would fight with Abby.

"I got rid of Kaylee."

"Before or after you fucked her?"

God, she had an imagination and she really didn't think much of me. That bit was clear.

"I got rid of her, OK? She's gone."

She narrowed her eyes at me as if deciding whether to believe me or not. She continued to give me a dirty look, till she finally sighed and walked toward me.

"Well, if I shot straight she would have been gone this morning," Kim said, frustrated with herself. A small smile spread across her lips. "Should have taken lessons from Abby."

It sounded like she was forgiving me.

"I can give you a few."

"Really?"

"Every girl should know how to shoot. Especially when you live here around this lot." I didn't know if it was a good thing to encourage Kim's ability with a gun. I didn't want her walking around shooting people. If she had a real concern, I'd take care of it.

Then again, if I had listened to her this morning, she mightn't have been as pissed off as she was.

"I'll take you up on that." She stood in front of me and then went on her tippy toes, putting her arms around my neck. "Don't disappoint me again, OK?"

I wrapped my arms around her. God, she was tiny.

"Yeah, you got my word, Kim."

She pulled back, looking at me. Why was she crying?

"You should have this." She stepped back, handing me an envelope. "Abby said to give it to you if something happened to her."

"Nothing has happened to her." I saw the pain in her eyes. What did she know that I didn't? "Kim? What's wrong?"

"Abby's not coming back." She wiped a tear from her cheek and crossed her arms. "You aren't going to get to her in time."

"What do you mean by 'in time?'" Did Abby contact her again? Without me knowing? Had Abby told her? I thought I was the only one she had messaged. Maybe I was wrong.

"Just call it a feeling," she muttered and dropped her eyes to the ground. "I know Abby. As much as I know she is strong, I know what I'd do. And we usually think alike."

I stepped forward, gripping her chin gently and making her look up at me. "What would you do?"

She took a staggering breath in. "I wouldn't let him win."

Sick. I thought I was going to be sick again. If Kim was thinking that, I knew then that Abby was serious about it. Abby was deadly serious. She wouldn't let him win. She wanted to go out on her terms. I had heard it. Fuck, I watched her say it. But now...

I needed... I had to...

"Here, Reaper, sit down."

"Do you think she will do it?" I muttered. I was hoping that Kim would say that Abby didn't have in her, that she would never do something like that.

But then Kim nodded her head. "I don't think. I know she would. She'd rather die at her own hand than let him get the pleasure."

"He would have to give her an opportunity to, though. It's not like he would hand her a loaded gun."

Kim pressed her lips together.

"What?" She was thinking something that I was missing.

"Well. She could just provoke him. She would already know his weaknesses. That's what I'd do."

Was that what Abby was thinking? Did she really want to be beaten to death? Of course she didn't want to be. She just saw no other option. Didn't she know I wasn't going to let that happen? I had already put the message out that I wanted to speak with Jake.

Now I was just waiting on one of his muppets to get the word to him.

The waiting was the worst. But it hadn't even been twenty-four hours.

***

Abby

I dropped the dishes in the sink. Another meal done. I was so sick of cleaning up after them. I'd rather be locked in my room but Jake liked having me in view. He liked reaching for me. He liked touching me.

Like I was the forbidden fruit and he was hungry for something that he shouldn't dare touch.

He was signing his own death warrant.

"Abby?"

I looked over my shoulder. "What?"

"Wanna play a game?"

Words I had been longing to hear since I sent Kade that video. Finally. I wiped my hands on a dishtowel. Jake was sick and twisted. He was doing it to torment me, to prolong my suffering. But didn't he realize when you take everything away from someone, they have nothing to lose? He was making me dance on the line of death. This time, though, I wasn't dancing on the line. I was going to jump across it.

I walked to the table. I could do this. I could totally do this. I wasn't nervous. I had thought it through. I didn't want to give him the pleasure of killing me. But if this plan failed, I had another one to back it up. I was ending this on my terms.

I took the seat across from him and smiled. "Always."

"See, boys, she looks forward to my games." Jake pulled the revolver out, putting in a bullet and spinning the barrel. He then handed it to me. "Let's see if you are as lucky as my wife."

I should be saying a prayer or something. Instead, I was thinking of one thing. One memory flooded back to me. I was getting a drink from the bar. It was a club party. And I felt him standing behind me, his arms locking me to the spot at the bar, his fingers wrapping over my hand clenching a beer. The coldness of his rings as they pressed into my fingers. The shiver he sent down my spine as he talked with me.

I left with him that night. Me. I left with the biker. I chose him that night. I chose the Reaper.

I put the gun to my temple.

I had thought about turning the gun on Jake and shooting him. But that plan would fail. I wouldn't get the time to get out alive. And then Andrew or Billy would kill me.

This was the better option.

I pulled the trigger. Nothing. Jake smiled, but I wasn't done. I pushed the chair away from the table so he couldn't stop me and I kept pulling, counting the chambers.

Jake's eyes widened and he lunged across the table at me.

But I had already reached the last chamber and I pulled the trigger.

Chapter 14

Abby

Nothing happened. A noise. That was it. You had to be fucking kidding me. I breathed heavily in and out. It was a blank bullet. I glared at Jake as he scrambled off the table and laughed.

"Now, sweetheart, you didn't actually think I'd give you a loaded gun." He stood up. "Billy, how about you get Abby something stronger than beer? Would have taken a lot of courage to pull that trigger."

He laughed. OK, fine. Plan B. I threw the gun across the table at him. It missed his head. I walked around. I was still ending this on my own terms.

"You said your wife had a painless death." I was standing beside him now, and he slowly got up and towered over me. From the edge in my voice, he knew I wasn't finished with him.

"You want to tell me different?" Jake was daring me to ruin his little bubble where his wife got a peaceful ending. The tint in his eyes told me I had him exactly where I wanted him.

"Just when Reaper got back, he told it a bit different." I had to lie. I would lie. I wanted this over. My cheek stung as Jake backhanded me. Bring it on.

"He didn't gloat about my wife's death. He was ashamed of it. Still is." Jake had me by the neck and pushed me backward till I was against a wall. My back ached as he slammed me against it. But this was only the beginning.

I laughed, mocking him. "Do you even know Reaper? He is made of stone. Heartless. He is no hero. And he's on the wrong side of heaven but the right side of hell. He is called the Reaper for a reason."

Jake let go of my neck, only to punch me in the stomach. I collapsed, gasping for air. I could do this.

I turned and looked up to him from on the ground.

"He said she screamed. She was terrified. But–" The air was squeezed from lungs. Jake straddled me. His hands tightened around my neck.

"What were you going to say?" Jake spat down at me, daring me to keep going.

I pried at his hands. Now for the knockout. This would make him go through with it. My voice was raspy and just above a whisper. I gulped down the tiniest amount of air. But it was enough.

"But that was nothing to when she screamed as he raped her." It was low but it was enough. He heard it. I saw the fury. The need for revenge. The despair. I saw it all flash through his eyes as he squeezed tighter. My eyesight became blurry and then bloody. Then I was choking.

It was an automatic reaction. I couldn't stop myself from prying at his hands, trying to get air.

"Boss, you got a message, something about the girl and cash." Andrew stood over us. "You sure you want to end it like this?"

My eyes closed. I fought underneath him, even though this was what I wanted.

I gasped. Nothing happened. I was going numb. Each body part was slowly stopping. First my legs stopped kicking. My arms got heavy and my hands, locked over his, went limp.

All energy gone.

I wasn't looking up at Jake anymore. My eyelids were too heavy to open. It was ending, on my terms.

Images flashed through my head. The first time I saw Kade. Him saving me in the alley. Crying into him. The sound of us laughing, shopping on the night of my eighteenth birthday. Him leaving. So much time we had spent apart. Then him holding Tyson, smirking at me like he had won the jackpot.

Then finally him at the hospital, giving me a lecture about driving. It was as if I was back there, standing at the car, watching him walk to his bike. It was my last memory of him and my last thought.

***

Kim

"I can't do it." I gave up and spun around. Brad had been working on Reaper's bike. He kept saying it was an embarrassment seeing Reaper on something that wasn't as mean as him. But Brad had stopped to watch the show. He was standing next to Cameron, who laughed every time I missed.

Lucky for me, a few other members were enjoying my lack of gun skills as well. They had all given their input. But basically, they put it down to me being a girl.

"Come on, Kim. Try again," Trent encouraged me.

It made it worse that he was witnessing this. It may also have been affecting my ability. I swear I was getting worse.

I pointed the gun and fired it. Missed the beer bottles that were lined up on the cabin of the truck and I watched the tire of the truck deflate.

Cameron burst out laughing again. I glared over my shoulder at him. Maybe I would do better with a human target. It didn't help that the other bikers sniggered.

"Kim, maybe you should aim for the truck and then you might get a bottle." Cameron stopped laughing for a minute to give his words of wisdom.

"That's it. I'm done." I turned back to face them. I was not doing anything more embarrassing. I had my limit for the day.

Reaper got up off the picnic table, leaving Tyson in his stroller and walked toward me. He reached into his leather vest, holding his cigarette in his mouth, and pulled a gun from his holster.

"Here, try this." He handed it to me. And he took my gun from me. "This is old." He gave me a look to say he wasn't impressed.

I rolled my eyes and gripped his gun. This was pointless.

"Both hands."

I brought my other hand around it. "Abby can shoot with one hand," I grumbled.

"Move this foot back." He kicked at my right foot, causing it to go back. I staggered back. "Now square your shoulders."

I pulled my shoulders forward.

"No." Reaper's hands were on my shoulders and he pulled them back. "Now bring your left hand underneath." I was gripping it with my left hand! "No, like this." He readjusted my grip on the gun. OK. I had that wrong.

"There is no point, Reaper. I'm useless."

"Lower the gun," Reaper said. Everyone in the background said he was wasting his time. I huffed and started to glare at them, but his hand went under my chin and redirected my head toward the bottles. "Don't listen to them."

"Easy for you to say." He didn't have everyone laughing at him!

"Alright. It is set up. Now breathe and shoot." He stepped away.

He made it sound easy.

"Come on, Kim," he said behind me.

For some reason, he hadn't given up on me yet. OK. The bottle was lined up. I pulled the trigger. And the bottle broke. That had to be beginner's luck. I aimed up a second one. I watched it splinter and the contents spill over the truck. Again, it must have been chance. I lined up the third one. A smile spread across my face.

I had never felt so much satisfaction as I did seeing those bottles explode. I turned to Reaper. OK, maybe he wasn't a bad teacher. I was so excited I jumped toward him.

"Did you see that I totally did it?!" I yelled and he caught me.

"Good girl." He held me with one arm.

"I'm competition now," I smirked at him.

He opened his mouth to say something, but someone else's voice interrupted us.

"Try doing that not set up by Reaper and with a man coming at you. Oh, wait. You couldn't."

I turned in time to see Trigger coming toward us, looking more furious than normal. Why was he glaring at me? I was mad with him last time I checked.

"She won't have to because I'll be doing it for her." Reaper put me on the ground. "Where have you been, Trigger?"

Reaper being protective of me just pissed off Trigger more. I think Reaper did it on purpose. Yeah, by the wink he just gave me, he did it on purpose.

"Off the grid." Trigger shrugged his shoulders. "Kim, can I talk to you?"

"No." I handed Reaper back his gun and gave him a smile.

"Come on, Kim." Trigger followed me as I headed toward Tyson.

"Not interested." I grinned at Tyson and put my arms out for him. "Did you see your aunty make those shots.?" I lowered to my knees in front of Tyson.

"Please, Kim."

Why was he bothering with me? I picked Tyson up and twirled around, right into Trigger. "God, back off." I sheltered Tyson from the blow. "Why are you up in my face? Did you not see I can shoot now?"

"Please, can I speak to you?" Trigger looked at me pleadingly. He pushed his sunglasses up and looked at me seriously. "Please. Don't make me beg." He looked over his shoulder. "In front of everyone..."

This wasn't like Trigger. He didn't do public. I tilted my head, studying him. What was so important that he had to speak to me now?

"Tyson needs his bottle." I moved around him.

"You alright, Kim?" Reaper asked as I walked past, giving me a look to say he would make Trigger go away if I wanted him to. Reaper had been waiting for a reason to lay into Trigger since he hit me. Trigger was following me. I might have told him no, but he wasn't listening.

Was I alright? "Yep. Tyson and I'll be inside."

He nodded his head but his eyes were on Trigger, who was being my shadow.

I ignored him and dodged Trent's eyes. I picked up my pace. What was Trigger's problem?

I pushed open the clubhouse door and didn't hold it open for him. But that didn't stop him from following.

"You know, I'm not going to stop following you."

I walked through the bar and out the back, into the kitchen. Ignoring him. I turned on the kettle. I didn't realize he was so close till I felt his chest against my back.

"Look at me."

Why? Why was he even talking to me?

"Kim?"

I slowly turned around. "What? What do you want?"

He gently lifted my chin and ran a finger across my cheek. A frown appeared on his face.

"It's still bruised."

"Barely." At first, I had tried makeup. But that didn't really cover it. So I just gave up and let it be bruised. It had faded now and was basically gone.

"Never heard you call me Lucas before." The corners of his lips twitched up.

"Yeah, well you never hit me before." The kettle boiled.

"Here, give me Tyson."

He was being nice. Trigger didn't do nice. Only when he wanted something. But if he thought he would get laid just for holding Tyson while I made a bottle, he was wrong. I handed Tyson to him.

"Make sure you support his head." I handed Tyson into Trigger's open arms.

"I have held him before, Kim." He rolled his eyes at me.

"Yeah, well, you have been gone for a while, haven't you?" I turned back to make the bottle, grabbing the formula.

"I expected you to call." His words were tinged with hurt.

I scoffed and kept making the formula. "That would mean I care." I added the boiling hot water to the bottle.

Trigger went quiet. Good, 'cause I was sick of him and his fake words.

"I fucked up, Kim."

I turned on the filtered tap and added cold water. I checked the temperature. Ouch. Too hot. I swear by now I should be better at this.

"Did you hear me?"

"I'm busy." I added more cold water.

"I fucked up, Kim, and I want you back."

"You never had me."

I turned around. Why was he looking at me like that?

"You were mine," he shifted Tyson and reached for me, holding Tyson in one of his big arms, "and I fucked up."

Why was he doing this? I might have waited for him. I might have been hooked on him for years. But he never cared. He used me and left me. I was good for one thing in his books. I knew that. Still I waited for years. I watched him with other women, and then as soon as he called my name, I would come.

Pathetic.

"I was yours, but you never wanted me. So now we are over. Well, I'm getting over you. Like I said, we aren't friends. We aren't lovers. So you should go find someone else to talk to. Now give me Tyson."

He wouldn't hand me Tyson. He muttered something under his breath. I swore it was something along the lines of how stupid he was.

He took a noticeable step closer to me and lifted my head to look up at him. "I want you. Hear me, Kim. I want you."

"Well bully bully for you! You want me, so what? I should just go back to sleeping with you whenever you feel like it? Fuck off." I was not desperate. I had learned my lesson.

"Nah, I don't want you like that, sweetheart." His hand cupped my face and he stepped in even closer to me.

Why did he have to get so close?

"I want you, all of you. Not just in my bed. I want you on my lap at every club party and I want to touch you whenever I feel like it and darn it, Kim, I want you to tell me your every problem and I want to fix it."

I took a slow breath and chewed my bottom lip. "You're just saying this because you have been on a bender."

"I wasn't on a bender."

"Right, you were 'off the grid.'"

"Yeah, thinking about you."

I slapped his hand off my cheek. "I'm not going to believe that you went off the grid just to think about me. Now, give me Tyson. I have a shitload to get done today, Trigger."

The softness in his eyes hardened. "You had time to play with Reaper."

Jealousy. I swore that was the only emotion he knew. "Tyson, please?"

"You two have seemed to have gotten even closer since I was gone."

I groaned. "The bottle is getting cold. And I don't know what you are talking about!"

"You basically jumped him, like he was your boyfriend."

Trigger's disgust with the situation was being heard loud and clear. "Reaper is family. You, on the other hand, are nothing. So fuck off and give me my nephew!"

"Not till you agree to giving us a shot."

Well, that wasn't going to happen. "Here, you give him the bottle." I shoved it at him. He smiled, like that was what he wanted.

"You had something to eat?"

"Why do you care?" I was hungry, but I wasn't going to tell him that.

"'Cause I'm making you my number one priority."

"Yep, sure, you." I nodded my head. "Till you see a pretty brunette tonight and decide, fuck it, I wouldn't mind having a piece of her."

I knew him too well. I knew his behavior. I knew what he was like. He couldn't fool me.

He looked at me determinedly and his thumb ran over my bottom lip. He looked at my lips as if he was dying to kiss me, as if he had never had kissed me before.

"I'm not touching another girl." His hot breath swirled around my face. It didn't smell of liquor and cigarettes. No, it was minty and fresh, welcoming. "All I want is you."

He was saying what I had always wanted a guy to say to me. No, not any guy to say to me. Him. All I ever wanted from him. To want me.

I didn't know if he was serious. There was only one way to find out. "Fine. Prove it."

"I will. But you have to promise me something."

Typical. He wanted something from me. "What?"

"Stay the fuck away from Trent."

"Why? Cause he actually treats me like I'm worth something?"

"No, because you're mine, whether you want to admit it or not. But I won't have him touching something that belongs to me."

"I'll do what I want."

"Fine then. Every time he so much as looks at you, expect my fists to get involved."

I narrowed my eyes at him. Was he serious? Would he really get in a punch out because of that? The look on his face told me he was dead serious.

"I won't let you make me wait for you," I blew out.

"Just give me a chance to prove it to you." His hand ran down my bare arm and he dipped his head to look me in the eye. "Please."

Why the hell did I still want him? I gritted my teeth. I was stupid. So fucking stupid. But I couldn't stop myself. "OK. But as soon as you touch another girl, and I know you will, the deal is off. You have a week."

A grin spread across his face. "That's all I need." He handed me the empty bottle. "I'm not leaving your side this week."

"Well, you are in for a boring week then because I have a shitload of errands to get done." I cursed. "Shit, I was meant to pay the boys last week. Surprised no one has pulled me up on it." Why hadn't Reaper mentioned it?

Usually, the treasurer made the payments but Reaper hadn't chosen one yet. So it sort of just became a job I did. But I was sure if Abby were here, she'd be doing it.

"I can do that. What else?" Trigger offered. Right, Trigger used to be treasurer when he was the VP.

Should I take his help? I knew he would let me down and I'd get upset. I was setting myself up for disappointment. Yet here I was, about to repeat all my mistakes.

"Thanks. And just other shit from washing to groceries."

"The club girls do the washing, don't they?" He frowned at me.

A smile spread across my lips. He most likely thought his clothes got magically washed. "Who do you think runs the club girls?"

"President."

"Usually the old lady does. But..." My smile dried up. Abby wasn't here to do it. Trigger must have seen it on my face. I quickly looked the other way. "Anyway, I do it. Now give me Tyson."

"Kim, I'm heading out. Trent is going to watch you." Reaper walked in, talking, and stopped when he saw Trigger with Tyson.

"I don't need anyone to watch me." I narrowed my eyes at him. I didn't need a babysitter. "I don't need a babysitter. So Trent can go with you."

"Not leavings you alone, Kim." Reaper gave me a look and I knew I was a fool to argue with him but I wasn't not going to.

"She won't be alone, Prez. I've got her." Trigger handed me Tyson.

"Thought you hated watching her?" Reaper crossed his arms and walked more into the kitchen. He wasn't happy, or accepting Trigger's offer. "You will fuck off and then Kim will be by herself."

"I'm not leaving."

"Again, I say I don't need anyone!" I stomped my foot. Why weren't they listening to me? They both looked at me, giving me a look to say I was going to lose this argument.

"It's alright, Prez. I've got it." Trigger walked toward him. "I'm not fucking off."

Reaper looked over Trigger's shoulder at me. "You OK with this, Kim?"

Was I OK with Trigger watching me again? Trigger or Trent. Decide, Kim. "I, um…" I stared at Trigger's back. I promised him a week. One week wasn't long. Normally he would screw up before the day ended. "Sure." Trigger would have a new girl under his arm tonight. "For today," I added.

Reaper nodded his head. "Fine. But if I come back to you two fighting, you'll be meeting my fist again, Trigger."

"Where are you going, anyway?" I asked, walking toward him with Tyson. "You said you raided all the houses."

"Found out the name of one of the guys who's at Jake's right hand. An Andrew Matthews. We just got an address for him."

I knew what this meant. Reaper was going out to reap.

"Well, at least ice your knuckles when you get back," I said, knowing him too well. He wouldn't be letting someone else do the beating.

"Will do. See you three later." He turned and left.

He was leaving me with Trigger. God, this was going to be interesting. I promised myself I would not open my heart up to him. He had destroyed it too many times. But at the same time, I wanted him to do something to prove he was worth the risk.

I just didn't know what he could do to make me trust him again.

***

I flipped the meat on the BBQ. Where were the guys? I expected them back by now.

"You cooked a lot."

I looked over my shoulder. Trigger hadn't left me all day. He had kept his word to Reaper.

"Normal amount." I turned back to the BBQ. All I was missing was the men.

"Tyson is still asleep."

"He'll wake when his dad gets here." I reached for my cider. The only ones around were the girls. Trigger still hadn't claimed one for the night, but I should give him time.

"Sounds like that is now," Trigger said, taking a steak off the BBQ. I listened more closely and could hear the dull roar of the bikes. The roar got louder.

I started dumping the meat onto plates and the girls started taking them out to the tables. It was a warm evening.

The bikes started to roar in. Men got off, the noise of the bikes slowly dying. Jeez, how many members did Reaper take with him? It looked like the whole mother charter. I then noticed the bikes lining up on the road. And it looked like other charters.

I still wasn't used to so many men.

The men flocked to the tables. I was guessing Reaper didn't let them have lunch by the way they were laying into the food.

The lot was backed up but the men parted. Then I saw Reaper taking his temper out on the bike he was riding, kicking it over and swearing.

What was wrong with him?

I watched him storm toward us with Brad following him. He looked furious.

I founde it very unlikely that Reaper, as angry as he was, would have taken his anger out on his bike. The sooner Brad got it back on the road the better.

"Kim, whatever you do, just keep your mouth shut," Trigger said, standing next to me.

I looked at him in disbelief. "No way." I dropped the tongs and met Reaper at the club door. "What's wrong?"

His nostrils were flaring. His fists were clenched at his sides.

"Move, Kim," he gritted out. He looked like he was barely keeping control of his temper to talk to me, and really just wanted to push past me.

"No. What's wrong?" I looked at his knuckles. They weren't bloody. I arched my eyebrows at him. "Something didn't go to plan."

"The house was guarded. Couldn't get closer than a block without being shot at."

"What, the house Abby's at?" My eyes widened. Hope. Hope filled me.

"No. Andrew's house."

My hope was shattered. "So, what, you couldn't get to him?" I was sure Reaper would find another way to get to him.

"Not with this fucking lot providing cover," Reaper yelled over his shoulder. I felt sorry for the boys. They were dealing with Reaper's stress.

"Did you at least get the message out?" Trigger asked. "Does Jake know you want to speak with him?"

"You want to talk to Jake?" I frowned. "Why?"

"Everybody fucking knows I want to speak to him. Even citizens," Reaper scoffed and ran a hand through his hair. "Still he fucking hasn't reached out."

"Maybe Abby killed him," Trigger said. As soon as the words left his mouth, I threw an arm into his stomach.

"Shut up."

"What? She's good with a gun." Trigger looked at me as if wanting me to fight him on it.

"He wouldn't be handing her a gun, now, would he?" Reaper muttered. "Move, Kim."

"Nope." I crossed my arms. "You need food."

"Not hungry."

"You haven't been eating." I noticed that the other night. He was avoiding food as if it was making him sick. He wasn't drinking liquor and wasn't eating. He would only get grumpier. He was living on cigarettes.

"So?"

I stepped out of his way and started dishing food up randomly onto a plate. And then I shoved it in his hand.

"Eat." I heard Tyson cry. I pointed a finger at Reaper. "I mean it. If you don't eat, I'll have you on lockdown."

Tyson crying had my attention. So I turned around and headed inside. The air conditioning was welcoming after standing in front of that hot BBQ. "Coming, Tyson." I picked up my pace.

***

I lit up a cigarette, inhaling the much-needed smoke. Reaper was at the bar, eating, and every so often giving me a dirty look. He didn't like being told what to do. Tyson was in his stroller and I was rocking it while he reached out and touched the toys hanging down from it.

I was standing next to the bar, watching Reaper. I swear he couldn't take much smaller bites.

Trigger dragged a stool up beside me. I glanced at him but my eyes were on Reaper. Why was he suddenly avoiding food? I watched him as he poked at the salad.

I gasped as I was dragged off my feet and onto Trigger's lap, his arms wrapping around me. I looked at the food in front of him.

"You're hungry," I stated and then looked back at Reaper. I was ignoring the feeling swelling in me as he positioned me on his lap. I put the cigarette back in my mouth.

"Not for me, sweetheart."

I frowned. Then why the hell would he dish up so much food? I looked back at him and my eyes darted between his face and the plate. "That's a lot of food."

"Didn't know what you wanted." He shrugged his shoulders while his hand rubbed up and down my thigh. God, that felt amazing.

Wait a sec, did he just say me? "I'm not hungry." I leaned into the bar and grabbed a beer.

"You are drinking on an empty stomach."

"I ate earlier."

"No, you didn't. I've been with you all day."

Darn, he caught my lie. I turned on his lap to look him in the eye. "I'm not hungry."

"Wait a fucking second." Reaper picked up on our conversation. "If you are making me eat, you have to fucking eat."

"You're not really eating," I challenged him.

"Fine, I'll stop."

We had a stare off. He was lowering his knife and fork.

"Fine. I'll eat." I pointed a finger at him. "You better fucking keep eating. I want that plate empty."

Trigger had cut up a piece of steak and had it on a fork for me. I snatched it from him. "You are not feeding me." I butted out my cigarette on the bar.

He laughed and kissed my bare shoulder, sending tingles through my body. "As long as you eat, babe."

***

Reaper

Zero, three, one, two.

The phone unlocked. I put my cigarette in the ashtray. I went to the photos and clicked on the first one. It was an ultrasound picture. I swiped across. It was a video. I pressed play.

"See this, Reaper. This is what I'm dealing with." Abby was pointing the camera at Brad, who looked to be buying something. They looked to be in a baby store. Abby turned the camera on herself. "Some fool gave him a bank card."

I smiled. I remembered telling Brad to go crazy.

"Three hours, Reaper. Three fucking hours. I think he just likes the girls talking to him. That and burning a hole in your bank card." She gave the camera a pointed look. "You owe me three hours. Actually, three and a half."

"I brought a crib."

The camera went from Abby to Brad. He was standing in front of her now. "Hear that, Reaper? He brought a crib."

"You filming this for Reaper?"

"Yep."

"He is going to regret ever giving me this bank card." A grin spread across Brad's face.

"I regret him giving you his bank card. Now, who is going to put that crib together? You do realize they are flat-packed, right?" I could hear the smile in Abby's voice as Brad's face was wiped of expression.

"'Course I did."

"So who is putting it together?"

Brad grinned. "Reaper. Hear that, man? You are. Now come on, Abby, we have to collect it from out back."

The video stopped. I swiped to the next one.

Roach was cursing on the ground with a piece of what looked like Tyson's crib.

"So, Dad, what were you saying about Reaper?" Abby's voice sounded amused.

"I told you! He is fucking useless. How the hell does this go with that? Fucking stupid instructions." Roach held two pieces up. "I'm telling you now, Abby. A father should be here doing this shit."

"You don't have to put it together, Dad," Abby laughed.

"What, you saying I can't do it?" Roach looked up, more furious. "What you doing with that phone? Are you filming me?"

"Yep. Proof for Reaper of what you really think of him."

Roach scoffed. "He knows what I think of him. Fucking knocking up my daughter, then fucking off."

The camera moved and Abby's face was on screen. "Hear what I have to deal with?"

"You sending that to him?"

"Maybe."

"Well, tell him to hurry the fuck up."

"Why, Dad, because you can't get the crib together?" Abby laughed and it was fucking music to my ears.

"Well, he is young. He should know how to do this shit."

"So, Reaper, you have to come back. Otherwise our child will have nothing to sleep in. So you have five months."

"Fuck that. I'll get it together," Roach barked and Abby rolled her eyes.

The video stopped. Why hadn't she sent me these? I had barely heard a word from her while I was gone. She never called. I always called her. I guess she didn't want to bother me.

I swiped to the next video.

Abby's eyes were swollen. Her cheeks were red. "You told me months today. Months." She gulped and wiped a tear off her cheek. "You're going to miss everything." The phone went black and the video stopped.

I did miss everything.

I swiped to the next video.

Abby's smiling face greeted me. "Guess what I did today? You won't be able to guess. I went to a store without being forced." She gave me a pointed look. "It was to print these." She held up an envelope. "I've forgiven you, by the way. I know you are doing everything possible to get back." She sighed. "Well, I hope you are." Her eyes lit up. "I've been working on this all week." The camera flicked to an open scrapbook. "I'm actually drawing again. Not very well. But I'm giving it a try. I'm doing this for It. Yes, I'm calling your son or daughter It. You can yell at me about it if you ever see this. Brad calls it Thing. So, It isn't really that bad."

The video stopped. She called Tyson It? For how fucking long?

I swiped to the next video.

Abby looked exhausted. I could hear the dull sound of a party. "This is your wife. I demand that you come back and make my stupid father's charter shut the hell up! It's a long weekend and the boys haven't stopped. I swear–" She stopped talking and a frustrated expression crossed her face. "You hear that? They turned the stupid music up louder! That's it." She threw the blankets back and got out of bed.

"I'm leaving."

The video stopped. She better fucking not have left. She knew she was on lockdown. Why hadn't someone stopped her?

I pressed play on the next video.

"So, I escaped. I bet you are pissed right now if you are watching this." She gave me a knowing smile. She had no idea how pissed off I was. "Before you go batshit crazy, you should know I didn't get out by myself." She rolled her eyes. "No, I had to bring the ringleader of the party with me."

The camera went off her face. Brad was pulling his boots off. "You messaging Reaper this late at night?"

"So you admit it's LATE?"

Brad rolled his eyes. "Harmless fun, Abby." He went to get up but wobbled on his feet, losing his balance and was forced to sit back down on the bed.

"I think your best friend is drunk."

"And stoned," Brad added.

"You really shouldn't have said that."

"I can still shoot straight! Now come to bed. For someone who was so tired, you sure are taking your sweet ass time to get to bed." Brad stretched out on the bed and grabbed a pillow.

"Wonder what Reaper thinks of you sharing a bed with me?"

They did fucking what?

"I'm sure I'll get a black eye for it. Now come to bed."

"Fine."

They shared a bed. They shared a fucking bed. He was right. He would be getting a black eye. Maybe a few bruised ribs as well.

"Reaper?" Kim poked her head in the door and I locked the phone.

"Yeah."

"Why aren't you up yet?" Kim let the door swing open. "Oh, Tyson's still asleep."

I glanced over my shoulder. He was. But that wasn't the reason I wasn't up yet. I had been too busy going through Abby's spare phone.

"Well, I can take over. The boys are all up and are looking lost without you." Kim walked in and sat on the couch. "Why aren't you dressed? Not like you to sleep in."

I grabbed a shirt off the floor. "Did you know Abby filmed videos when she was pregnant?"

Kim scoffed. "Do I? I swear that phone was glued to her hand. You must have gotten sick of them, right? Why are you rewatching them?" She twisted on the couch to look at me.

So she knew. Brad knew. I didn't. Why didn't Abby send them?

"Something like that." I put my rings on and walked toward Kim.

Kim put her hand out, holding my vest. "Oh, and I don't want to put you in a foul mood but..."

"Spit it out, Kim."

"Your parents are downstairs. With Dad."

Fucking Roach. Stirring shit up. "I'll handle it." I put my guns in my holster. "You alright with Trigger watching you today?"

"Yep."

"You two seem to be getting close."

She laughed. "In order for him to be watching me, he would have to get out of bed. So I doubt I'll see him." She shrugged and stretched out on the couch.

My phone starting ringing on the bed. I walked toward it. It would be Brad wondering where I was. I answered, barking a hello into it.

"It's Jake." His voice was dark and I could hear how amused he was with himself.

"Is Abby alive?" That was my only question. All I cared about was her. I needed to know she was still breathing and hadn't done something stupid before I could get to her.

Chapter 15

Jake

Didn't know how it happened. Couldn't explain it if I wanted to. Somehow Abby turned into someone I didn't just want to kill. At the time all I could think about was ending her life.

Now that I was starting to get to know her. I found myself not being able to go through with it. There had to be another way to punish Reaper for taking my wife.

Maybe I should just take Abby from him completely. But keep her in my life.

She was testing my limits today. And I did nearly kill her.

As soon as she blacked out, I knew then. I couldn't kill her. Not now.

I was attracted to her. I could see what Reaper saw in her. And I could also understand why he loved her as much as he did. Any man would love Abby. Wasn't just her looks either.

So what do I do now?

Reaper wanted to speak with me. It was all over town. Maybe I should have a conversation with him.

There was another way to punish Reaper and that wasn't just taking Abby's life. A death would be final. But if I kept her alive and under my control for the rest of her life. Living Reaper to be forever looking for her, he would never get closeure. And I was liking that idea more and more.

Abby

Why the hell was I still breathing? I had baited the shit out of Jake. I remembered blacking out. I thought that was death. But when I woke up in this cursed bedroom, I knew my life hadn't been taken yet.

What the hell stopped him? Why couldn't he just get it over with? I sat up, putting my feet on the floor. How long had I been out for? I had a feeling it was longer than a few hours. I looked outside. It looked like morning.

There was a knock on the door and my head snapped to it as it opened.

"Jake wants you downstairs." Andrew looked over at me. "Finally awake, I see."

What did he want? I pushed myself off the bed. Andrew had left the door open. It wasn't like Jake to send someone to get me. He usually liked to personally annoy me. I walked down the stairs.

"Why aren't I dead?" I demanded as soon as I hit the last step. "Why couldn't you go through with it?"

Jake smirked, dropping his cards on the table. "Just be thankful you are still breathing."

"Can't you fucking tell? I'm fucking jumping for joy." My tone was as sour as my expression. I wanted this over with. Why couldn't I get it my way? I wasn't going to let him win. This was a game and I was ready to play till the death, literally.

Jake pulled out his phone. "Come here."

"Do I have to?"

"Yes."

I dragged myself around the table and stood next to him. "What? What do you want?" Why had he gotten me out of bed? Why did he want me down here?

He handed me his phone and my eyes widened. Why would he willingly give me a phone? Had he lost his mind?

"I want you to call your husband." He reached out for me and pulled me onto to his lap. "I'm assuming you know his number."

"Why?"

"He wants to talk to me. Guessing about you." Jake gestured with his head for me to hurry up. "Go on. Call."

"I know he wants to do more than talk to you." If I knew Reaper at all, I knew he wanted blood by now.

"He is the one going around town, demanding I call him. So dial his number and I'll talk to him."

Did I do it? Why was Reaper hellbent on talking to Jake? More importantly, why hadn't he found me by now? Because Jake had me hidden in this mansion. I sighed and my fingers dashed across the screen. I handed him back the phone. I had to trust Reaper. He must have a reason to speak to Jake.

Jake put the phone on loudspeaker and placed it on the table in front of us. My heartbeat was going a million times a second hearing the ringing. I tried to get out of Jake's lap but he just wrapped an arm around me, making me stay put.

"Hello?" Reaper was rude and basically barked into the phone. Now that's my husband. I smiled.

"It's Jake." Jake looked at me, smug.

Reaper went silent for a second. "Is Abby alive?" I could hear the panic in his voice, the nerves of the unknown. He should know by now, this wasn't going to end with me alive. I mightn't be dead today but if I had it my way, I would be as soon as possible.

"Maybe," Jake answered. "What do you want? Heard rumors on the street you want to give me back my money."

This was over money? I rolled my eyes. Of course it was. Jake loved his money.

"Is Abby alive?" Reaper demanded.

"Yes." Jake looked at me. "Don't think your wife is happy about that."

"You want your money back?"

"Let me guess. I get it back if I give Abby back?" Jake's hand ran up my thigh. "Not going to happen, Reaper. I can make more money."

"It would take you a while to make that much. Just give her up, Jake."

"Not happening."

"Fine. You promise me you keep her alive for a month. Give me more time to find her." Reaper was desperate and I wanted to tell him I was fine with what was going to happen. I opened my mouth but Jake's hand quickly wrapped around it, stopping me from talking.

"And I get my cash back?"

"Yes," Reaper gritted out, "if you can prove Abby is still alive. And she has to be kept breathing for a month."

I bit Jake's finger. He cursed and shook his hand. "Don't be stupid, Reaper. Like he is going to keep his word!"

"ABBY!"

"Yes, I'm here and I'm fine. Don't give him his money. He will only kill me anyway. His word doesn't mean shit."

"I always keep my word. I said I'd kill you and I'm still firm on that," Jake said and his hand was back on my thigh.

I squirmed on his lap. But he just held me in place.

"So, you keep her alive, I give you the money and we have a deal?" Reaper was crazy. As if this was going to work.

"How much money are we talking about?" I asked both Reaper and Jake.

"Nearly four mill." Jake looked at me. "Your husband is willing to pay me a large amount to keep you breathing."

"Keep it." Was I the only one seeing that ripping Jake off was the best possible outcome of this situation? "Seriously, Reaper, don't give him a fucking dollar."

"Jake, you promise to keep her breathing for a month?" Reaper ignored me altogether, even though I was the only one making sense right now.

Jake looked at me, torn. "One month?"

"One month."

"OK, I'll send one of my guys to pick the cash up from you."

You had to be kidding me! I was going to be forced to keep breathing for a month! I wanted this over with. I was ready! I had never been more ready for my own death.

"Fine. But I want to know one other thing," Reaper said.

"What?"

Yeah, what was it that Reaper wanted to know?

"What's this game you and her play?"

I clenched my eyes shut. He had watched the video. Did I not make it clear to him not to watch it till I was dead? I suddenly knew the reason Reaper was so desperate to get hold of Jake. And why he was forcing Jake to keep me breathing for a month. He wasn't just ensuring Jake didn't kill me. He was making sure I didn't kill myself.

"Been talking to our little cherub, have you?" Jake looked at me, amazed. "Here I was thinking I had been careful around you."

"WHAT'S THE GAME?" Reaper roared from the phone.

I cringed. I hated it when he used that tone.

"I think your wife has been baiting me, Reaper. Only now, her little scene with the gun is making sense." Jake looked at me, seeing right through my outbursts and seeing the cause. I wanted to die. He knew that now. "I think your wife has a death wish. Maybe she should be the one to decide if she lives for another month."

"YOU GAVE HER A GUN!"

Jake laughed. "You can't play Russian roulette without one."

"I'm going to kill you, Jake."

"You say that, but I'm still breathing." Jake leaned over the phone. "In fact, I'm the one with your girl on my lap. So I think it is fair to say I've got the upper hand."

"Let me talk to Abby."

"Not happening. Whatever you have to say, you can say it in front of me."

"Fine. Abby, you listening?"

I opened my eyes. Of course I was listening. Jake wanted to torture me. But did I let Reaper know I was listening? If he had watched the video, he would know my plan. But I couldn't not talk to him either. Regardless of whether he knew I was going to kill myself or not.

"Yes," I finally sighed. "I'm here."

"I need you to trust me."

"Kade–"

"Abby, I need you to have faith in me," he cut me off. "You have to keep breathing for me and your son."

Tyson. I knew what it was like to not have a mother. That was what caused the tears to well in my eyes.

"Abby, just have faith I will find you."

I knew the chances of him finding me were slim. But I also knew that Kade didn't give up on things. He would find me. I just didn't know if I would still be breathing by the time he did.

"OK," I blew out. "I trust you, Kade."

"You won't do anything stupid? You'll keep breathing for me?"

"I have faith in you."

"OK, now you have had your heart-to-heart, I want my money. I'll send Andrew to get it this afternoon. You have a month from today." Jake hung up.

Just like that, it looked like my plan of dying early was over. And now, somehow, I had to manage to keep breathing for a whole month. God, did Kade know how hard that was going to be for me?

Chapter 16

Abby

I had taken the notepad and pen from the kitchen and was sitting on the bed, drawing. It was calming and, for the first time since I was taken, I wasn't thinking about dying. Instead, I was sketching pictures of Tyson.

"You disappeared."

I looked up at Jake, who was standing at the end of the bed. How long had he been there? Why did it look like he was studying me?

My eyes went back to my sketching. "Didn't see the point in hanging around. You got what you wanted."

"Are you going to eat?"

"Is that your way of saying you want me to cook?"

"No. I ordered in."

I looked up. OK. What was going on? He was being nice again. He walked around the bed and actually sat down next to me, pulling his legs up on the bed and sitting beside me like it was normal.

He nodded his head at my sketching. "You're good at that."

"How would you know?" It wasn't like he had seen my work.

"I've seen your sketches you've left in the kitchen."

"Oh."

"What you working on?"

Again, I was thrown. Why was he being nice to me? Maybe it was because he would have to put up with me for another month. That was if he didn't go back on his word and kill me before that.

"Um, sketches of Tyson. When I last saw him." Before I was ripped away from my son.

"If he is anything like your sketches, you have one cute son."

"The sketches don't do him justice." I smiled for the first time at Jake. I guess talking about my son would bring a smile to my face. He was so little. So fucking perfect. And, as I looked at my sketches, he was the spitting image of his dad.

"What made you have kids?" Jake sounded genuinely interested. I frowned at him. Wouldn't it be better if he didn't get to know me? He was going to kill me. He arched his eyebrows, waiting for an answer. I guess I was just staring at him.

"Well, Tyson wasn't our first."

"I didn't know you had another kid. How old are they?"

"He died. I, um, had a complicated labor. In the end, he didn't make it."

"Sorry." He looked at me with sadness. "I know what it is like to lose someone you love. That loss eats you up."

"Yeah, it does." I nodded my head. "Nothing compares to losing a kid, well, apart from losing a parent, or in your case, your partner. But even when I lost Mom, I didn't feel as numb as I was when I lost Matthew."

"Your mom died?"

"When I was young, to cancer."

He looked at me again with a glint in his eyes I couldn't explain. As if I was a mystery and he wanted to know everything, like he was seeing me for the first time.

"Sorry about your mom."

I shrugged. "It's history. It made me stronger. And she would hate for me to stay stuck in the past." It was funny. When it came to Mom, I never spoke about her, not even to Kade. So why the hell was I speaking about her to Jake?

It comforted me to think Matthew was with her. If he couldn't be with me, he was with his grandmother, and Mom would have made a great grandparent. She loved with her whole heart. Even the badness. Especially the badness. She would love every side of me. She wouldn't care about me taking lives.

Even when it came to Dad, she would love every side of him. She accepted the fact he didn't come home for days because she knew he would be with her as soon as he could.

I had barely any memories of them together, but in the ones I did their love always shone through all the bullshit of the club. Mom always had a way of making you feel complete. I hoped one day I would be half the mother she was to me. That was, if I ever got the chance.

"So I'm guessing you and Reaper tried again?" Jake said, snapping me out of my thoughts.

"No. Um, Tyson wasn't planned. When it happened, I was set on having an abortion. After Matthew, I wasn't ready."

Jake looked at me, shocked. "But you love him?"

"Unconditionally."

"So what changed your mind? I mean, I've never lost a kid but I imagine to go again, you have to be fully convinced."

"Kade, I mean Reaper, changed my mind." And if it hadn't been for Kade being so determined on me keeping Tyson, I wouldn't have a son today. If he hadn't found that pregnancy test and it had been left up to me, we wouldn't have a son.

"Do you regret it? Bringing a life into the world?"

"No. Not at all. As soon as I saw Tyson, all the shit I'd done in my life, all the badness and the death, it didn't matter anymore because I got this perfect, healthy little boy. And if it wasn't for all those dark paths I took, I wouldn't have a son."

"Dark paths? As if you have any."

I looked him straight in the eye. I doubted I had to worry about him going to the police. "You know the Hellbound?"

"My competition."

"Well, I was Blake's personal hit man."

"Wait, are you the one that took out the board?"

I nodded my head. "Yep. Like I said, his personal hit man."

"But everyone thought he had hired a professional. Even I admit those kills had talent behind them."

"Thanks for the compliment."

"Got Blake sentenced to six months. He is out next month."

"Is he?"

"Yep, gotta keep eyes on the competition. I'm sure when he gets out they will be running at full speed again."

"He needs new members. It will take him a while to rebuild the gang before he even looks at taking over your market."

"Do you know much about them?"

"A lot. I used to wear their tattoo. So you can say I know a lot about their operation."

"Anything you would share with a friend?"

A friend? Was he joking? A friend doesn't kidnap with the intent to kill. "No. I'm loyal."

"Well, will you at least tell me if I should be worried about them coming into the ice business?"

I narrowed my eyes at him, knowing he was testing me. "You mean, do you think they will expand their ice business?"

He smiled. "So you do know about their operation."

"Like I said, I was one of them."

"Well, will they expand?"

I really shouldn't help him. But at the same time, I didn't want to do Blake or Daniels any favors. Not after what they put me through.

"When I was with them, I helped them secure a gun deal. So they have the gun power to take you and the money to recruit. All they are waiting on is Blake to come and take charge. But if I were you, I'd focus on their weakness."

"Which is?"

"Well, Blake depends on petty crimes. His main market is young kids who like to steal and get off raiding businesses. If you focus on getting to those kids before he does, his market will dry up. He also doesn't have a contract shooter. I was it. He hasn't replaced me. So if he has a problem with someone, he has to deal with it himself. If I were you, I'd take up the opportunity as soon as he is out of prison. Sure, he is untouchable in prison. But once he is out, a contracted shooter could take him out with ease."

"You're smart." Jake looked at me, shocked. "How did you get to be so beautiful and smart? Normally a girl is either smart or beautiful, not both."

"Your Rebecca was beautiful and would have to be smart to be a schoolteacher," I pointed out.

"Nah, she wasn't your type of smart. She didn't see people's weaknesses like you. She couldn't put a plan together like you just did. Hell, she would never be able to pull a trigger. Never had guts when it came to this life. Clearly, you do."

I didn't know if he was complimenting me or not. Was he actually saying I was better than his wife?

"Thanks, I think," I said, arching my eyebrows.

"It's a compliment."

"OK."

"So Tyson made up for all that shit?"

"Yeah, he did." I smiled. "Like I said, it makes up for all the bad, makes you realize the world is bigger than your mistakes, you know?"

"I've always wanted a son. Someone to shape. Someone to carry on my name."

"Well, girls can do that too."

He grinned. "Yeah, I'd settle for a daughter."

"Have you dated anyone since Rebecca?"

He shook his head. "Never wanted anyone but her."

I knew what that felt like. I had only ever wanted Kade and it would destroy me to live without him. Hell, I had lived without him. And my life had turned to shit. Was he going to be OK without me? He had Tyson now. He had to pull himself together. Tyson needed him. Surely Kade wouldn't let grief make him turn his back on his son.

"Well, I can't give you any advice because I honestly don't know what it is like to lose your partner."

"You've lost Reaper."

"No. He has lost me. I'll have him till I die."

"How much do you miss your son?"

Was that a loaded question? I looked him in the eye, not understanding what he meant by that.

"You ripped me from the love of my life and a whole new life I had just created. You stole me from my son's future. Is that what you want to hear? That I'm suffering?" I gritted out, gripping the pen tighter. "You don't have a child so you have no idea what it's like to lose that."

He smiled. "I didn't want to know if you were suffering. But you have given me an idea." He leaned forward and before I knew what he was doing, he kissed me. "I've got to go. Like I said, you've given me an idea." He got up and then turned around before he got to the door. "You're drawing. I'll make sure you get more supplies than a notepad and a pen. After all, you need something to do in your time." He turned and left.

I was panicking, completely and utterly panicking. He had kissed me. That was what I was afraid of. I could handle being beaten. But I couldn't handle being raped. I knew that would break me. I touched my lips and the tears welled in my eyes. I was too busy panicking to even fully understand what he meant by me 'giving him an idea'.

Chapter 17

Kim

I wouldn't say that the depression that had blanketed the club since Abby was taken had lifted completely. But the boys were more positive knowing they had a month. I looked around the bar. It was covered in guns. There was no room to move.

The boys were going to war. And Reaper had made sure when it came to guns, well, we had enough for the war and then some. Normally the boys carried but now they had machine guns strapped to them. And they were using them.

I personally hated having Tyson around all this crap. But it was his home. I walked into the living room and put my feet up on the crib. Tyson was slowly waking up and once he was awake we had a doctor's appointment.

I sipped my cup of coffee and watched the last bit of Elmo on the television.

"You ready to leave?" Trigger walked in.

Why was it when he was near, I couldn't tear my eyes off him? Admiring all his good aspects and loving the bad.

"Tyson is waking up." I tried to focus on the television. It would have worked too, if Trigger hadn't chosen to sit down next to me, his hand running up my leg.

"So, how are you?" he asked, sounding like he really cared.

"Fine."

"You're not sleeping."

I turned to look at him. I knew it was starting to show. But I had put makeup on today to look more human. "How the hell did you know that?"

He just grinned. "I know you, Kim." His hand ran up the inside of my thigh. "How about tonight you try and sleep with me? Last time I checked you usually sleep great in my bed."

"Nice try." I looked away from him. Just because he hadn't been screwing girls didn't mean I was about to go back to him. It was only a matter of time till he got drunk enough at a club party and gave in to the need for sex.

"Come on, Kim. You need sleep." His hand was making my breathing come out sharp. Why did his touch do that to me?

"I'm not sleeping in your dirty bed. I would put all my money on the fact those sheets haven't been changed since I did them last." I looked him in the eye. "And before you even lie and say you have, remember, I know you."

"I'll change the sheets."

"Still not happening." I looked at the time. "OK, I better get moving."

"You know I'm coming, right?"

"Considering you have become my shadow, I was actually counting on you driving." I finished my cup of coffee and got up. I smiled and laughed at Tyson as he woke. "Do you think he can get any more adorable?" I said, picking him up and holding him up. "You are killing your aunty with your smiles."

I turned and looked at Trigger. Why was he looking at me like that? I frowned, not understanding the look in his eyes. If I had to take a stab at it, it was as if he was looking at me with love, which I knew was impossible.

"Where's the, um, keys?" He stood up, not sounding like his confident self. What was wrong with him?

"In my handbag."

He just stared at me again with that look. I laughed, not understanding it but enjoying seeing him frozen. Why he was frozen I didn't know. But not seeing him oozing confidence, well, it was nice for a change. It was like he and I swapped places and, for once, I wasn't the one gawking.

"OK, seeing as you've turned into a statue, I'll get the car keys." I walked to the table and searched through my handbag, getting the keys out. Trigger was still standing there. "Are you coming or not?" I asked.

He blinked and then snapped out of it. "Yep. Give me the keys."

I threw them at him. I didn't know what was wrong with him. I looked him in the eye as he walked past. What was wrong with him?

***

Tyson's checkup went perfectly. He was nailing all the health scores. I called Reaper and told him how well Tyson did. He told me off for not telling him about the appointment. But I knew he was busy. And I could handle an appointment.

Trigger was collecting rent off the last business on the list today. Reaper had enough on his plate and picking up rent wasn't a big deal. It was actually one of the safest jobs to do for the club. I was getting Tyson out of his stroller and putting him in the car. I was about to strap him in when I felt it. My eyes went wide.

"Just give me the kid," a man's voice whispered calmy in my ear.

Panic. What the hell did I do? I felt the gun press firmly into my back.

"You will have to kill me before I give him to you."

"Easily done."

Without even thinking, I elbowed him in the stomach and the gun went off. But it didn't get me. I dropped to my knees and my hand went in my handbag and I gripped Abby's gun. I had moved so quickly he hadn't noticed till I was back in his face. I just started firing. Aiming for his body. People started screaming around us. I fired again at him. I didn't know if I was hitting him but I was firing.

He staggered back but he must have been wearing a vest. Fine. I lowered the gun and fired into his leg. I got one shot off before pain consumed every blood vessel and I collapsed backward, my head smashing back into the concrete.

From the corner of my eye, I saw Trigger coming out.

"KIM!"

"GET TYSON!" I yelled. I didn't give a fuck about me. I wanted to pull myself up to see if he was still there. But the pain I was in was all-consuming. I couldn't move. Trigger was at my side. His hand went to my stomach. "GET TYSON OUT OF HERE," I yelled at him.

"I'M NOT LEAVING YOU!" Trigger's hands pressed firmly into my stomach.

"GO, TRIGGER, NOW. BEFORE THEY COME BACK." I didn't care if I bled out here on the sidewalk. What mattered was my nephew was safe. That was when I heard the shots. Trigger was up and I saw him firing, but I also saw that there were two of them.

"TRIGGER, LEAVE ME AND GET TYSON OUT OF HERE!" I was yelling and I didn't know if he was hearing me. My vision was getting blurry. I knew I was minutes away from being out of it completely. So this was what it felt like to be shot. My hand was shaking as I took it away from my stomach. So much blood. Was it all from me?

Trigger was at my side again, still firing. They weren't giving up. I heard the sirens coming. Someone must have called the police. Police meant ambulance. I would be fine, which couldn't be said for Tyson if they got him.

"TRIGGER. NOW. GO."

"I'M NOT LEAVING YOU!" He was leaning over me, pressing into my stomach.

"Tyson comes first. Go." That's when the firing started again. They must have reloaded. "GO!" They weren't stopping. They wanted Tyson. They had come for him and weren't planning on leaving without him.

I saw his torn expression. He knew what he had to do and then there was what he wanted to do.

He placed my hand over the bullet wound. "I'll meet you at the hospital." He was saying it like it was a date. I smiled.

"Go."

I turned my head, watching my car pull away from the curb abruptly. It was replaced by a police car immediately. Tyson was safe. I hadn't failed Abby.

The firing stopped. I was guessing it was because of the police; that and what they were after was gone.

Chapter 18

Trigger

Tyson was wailing and it wasn't helping that I had covered him in blood. I pushed open the clubhouse door. Thank fuck they were back.

"They shot Kim. I have to go to the hospital." I walked straight to Reaper. He looked at me, confused. When he didn't take Tyson from me, I yelled, "DID I FUCKING STUTTER? THEY SHOT KIM!"

He looked from me and the bloody shirt to Tyson, who was covered in Kim's blood. "What the fuck is going on?" Reaper roared, only now understanding the situation. "Who shot Kim? Where is she?"

"I left her on the sidewalk." I had left her to bleed out. I had left her to die. "Here, take your son. I have to get to the hospital!"

"YOU LEFT HER!"

"THEY WERE AFTER TYSON, REAPER. IT WAS LEAVE HER AND GET OUT OR LET THEM TAKE HIM!"

"Did you see who it was?"

"It was that Andrew prick who picked up the money. Look, I can't talk. I have to go!" Didn't he understand? KIM HAD BEEN SHOT! On my watch! I had left her bleeding out on the sidewalk. I chose to save his son over saving the woman I love.

Fuck, I only realized this morning that I loved her. I hadn't told her. All this time and I realized today I love her and it's the same day she was taken from me? How the fuck is that fair!

"Brad, look after Tyson. Call Roach. Tell him Kim's at the hospital." Reaper looked at me. "Do you want to change?"

"I don't give a fuck what I look like."

All I cared about was Kim. Didn't they get that?

"Shit, she's lost a lot of blood." Brad took Tyson from me. "Where did they shoot her?"

"In the stomach. I couldn't see if the bullet went through." I ran my bloody hands through my hair. Brad didn't know how right he was. There was so much blood.

"Well, let's go. Brad, start calling and get the security footage. I want a fucking number plate." Reaper whacked me on the back. "You alright?" He looked at me like he knew what it was like to have your woman shot in front of you. Then I thought of it. He did know exactly what it felt like.

I never thought I'd love anyone. But I knew this morning I loved Kim, seeing her so happy with Tyson. I wanted her to be that happy holding my child. I wanted her to be looking at me with that much love.

"Let's go." Reaper gave me a solid push in the back.

I had never been in shock. Never had anything happened to me that put me in shock. But seeing Kim lying there, bleeding, and having to leave her, that had sent me into shock.

I followed Reaper, pulling my bike keys out of my pocket. She would be fine. I kept repeating that to myself as I straddled my bike. She would be fine.

***

"Kim Harrison. Bullet wound to the stomach. Would have come by ambulance," I basically shouted at the emergency nurse. "Tell me where she is?"

Panic. Red, raw panic was flooding my body. I had to know she was breathing.

I saw the nurse type Kim's details into the computer. She looked at me, her eyes lingering on my shirt. Maybe I should have taken Reaper's advice and changed.

"Relationship?" the nurse said, being professional.

"Husband," I gritted out. Never in my life had I wanted to be married, but right now I wished I had fucking realized sooner I loved Kim and been a man and married her. But fuck it. That wasn't helping me now. Now I needed fucking answers! If it wasn't for the security glass in my way I would have reached around and looked at the computer screen myself.

"She came in as a Miss."

Reaper pushed me out of the way. "I'm her brother-in-law. Can you at least tell us if she is alive?"

The woman opened her mouth and I would bet she was about to give Reaper the same treatment she was giving me.

"I'M HER FUCKING FATHER! NOW WHERE IS SHE?" Roach pushed both Reaper and me out of the way.

How did he get here so quick?

"She's in surgery. She will be discharged to Four South," the nurse gave Roach the details. "From the notes on screen, she just went in."

"Was she stable?" Reaper asked, like it was his heart on the line.

"No."

Fuck.

"There is a waiting room on the ward, Mr. Harrison. I'll let the nurses know you're waiting for news." The nurse picked up the phone.

Roach grunted and turned, heading for the elevators.

Wait. We had to wait.

Normally, I welcomed the unknown. I lived for not knowing what I would be doing tomorrow. But the unknown of facing a world without Kim, well, that unknown scared the shit out of me.

"So, what were you doing while my daughter was being shot?" Roach barked at me as we got in the elevator.

"Clearly not his fucking job." Reaper was glaring at me.

It didn't matter what they said. They couldn't make me feel any worse.

"So?" Roach snapped at me.

"Like Reaper said. Not my job," I muttered, getting out of the elevator. "I fucked up, alright? Is that what you want me to say?" Wasn't it obvious? I HAD FUCKED UP!

"You saved Tyson, Trigger. You didn't fuck up completely." Reaper closed the waiting room door after us. "I shouldn't have let Kim go to that appointment by herself. If she had fucking told me Tyson had an appointment, then I would have been there."

"We were collecting rent." I ran a hand through my hair. "We weren't anywhere near the hospital."

The look on Reaper's face was as if I had just slapped him.

"You were doing club business?" he gritted out. "ARE YOU FUCKING STUPID?"

"We were collecting rent, Reaper! We weren't taking risks! Fuck, it didn't matter what we were doing. They clearly followed us. They waited till I was out of sight. Then they fucking made their move." I shouldn't have left Kim by herself.

Reaper's phone started ringing.

"Yeah, Brad? Right. Yeah, we are fucking making a move. I don't care how guarded his house is. We are getting in."

We knew Andrew's address. We just could never get close enough. Clearly Reaper was planning on making sure that wasn't the case when we made a move now.

"Trigger and I are coming." Reaper looked at me. "Get the boys ready."

"I'm not leaving the hospital," I said as soon as Reaper hung up.

"Yeah, you are," Reaper said, like I couldn't argue with it.

"Are you ordering me to leave?" I stood up, ready for the challenge.

"Would you rather sit here and think the fucking worst or shoot at the bastard responsible?"

"I told Kim I'd be here for her." It was the very last thing I told her. I wasn't letting her down, as much as I would love to live up to my name.

"We'll be back before she is out of surgery. Let's go."

"Make the bastard pay, Reaper," Roach said, and then looked at me. "Trigger, I'll call you when she is out."

I nodded my head and followed Reaper out.

"I know you want to torture Andrew to get an address out of him. But I want to finish him." I hit the elevator door. "Hear me, Reaper? Andrew is mine." I looked him squarely in the eye. "Don't fight me on this."

Reaper nodded his head. "As soon as I get an address, he is all yours."

Good. He was going to pay for shooting my woman, slowly and painfully. I had gotten a taste of what Reaper must have felt when Abby was shot. Fuck, he must be going through hell now. All this time I thought I got it. But only when I got a taste of what it was like to possibly lose the woman you love did I understand what Reaper was going through.

Chapter 19

Abby

I was in the bedroom when I heard it. The cursing and shouting. I had been by myself all afternoon so I was curious when I heard it.

I walked out of the bedroom and down the stairs.

"Shit, Andrew, are you OK?" I asked, my eyes widening when I saw the blood coming out of his leg. "Here, sit down." I dragged a chair out for him.

He was still cursing as he sat down. I went to the kitchen and grabbed a dishtowel and went back to him. I started to apply it to his leg.

He ripped his top off and I saw the vest with several bullets in it. He unstrapped it and took it off, dropping it on the floor.

"So, you've had a busy afternoon," I stated the obvious.

"Fucking Jake," he gritted out.

I smiled. "Yeah, I know what you mean."

I picked up his vest and pulled a bullet out of it. I knew that bullet. I had personally bought it. How the hell would a bullet from my gun, which I had left under the floorboards in my wardrobe, get used?

"Decides he wants a fucking kid and sends me out to get it. Fucking sick of his hormones."

"Wait, you went to kidnap a kid?" I looked at him, shocked. "You're joking, right?"

He shook his head. "Not any kid. He wants your kid."

"You went after Tyson?" I suddenly applied more pressure to his leg, causing him to swear. "HOW FUCKING DARE YOU?"

He scoffed. "Don't worry. Your sister made sure I didn't get him. Winded me by shooting me nonstop in the chest."

"So you didn't get him?"

"Does it look like I have your kid right now?"

"No." Thank fuck for that. But Kim didn't know how to use a gun. She must have had a member with her.

The front door opened and Jake walked in, laughing, with Billy.

"What the hell is your problem?" I yelled at him. How dare he go after my son! Didn't he have me? Wasn't that enough? "What was your plan? Kill me, keep my son?" I strode toward him and as soon as he was in reach I shoved him hard. "I can't wait till Reaper kills you."

"You gave me the idea." His hands locked around my wrists and he stopped me from pushing him. "You went on about how a child fixes all your problems. You made me realize how much I wanted one."

"THEN HAVE ONE OF YOUR OWN! DON'T GO AFTER MINE! JEEZ, I'M SURE YOU CAN GET A GIRL PREGNANT!"

Jake looked around me. "Your house is being shot up, Andrew. Guessing Reaper didn't take kindly to the fact you tried to take his kid."

Andrew scoffed. "Means I'm staying here. I loved that fucking house. You, Jake, will be paying for the repairs."

"Yeah, when we went past they were raiding it. Heard your alarms going off a block away."

"Well, they will be hunting for you, Andrew," I gritted out. "I hope you like the idea of being locked up here with me, because Reaper will be hunting for you too." I looked between them smugly. "I cannot wait till Reaper gets a hold of one of you."

"Like that is ever going to happen." Andrew limped toward us. "Now call Jeff. I have a bullet in my leg."

"I think it should stay there." I smiled smugly at him. "I'm happy that a Satan's Son put that bullet in your leg."

"It wasn't a member," he gritted out.

"Who was it then?"

"I already told you."

"No, you didn't."

"Your sister stopped me." He looked at me like I was stupid. "By shooting me."

So Kim had my gun. And someone had taught her how to use it. I smiled. If Reaper had taught her, then that would explain why she had gotten so many shots right into his chest. He was lucky to have been wearing a vest. "Well, I can't say I'm sorry."

"Well, she was when I shot her in the stomach." Andrew limped off.

"DID YOU SHOOT MY SISTER?" I gripped his arm and spun him around. "TELL ME YOU DIDN'T HURT HER!"

"When I left, she was bleeding out on the sidewalk." Andrew looked at me smugly. "Not so happy now, are you?"

I gulped and turned to Jake. "You have to find out if she is OK."

"No." He walked around me.

"You can't do that to me!" I followed him. The panic I was feeling was suffocating. "Jake." I gripped his arm and forced him to look back at me. "Please find out if she is OK?" I never thought I'd beg Jake for anything. But I had to know that Kim was OK.

Jake looked at me, then my hand, frowning. "Fine. I'll make a call."

I sighed in relief. "Thank you." I let go of his arm.

"You should go back to your bedroom, Abby. I need to talk to the boys." Jake was actually speaking nicely to me. He even looked half torn as he gently pushed me toward the stairs. "Go."

"And you'll find out about Kim?"

"Yes. I'll come tell you as soon as I know something."

I nodded my head. I'd settle for that.

***

Kim

How many times did I have to say I was fine to Dad in order for him to leave? It would have to be a thousand. I was stable. I was out of surgery. The bullet had missed my organs and, apart from being in a world of pain that the drugs weren't even touching and the extreme blood loss that I was still lightheaded from, I was fine.

So Dad left me to sleep.

Which I would have loved to have done, if it hadn't been for the beeping of machines, the IV in my hand, the fact I was getting a blood transfusion and every few seconds it was like someone had taken a hot poker rod and stabbed it through my back and into my stomach. I couldn't get comfortable.

I was so tired. My eyelids were heavy. But my body was fighting me. Everything in this room was fighting me.

The door opened. Surely they couldn't be wanting to check my blood pressure again? That was another reason I couldn't sleep: because the nurses kept coming in and checking on me.

I had been told the police would be by in the morning for a statement. I still didn't know what to tell them.

I was glaring at the IV in my hand, not caring that I was ignoring the nurse.

"You should be asleep."

My eyes bounced up. What was he doing here? It was after two in the morning. "Trigger?" I looked at him, completely surprised. I could honestly say he was the last person I expected to see. Hell, Dad being here and annoying the shit out of me, I got. Reaper, I was expecting in the morning. But Trigger, he didn't have to come up, unless he felt guilty.

I watched him drag the plastic chair to my bedside. He took the hand that didn't have an IV needle in it.

"I thought I lost you today." His eyes moved from my hand till he was looking me in the eye. "So fucking sorry I had to leave you."

"I'm fine." I wanted to ease the pain that was so clear on his face. Guilt. He must feel guilty.

He got out of the chair abruptly and leaned over, cupping my face. "You might be but I'm nowhere fucking near it."

I ran my hand down his jaw. "You did what had to be done. And there wasn't anything more you could have done for me."

"I should have–"

"Stop." I put my finger over his lips. "I told you to leave. I stand by my decision. Now I'm telling you I'm fine."

"You're lying to me, Kim. It's after two in the morning. I was expecting to be watching you sleep. So tell me, why are you awake?"

"Pain and I can't get comfortable and these machines won't shut up." All my problems just rolled off my tongue.

I might as well have slapped him because the look on his face, well, it was as if I had.

"Sit up." He gently pushed me across the bed. I didn't understand what he was doing till he lay down beside me. He put an arm around me. "You OK? I'm not making it worse, am I?"

I curled in to his side. "No, the complete opposite." I laid my head on his chest, hearing the familiar beating. How many nights had I fallen to sleep listening to it?

His hand undid the ties on the back of my hospital gown and then his hand ran up and down my spine.

"I want to tell you something, Kim."

"Is it important? Because you are kind of putting me to sleep." I enjoyed his hand on me way too much. It was relaxing and I was so focused on how his fingers were running back up to the top of my back and down again that I had tuned out the beeping of the machines.

"I love you."

My eyes went wide and I pushed myself up to look at him. "Why would you say that?" Did he not know by now that he couldn't just throw that word at me? I couldn't handle it. Though this was the first time he had said those three little words to me. I used to be the one saying it to him, till I gave up on him, till my heart realized enough was enough. There was no possible way this man was capable of love.

He dipped his head, his eyes deeply calm. "I love you, Kim. I don't know why the fuck it took me so long to realize it. But today, I did."

"Why, because I was shot? If you are saying this out of guilt, you don't have to."

"No, I realized it this morning, well, yesterday morning. When I saw you holding Tyson and I wanted you to be looking at me with that type of love." He cupped my face. "I want you to hold my son or daughter with that much love. I want you, Kim, all of you. And I won't stop till you are mine."

I swallowed sharply. Was it possible I was on so much pain medication that I was hearing him incorrectly? The shock I was feeling was clear on my face and he must have seen it, because he smiled.

"You don't have to say anything." He kissed my forehead. "I just wanted you to know. I'm making a claim on you."

I opened my mouth. I shut my mouth. I started to say something and then stopped and frowned. Never in my life did I expect Trigger to actually feel something for me, let alone tell me, or want to tell anyone, for that matter.

"How about you try and get some sleep?" Trigger ran his hand down my spine again. "If I remember correctly, I was putting you to sleep."

"Um, you, um, don't have to stay." I found words and spoke for the first time since his bombshell. From the expression on his face, it wasn't what he wanted to hear. "I mean, I'm fine. And you should, you know, get a good night's sleep and I–"

"Stop, Kim. I'm not leaving."

Right. I knew better than to argue with him when he had set his mind on something. But had he meant it when he said he had set his mind on me? That he loved me? I had never heard the word 'love' come out of his mouth about anything.

I lowered my head to his chest and his hand went back to stroking my back. It was going to be impossible to sleep now. My mind was racing. And his words, *I love you*, were repeating over and over in my head, getting louder. I hadn't said it to him. He had said it to me.

Was it because I had been shot?

He said it wasn't, but why now, then?

It was way too late to even be having this conversation in my head and never in my life had I been able to understand the reasons behind why Trigger did something.

So why was I going to start now?

***

Abby

I rolled over in bed. I couldn't sleep. I was worrying about Kim. I was dying for answers. But Jake hadn't come to me. I rolled over again when I heard the bedroom door open.

I automatically sat bolt upright in bed.

"Jake?'

"Yeah, it's me."

I exhaled slowly. Never in my life did I expect to be happy to hear Jake's voice. He walked into the room.

"Do you know if Kim's OK?"

"She's out of surgery and is stable." Jake walked to the other side of the bed. "She's going to be fine."

I fell back on the bed. "Thank god."

Jake sat down on the other side of the bed, putting his legs up and leaning back against the head of the bed. "Took me fucking hours to get answers out of the hospital, getting passed around," Jake groaned. "I hate policies."

He didn't have to do that.

"Thanks." I knew it was asking a lot of him to find out if Kim was OK. "I know I was asking a lot of you. Considering I'm your prisoner and you intend to kill me, you didn't have to give me an answer." I turned on my side to face him.

Jake slid down the bed. His hand ran down my arm. "You gave me another idea," he said, his fingers running up and down my arm.

"Well, seeing as my first idea made you think I wanted you to kidnap my son, I don't think I want to know what your new idea is."

"I'd tell you but I think it's better if I show you. Just not tonight." His arm went around me and my stomach twisted as he pulled me to him. "You should be asleep."

"I couldn't sleep when I was worried about Kim." I swallowed sharply. *Please don't touch me.* But he just held onto me tighter and pulled me against him, tucking my head under his chin.

"Well, you can sleep now."

"Why do you care if I sleep or not?'

"I don't know," he sighed. "Doesn't make sense. Jeez, I never thought I'd sleep in this bed again."

"I'm guessing the last time you were in it, you were with Rebecca, right?" I attempted to pull away from him but he just held me in place.

"Yeah." And his hand ran down my back. "And now I'm in it with you."

"Well, you don't have to stay." *Please don't stay. Please don't stay.*

"Just go to sleep, Abby."

I needed Kade. God, I needed him right now. How the hell could I sleep while the enemy was lying beside me, touching me and treating me like I was his?

"Stop panicking, Abby, and go to sleep." Jake kissed the top of my head. "Or I'll force feed you sleeping tablets."

I gulped. And there it was, the fact he was in control of my life.

I closed my eyes. And I forced myself to think of Kade. And I promised myself Kade would never know I shared a bed with Jake.

Chapter 20

Abby

I woke up alone. Thank god. I hoped that that was a one off. I ran a hand through my hair and sat up.

I was stretching when the bedroom door opened up.

Jake.

"Morning," I forced out. I noticed he was carrying bags.

"Got you those art supplies and clothes." He put the bags on the bed. "Did you sleep alright?"

"Fine," I yawned. "Um, why did you get me clothes?"

"Because you are going to need more than two sets if you are planning on living here for a month."

"You didn't have to." I walked toward him, looking at the bags. "I wouldn't have complained."

"You've got a good figure and shouldn't be wearing a baggy shirt and shorts for the rest of your short life." He pulled on my top, bringing me close to him. "Plus, this way I get to see that figure."

Sick. I felt sick. "Um, you going out today?" I wanted so badly to change the subject. I didn't want him to find me attractive. If he was going out today, I might be able to break back into the study and call Reaper. I wanted to make sure Kim was OK.

"No."

Well, that caused my plan to end before it began.

"I got you breakfast downstairs. Get changed and come down." Jake let go of me. "Wear a dress. I want to see your breasts."

Reaper. I needed Reaper. I was shaking when I looked in the bags, hoping that there was something in here that would make sure my breasts were covered. I didn't want to give Jake what he wanted.

But it looked like every dress he picked would show off my cleavage.

Maybe I could just stay here?

"I'll go so you can change. If you're not down within a few minutes, I'll come back up." Jake gripped my hand. "And maybe I will get a glimpse of what you look like free of clothes. Because I don't think my imagination is doing you justice."

He let go of me and left. Suddenly I didn't care if these dresses didn't cover me completely, as long as they covered me enough.

***

I walked down the stairs. Jake and Andrew were at the table eating. Jake's eyes lit up when he saw me and he whacked Andrew's arm.

"Looks like I've got good taste when it comes to women's clothing." Jake grinned, "Come here, Abby."

I didn't want to. But I wasn't given a choice.

I walked to him and was going to take the seat next to him. But he reached out for me, grabbing me by the hips.

"Sit." He pushed himself away from the table and made room for me.

"I thought you wanted me to eat?" I didn't jump at the chance of sitting on him.

"Andrew, get Abby a plate."

"I can get it."

"No. I want you to sit." He pulled on me. "Now."

I sat down on his lap. His arm wrapped around me. I watched Andrew limp to the kitchen.

"I thought I'd show you the rest of the house today." Jake's hand ran up my outer thigh. "Make you feel at home."

"Trust me, this place will never feel like home." Home was Kade. Home was being held by him. Knowing he was always there. Home was my husband.

"Still, I will make sure you are comfortable. I'm kicking Andrew out this afternoon."

"Why?" I frowned. I didn't care if Andrew was here.

"I don't want anyone in the way of us."

Us. US? When the hell did we become an 'us'? I gulped and I don't know if my expression showed my surprise or not, but the look Andrew was giving me told me I hadn't exactly hidden it well.

"Reaper's on a manhunt for me," Andrew grunted, dropping a plate in front of me.

"Well, you might think he took it personally when you attempted to take his son." I did not feel sorry for Andrew. As far as I was concerned, Reaper could kill him now. I was hoping once this was all over, Reaper wouldn't just settle for Jake but would take out Andrew and Billy as well. Now that he knew Andrew existed, I just had to make sure he knew about Billy as well.

I really needed access to that phone.

"It's your fault, Jake. He took out my security, trashed my house and now I have nowhere to go," Andrew was complaining. He looked dryly at Jake. "I'm not going back after her kid. It isn't worth the risk."

"I won't need you to. I've come up with a better idea." Jake was looking directly at me, smiling.

I gulped. Why did I have a feeling I wasn't going to like his new idea?

"You aren't eating, Abby." Jake pushed the food on the plate toward me. "You haven't been eating right all week."

He had noticed? Maybe Jake was watching me more than I realized.

"I'm not hungry." I pushed the plate away.

Jake frowned. "Are you going to make me make you eat?"

I sighed. He would force me. "Can't you just respect me when I say no?" I knew what the answer was. He didn't care what I wanted.

All he cared about was what he wanted. And right now, he had decided what he wanted was me eating.

He reached out, tucking my hair behind my ear. "OK."

I looked at him, shocked. Did that mean he wasn't going to force me to eat? "So I don't have to eat?"

"No." Jake brushed his lips against mine. "Let's just say I'm going to force you to do something later and if you don't want to eat, you don't have to."

I nodded my head. "Thank you." I didn't know why, but when it came to food, I just couldn't eat. Even if I did eat, I ended up being sick.

"Alright, Andrew, get lost. I want to show Abby the house." Jake gently moved me off him. I stood up.

I thought I could escape his grasp, but he wrapped an arm around me, pulling me back to him.

"Andrew doesn't have to go anywhere," I found myself saying, not wanting to be alone with Jake. Something inside me was screaming a warning, like *at all costs, don't be alone with him*.

But that wasn't going to happen. I watched Andrew pick up his keys and walk to the front door.

"I'll leave you lovebirds alone," Andrew smirked over his shoulder at me, knowing I was hating every second of being alone with Jake. "Jake, if I get killed, remember what you promised."

"Yeah, yeah, I know. No open casket," Jake grumbled. "Now get lost."

The front door shut and Jake spun me around.

"You ready to see the rest of the house?"

Why did he sound excited to be sharing something with me?

"Sure." I was half interested in what room followed the formal room and what was behind that door near the stairs.

Jake linked his hand with mine. "I have something I want to tell you later. Remind me if I don't tell you."

"And I should say what to prompt you?"

"Just say, 'hey Jake, don't you have something you've been dying to tell me?' And I'll know." He smiled. "Come on."

I didn't move and he pulled on my hand, forcing me to follow him. Why was he staying here to begin with? He never used to be around, only to torture me. I guess he was still torturing me, just now with his presence.

***

I was lying on the bed, still dressed. Jake's house was more impressive than you would think. He showed me a gym, a cinema, more bedrooms and a games room, which stumped me because if he had a games room, why was he always gambling in the open living room?

I was sketching one thing over and over. Tyson. Those blue eyes of his, but it was his dark hair that set them off. Kade's hair. I sucked on the end of the colored pencil. Thinking of what he might look like now. He would be bigger. And I would bet everything I owned, he would look more like Kade.

"You look deep in thought."

My head snapped up.

Jake.

He had disappeared this afternoon into his study and I was hoping he would stay there and away from me. He did for the rest of the day, but it seemed now he was finished for the night. I had no idea what the time was, but I knew it was late. I had been taking in the full moon earlier.

"Just thinking." I closed my sketchpad and sat up, putting my legs over the side of the bed. I was ready to bolt if he went to the other side of the bed to sleep. I would happily sleep on the couch downstairs.

"Yeah, I've been doing a lot of that today as well." He moved into the room. I thought he was going to go to the other side of the bed, but he didn't. He came to my side.

I had my legs over the side of the bed and he went and stood in front of me. His legs went to either side of mine, locking mine in between his.

"Remember how I wanted to tell you something earlier?" He tilted his head, making sure our eyes were locked.

I nodded. I was meant to remind him.

"There was always a rumor that Reaper married a pretty woman." His hand cupped my cheek. "But they didn't say how incredibly stunning and beautiful you are. You're more beautiful than Rebecca ever was." His thumb ran over my bottom lip. "I gave more thought to what you said."

Why was he telling me that? Surely he wasn't really saying I was prettier than his wife, the wife he was going to kill me over. I frowned, finally registering his words. "What do you mean about something I said?"

His hand ran down my cheek. "About having my own children."

Oh, that. "Well, I'm sure you will find someone to share the rest of your life with. And when you do, I'm sure you will have kids with her."

"I've already found her."

Well, he hadn't wasted any time. "What do you want me to say?" I honestly felt pity for the girl because he was controlling and ruthless. I guess Reaper was both those things. But at least I knew he had a heart. When it came to Jake, I doubted he did.

He smirked. "You haven't worked it out yet, have you?"

My frown deepened. "Jake, you are confusing and it's late. I should really go to bed." I went to push him away from me but he gripped my hands, pulling me up.

"You're it."

"I'm what?"

"The woman I'm going to spend the rest of my life with. Be the mother to my kids. You're it."

I opened my mouth and then I shut it. That couldn't be. In a few weeks, I'd be dead. I wasn't spending the rest of my life with him. I wasn't being forced… The shock hit me hard and fast. If he wanted kids, that meant one thing. Sex.

He kissed my neck. I stayed still, too frozen in shock to move or push him away.

"I think we should start right away, you know, trying for a baby. Nothing is stopping us."

I gasped and my brain clicked on. I pushed him off of me. "How about me? I'm stopping us!"

"Abby, I'm going to give you two options. You have sex with me. Or I find Tyson, and this time I don't take him, but I kill him. And then I keep you alive. So you feel how much that hurts. Knowing you've ended your own son's life."

"And if I have sex with you?"

"I won't go near Reaper or Tyson. In fact, I'm not planning on bringing up my family here."

"If I don't have sex with you?"

"Did I not make myself clear? I kill your son. 'Cause we both know Reaper can't protect him forever. I got you, didn't I? And then I keep you alive, to live the rest of your life knowing you caused your son's life to end early. All over sex."

I am positive there are life decisions. You know, decisions that will frame the rest of your life. The night I left the club with Reaper, that had been a life decision. It shaped the rest of my life and right now I was being faced with another life decision. My first life decision led me to my second life decision.

Though this one was going to ensure I never saw Reaper again.

An early death would have been a gift now. Jake was going to keep me alive, and worse, he was going to rape me.

I took a staggered breath in. "Reaper won't let Tyson out of his sight, not after you nearly took Tyson. I can guarantee that."

"You're right that he mightn't right now. But one day, Tyson is going to have to go to kindergarten or school. I have no problem waiting till he is older."

"What is stopping you from doing that if I do sleep with you?" I couldn't believe I was even considering it. But I would do anything to protect Tyson, and Jake was counting on that.

"My word. Believe it or not, Abby, I don't want you hurting." His hands ran up my sides. "I don't want the mother to my children unhappy or hurt. Heck, once we get overseas, I'm planning on you getting that tattoo covered and taking off his ring and putting on one from me."

"You can't do that to me!"

"You'll come around." He lowered his head to mine. "I'm counting on that. I know once you have my child, you'll love him or her more than you love Tyson. And then love will naturally start for me."

He wanted a happy ending? With me? This was insane. "What about your promise to keep me alive for a month for Reaper to find me? Do you expect him to just give up on me?"

"About that. I need you downstairs."

"Why?"

"Jeff's here. He needs some of your blood to have on record." He shrugged.

"That makes no sense."

He took my hand. "Come on, Abby. It's in your best interest. And you can think about your answer while it's being taken." Then a smirk spread across his face. "And maybe we can start trying tonight."

Sick. I felt incredibly sick. But Tyson's life was more important. I would do anything to protect it, to keep Jake away from him. So I already knew my answer.

***

I stared at myself in the mirror, hating the reflection. I ran a hand through my wet hair. I didn't know it was possible to hate yourself as much as I did. I hated everything about me, right down to my looks.

It was because of my looks that I was being raped.

I was standing in my underwear trying to come up with the courage to face another day. Here. With Jake. Forced to be his pretend wife.

He told me over and over again he wasn't letting me go. He even said he was starting to love me. He loved the way I was around. He loved that I didn't push him away anymore when he went to touch me. I didn't push him away because I didn't see the fucking point. His grip on me would just tighten anyway.

So I stopped pushing him away.

I stopped doing a lot of things.

Like drawing. I stopped that. Because I couldn't look into Tyson's eyes anymore without wanting to cry. And I wouldn't cry. Nothing would crack me to the point of crying. Not even being raped. I wouldn't let myself cry.

I think my heart was broken.

I was so determined to not let Jake break me. But, as more days passed, I couldn't say he hadn't. He had broken me. As soon as the raping started, I became a walking, breathing shell of the woman I had been.

I didn't think I'd ever get back to who I used to be.

My eyes darted to Jake as he entered the bathroom, grinning like normal.

I looked back into the mirror. It was only when I felt a sting on my thigh that I looked at Jake. He had a razor and he was digging it into my leg. I never thought I would be thankful for pain. But I was because, for once, I was feeling something else other than the broken mess, the crumpled, breathing shell that I was.

Jake pulled the razor away and put it in my hand.

"I heard it helps when you are hating yourself," Jake said, planting a kiss on my shoulder. "Just don't do your wrists. I don't want people to know you do this to cope being with me." He turned and left.

Leaving me with a razor. Like he had just solved my problems or, at the very least, given me a way to cope.

I turned it in my hand. I had felt release when he cut me. I had felt pain instead of sadness and self-loathing. So I put the razor to my outer thigh and cut underneath the line he had just done. And I felt it again. The pain. It was welcoming. And I didn't stop with just one cut.

***

Jeff had just finished taking more blood from me. I gave up asking why a long time ago. They wouldn't give me a straight answer anyway. Why did they want to have such a large supply of my blood?

I got up, leaving Jeff with my blood, and walked into the dining room. Dinner was the next thing I had to do.

Jake got up, taking a gulp of his beer, and looked at me with regret. "Sorry about this, sweetheart."

I frowned and then his fist connected with my jaw. The pain was overwhelming. I think he broke my jaw! My hand went to cup it, as I spat out blood and a back molar.

Jake picked up my tooth and threw it at Jeff. He then came to me. Tears were stinging my eyes but I wasn't letting them drop.

"I'm really sorry about that. Here, let me get you some ice." He took my hand.

"What are you? BIPOLAR?!" I yelled at him, pulling my hand from his. What happened to his speech about how he never wanted to and never would hit me again?

Yeah, I had sat through that speech, not believing he would stop hitting me. Now he had just proven it to me. He didn't keep his word.

He handed me ice. "Trust me. I didn't want to do that."

"Then why did you?" I snapped, in a world of pain.

"Because I had to."

"You're insane." And that was an understatement. "And a complete jerk! What happened to never laying a finger on me while we are trying for a baby?"

"Trust me, Abby. I won't ever hit you again. That had to be done." He stood in front of me and, when I didn't put the ice to my jaw, he took my hand and made me apply the ice. "Ice it. I don't want to see you bruised."

"I think you broke my jaw," I said, blood still coming out of my mouth.

"Jeff, can you check her before you leave? I wanted a tooth. I didn't want her to have a broken jaw," Jake said, stepping around me. When I didn't follow him, he put his hands on my hips and made me turn around so Jeff could check my jaw.

Why did he want a tooth to begin with?

Chapter 21

Reaper

One week.

I had one week to find Abby.

I was pulling every string I had to find her. But I wasn't getting any closer. There was a knock on my door. I didn't jump up to get it.

Today was going to be harder. Because today, was, well, it was her birthday.

There was another knock on the door. "Reaper, it's Kim. The police are here, wanting to talk to you."

The police? I hadn't done anything to warrant their attention. I opened the door, meeting Kim's upset face.

"I think it's about Abby," Kim said, with tears in her eyes. "I think it's bad."

"Kim, I still have a week." It wasn't about Abby.

"I'll get Tyson. You go down." Kim stepped into my bedroom and I headed downstairs.

It wasn't about Abby. It could be about the number of guns we were currently running. It could be about the fact we were raiding drug house after drug house, looking for Abby.

I walked into the bar, seeing the two cops. I was used to seeing officers normally. I was used to being questioned by them. But these two were in plain clothes. Detectives.

"You wanted to see me?" I said, coming to a stop next to them.

"Mr. Wilson?" The man extended a hand. It was something in his voice that had my inner warnings going off. Normally cops and detectives weren't friendly toward me. So a handshake was out of the normal.

I shook it. "Yep."

"I'm Detective Woods and this is Detective Harlot. We have been investigating your wife's disappearance."

It was about Abby.

"Didn't know you lot were even looking." I didn't hide my surprise. As far as I knew, I was the only one making it a mission to find Abby.

"We have been. Yesterday, remains were discovered. At the time, we couldn't confirm if they were Abby or not. But this morning we got a confirmation."

"It's not Abby." I didn't need to hear whatever they had come to say. Abby wasn't dead. I would know. I still had a week.

He smiled grimly. "We have a positive match on blood and dental records. Unfortunately, we can confirm it is Abby Wilson."

"No, it's not." Abby was not dead. I would fucking know! Somehow I would know! "She isn't dead."

"Denial is normally the first stage," his partner said. "We are sorry for your loss, Mr. Wilson. We wanted to notify you as soon as we got a confirmation. This was found with the body."

They handed me rings in a plastic bag. Sure enough, they were Abby's engagement and wedding rings.

She wasn't dead. Kim stepped around me.

"When will the body be released?" Kim said. I looked at her like she couldn't be serious. Body. Abby wasn't a body. She wasn't dead to begin with! This was a sick joke.

"Within a week we can have the body released to a funeral home," the detective said.

"Do you have a card so I can let you know which funeral home to release it to?" Kim said, still holding Tyson.

The detective handed her a card. "We are sorry for your loss." I watched them walk out. This was a sick joke. Jake was going to a new level to torture me.

The clubhouse door shut. I hadn't spotted Roach at the bar. But he got up as soon as they left.

"I'm burying my daughter. You hear me, Reaper? I'm in charge of this funeral. I always knew you would be the death of her." He looked me in the eyes, tears in his. "You killed her. I hope you never sleep a peaceful night for the rest of your life. As for your son, I'll be fighting to take him from you."

"Oh shut up, Dad. Reaper just lost his wife. I just lost my sister. And Tyson just lost his mom. So don't stand there and say you are taking Tyson away from his dad as well." Kim might have been calm before but she wasn't anywhere near it now, tears running down her cheeks. "Tyson will be staying here with his father. And you can go on a bender as soon as the funeral is over."

"Reaper leaves a trail of death in his wake. I'm not letting my grandson become another headstone! He already took my daughter."

"ABBY'S NOT DEAD! I WOULD FUCKING KNOW!" I yelled at both of them, finding this whole situation ridiculous! "I WOULD KNOW!"

Kim went silent. Roach looked at me with disgust and walked off. His lecture and threats disappeared with him as he stormed outside.

"I'll handle the funeral," Kim said, breaking the silence in the room.

I turned to look at her. "Abby's not dead."

Kim smiled sadly up at me. "We lost Abby weeks ago."

"What do you mean?"

"I can't explain it. But all I know is something happened to her and, since then, I felt like I was living without her already. I thought she had died weeks ago. They only just confirmed what I was feeling." Kim moved Tyson in her arms. "Abby has everything set up for the funeral. All it will take is a few phone calls. I can do that."

I looked down at Abby's engagement and wedding rings. She wasn't dead.

"She's not dead."

"Reaper, I'm going to let you come to terms with this in your own time. But if you won't accept it, I will just take over. I'm not letting my sister's remains just sit in the police morgue."

Remains? Abby wasn't just remains. I would know if she was dead. I would feel it. I looked at Kim. She was saying she had felt it weeks ago. Jake said I had a month. I still had a week.

Kim wiped tears away. "Abby knew this was going to happen. So before you go on a rampage, remember she accepted that it was going to end like this."

She was not dead. She was not dead. I clenched my eyes shut. I'd know. Somehow something would change. I would know if she was dead.

"Abby's will, do you still have it? If not, I have a copy. I have a feeling Dad was serious about trying to take Tyson. So we will have to handle that soon. Abby would want you to keep Tyson. But if you can't, I'll take him."

I looked at her. She couldn't be serious? "No one is taking Tyson from me. And Abby isn't fucking dead!"

I took Tyson from her.

"Reaper, where are you going?"

"To give Tyson his bottle, and then I'm going out to look for my wife." I wasn't giving up on her. I knew she wasn't dead. Something would change. Something would happen to me if she were.

My phone started ringing. I didn't even look at the caller ID. I just answered it, needing a distraction.

"Hello?" I barked into the phone.

"Guessing you've heard by now?"

Jake. I froze. "Of all your sick torturous jokes, Jake, this one tops them," I yelled. Kim was at my side immediately, taking Tyson from me. I let her because I was a second away from letting my temper snap.

"Not a joke, Reaper. If it makes you feel better, she wasn't in pain."

"She isn't dead. You said a month. I still have a week."

"I gave you three weeks. I wasn't going to prolong her death any longer. I actually was starting to feel sorry for her. So it was short and it was sweet. Nearly as sweet and painless as Rebecca had."

"You didn't kill her."

"Did you get her rings? Because she asked me to make sure you got them. I guess, call it her dying wish."

"She's not dead." I looked at the rings.

"Whatever makes you happy, Reaper. But I'm flying out this afternoon. My work here is done."

"You didn't kill her."

He laughed. "Denial. Yeah, I had the same. I expected Rebecca to walk through my front door, every day. Wasn't till I saw her body that I accepted she was gone. But you aren't going to get that pleasure. I think you deserved it, being left not knowing. Yeah, I would say that was payback enough. Bye, Reaper."

He hung up.

"What did he say?" Kim snapped at my side. "Is it Abby or not?"

He was telling me it was Abby. The detectives were telling me it was Abby. But my heart was telling me it wasn't. Did I not want to believe it? Was I in denial? Something just told me I would know, deep down, if she was dead. I would know. Something would die inside me.

I was sure if she was dead, my heart would stop as well.

"It's her, isn't it?" Kim said.

"He told me it was." I still didn't believe it.

Kim's eyes welled up with tears. "I knew it happened weeks ago."

"She's not dead." I went to take Tyson again but Kim stepped back.

"I need Tyson right now. You can go blow off steam or something. But I need Tyson." She was holding him close to her chest. "He is all of Abby I have left."

She was not dead.

She just wasn't.

But if Kim really needed Tyson right now, then I would let her have him.

"Fine."

"Go over her will, Reaper. I know you're in denial. But we have a funeral to plan and Abby left instructions about what she wanted."

I nodded my head. I wasn't looking at the will. I wasn't accepting the fact she was dead.

I would fucking well know. Wouldn't I?

***

"OK, Kade, look at me. I'm huge." Abby showed off her perfect stomach in the mirror. "Be proud of yourself, Kade, because you did that." She flicked the lights off and walked into the bedroom.

"Guess how I've spent my day?" Her face lit up. "This." She showed me a scrapbook. "Also, I've been drowning your poor baby in my music. I hope he or she gets my taste in music."

She flicked the page. It was of a half-drawn picture. "Now I don't know when you are coming back. But if something does happen to me, I want this to be a standing memory." Abby switched the angle of the camera and her face lit up the screen. "Sometimes things happen that are out of our control. And if history repeats itself and I lose this baby as well as my life, I don't want you to blame yourself." She frowned. "Like I said, sometimes things are out of our control. This might be one of those times."

Her frown deepened. "You'll call me stupid but I just have this feeling that I won't be around for this baby. Call it a bad feeling. But I'm not going to worry you about what might happen. Like I said, some things are out of our control. And I think this turns out to be one of those times."

The video stopped. I put the phone down and opened up the scrapbook. God, she was talented at drawing. She was also talented with a gun. But I never gave her credit for either.

I flicked over the page. Where did she get these pictures from, if we were both in them?

She had written notes beside the pictures. There was one of me being pissed off, with a note beside it saying, *this is the face you pull when I've annoyed you.* I smiled at that. Because if there was one thing she loved to do, it was to annoy me to the point of pissing me off.

I went through the whole scrapbook. She had basically documented our relationship from the beginning. But the last page had drawings all around a blank square. Written in the middle was *our baby's picture goes here.*

She wasn't here to put it there.

And it had been days since the detectives and Jake had told me she was dead.

The first few days, I ignored it, not believing them.

The third day, I caught Kim crying in the kitchen. She wasn't doing too well. She was pushing everyone away from her, especially Trigger. She wouldn't even speak to me because she said it was harder for her to watch me in denial.

The fourth day came and I woke up alone in bed. Again. The routine was the same.

Then last night I had a dream about Abby where she was telling me over and over to look at the scrapbook.

So I did.

And now, on the fifth day, it hit me.

She wasn't coming back to me.

I wasn't going to find her. She was gone.

I looked at her engagement ring and her wedding ring. They belonged on her hand. I got up and just let my feet lead me to where I needed to go.

I knew Kim was planning the funeral. I had been ignoring that too. While she planned my wife's funeral, I was still raiding cookhouses. One of the men I got my hands on yesterday said Jake had flown out days ago. He'd headed overseas, leaving his business with Andrew.

Jake had left.

His business here was done.

He had killed my wife. Nothing else was keeping him here and he wasn't staying around in case I found him.

"Kim?" I came to a stop in one of the living rooms. Kim was on the floor. So was Tyson. She had become more protective of him than ever. She wasn't letting him out of her sight. She was even sleeping on my couch at night.

Not wanting to be away from him.

"What, Reaper?" She looked up from the paperwork. "If this is about it being late and Tyson not being in bed, it's because he won't sleep. I've tried him in the crib for hours and he won't go to sleep."

"It's not about that." I went to her and sat beside her.

She and Abby may have had similar features, being twins, but Kim was nothing like Abby. And Abby was nothing like Kim. But together they were a powerful a force. Right now, Kim was grieving for her other half and only today I started to feel what she had been going through all week, since those detectives came.

"What, then?" She picked up a brochure on coffins.

"I want to help." I was positive that this morning my heart had stopped beating properly. I was positive I would never be the man I was before she was taken from me. Abby had wanted me to move on. Abby wanted me to not become heartless. Abby wanted me to find another woman to be Tyson's mother.

All that wasn't helping.

I could never love another woman, because I would always love her. I didn't know how Tyson was going to cope not having a mom. Somehow I'd handle it. Somehow I would give him what he needed.

"With the funeral?" Kim looked at me, shocked. "Does this mean you've finally come to terms with it?"

The tears just fell. Come to terms with it. Was that what I'd done? "No and yes, I guess," I said.

Her hand went to my knee. "You don't have to help."

"I want to. She was my wife. I need to know she is at peace." She deserved peace. She deserved to still be breathing. She deserved a hell of a lot more than she got. I had caused her life to end. It was all my fault and now all I could ensure was that she was at peace.

"OK."

"Was it hard?" I asked her. "Living without a mother? Was it hard?" She had lost her mom. She had gone through what Tyson would go through when he realized he had lost his mother. I could bet everything I had he would hate me for it. Because when he was older, I would tell him the truth. I was the reason he didn't have a mother.

"It was. But Tyson will be OK." Kim looked me in the eye. While my eyes blurred, I could still make out the pain in her eyes. "He has something I didn't. He has an aunt who will always be there. You don't have to worry about him not having a mother figure because I'm going to be it."

"You don't have to, Kim. I don't expect that of you."

"Abby would. And I do. So don't fight me on it. Tyson will have a mother figure in his life. He mightn't have Abby, but he will have me." She nudged me on the shoulder. "And you."

Would that be enough? My heart had gone so cold that I wasn't sure if I could give Tyson what he needed. A drunken, wasted, useless father. Maybe I was better off letting him go, letting Kim have custody.

Abby had made it clear. She didn't want him to have a shadow of a father. She told me to man up. She told me to pull myself together and be there for him. But that wasn't possible. I wasn't capable of functioning without her.

I wasn't capable of being a father. The father to her son. I couldn't do that without her.

"I was thinking black for the coffin. She loved black," Kim said, flicking the pages of the brochure. "As for the service, she didn't want one."

I nodded my head. "I know. I reread the will and what she wanted."

"She picked the cheapest coffin. I'm ignoring that request of hers."

"She always hated spending money."

"Which is stupid because you're loaded and she has more money under her floorboards than guns. Blake must have been paying her for those hits because that is the only way I can explain her having that much cash."

"Yeah, I think he was too." I ran a hand through my hair. "Has your dad shown his face since the other day?"

"Nope, and it's a good thing because I'm not in the mood to deal with his mood swings."

"Custody of Tyson, is that something you still want?" I looked back at her. She had to know I wasn't capable of being a father now. I couldn't love him like he needed. Not when I took his mother from him.

"You aren't thinking what I think you are thinking, are you?" Her words were as sharp as knives. "Because Abby would want you to be the one to take care of him. You need to man up, Reaper. Tyson just lost his mother. He can't lose a father as well. I can't be a father."

"You can leave the club. I'll set you up. I'll pay for everything. All I want is for him to have a normal life and I can't give that."

"NO!"

"Come on, Kim. It makes sense. I can't give him what he needs."

"All he needs is you!"

"And love, Kim. He needs that. And I'm not capable of that."

"You love him. Unconditionally. You're just freaking out because today you realized you lost your wife. So you are thinking you aren't capable of loving something or someone as much as you loved her. But I'm telling you, holding onto Tyson will help you get through this. Abby gave him to you. Don't turn your back on that."

I didn't say anything.

"He only has you and me, Reaper. So don't take yourself out of the picture."

"The father he needs, I'm not capable of being that. The father Abby wanted me to be. I'm not capable of that either. Not without her." Didn't anyone get it? When I lost her, I also lost my son because how could I look at him and not be eaten up with guilt for costing him his mom?

How the hell was I meant to live without her? I didn't know how to. Today was the first day without her. The first day I accepted she was dead. Yeah, that had stopped my heart beating. The man she loved and the man Tyson needed died when she did.

"You'll get through this, Reaper."

"How can you be so sure?"

"Because Abby would want us to," she said firmly. "And I'm not letting her down and neither are you. Running from Tyson. Giving him up. That isn't happening."

I scoffed. "Kim. The biggest part of me died when I realized she was gone. When I realized I'd never see her again. I'm capable of running this club. But I'm not capable of being a dad. Not without her."

"Reaper, you've been doing it without her from the start, when she was taken. You have been on your own since then. And you've managed fine. Just because the dream of getting her back is dead doesn't mean you aren't capable of continuing to love her son. Your son."

I ran my hands down my face. "I just want to wake up from this nightmare."

Kim's face twisted in sorrow. "You know what's been helping me get up in the morning? Knowing I'll never see her face again, or laugh at her stupid jokes, or tell her off for doing something completely stupid?"

I shook my head. Because today was my first day without her and I was managing it. I doubted tomorrow I would even see the point in getting up. I had been living to find her, to get her back. I had been living for that.

"She said once she would rather die quickly than to suffer like Mom. And if she was given a quick and painless death, I didn't have the right to wish her back. Because she would be at peace." Tears welled up in her eyes. "So don't wish her back. Let her be at peace. I'm letting her have the peace she wanted. So now you need to give her that as well."

I couldn't just let go of Abby. Never. I would never let her go. It didn't matter if she was breathing or not. I still wasn't letting go of her.

I nodded my head. "So where are you up to with the funeral?"

Kim started telling me details. I was only half listening, even though I knew she needed my full attention. I just couldn't give it to her. Because my heart was bleeding. I had died inside. My heart had stopped beating along with Abby's.

Tears welled in my eyes. Jake said it had been painless. She hadn't suffered. But I knew that to be a lie because knowing you're dying and waiting for the day to come for your life to end was torture enough. That wasn't painless. Waiting for your death.

Even in that video she had sent me saying goodbye, she had accepted the fact she was dying. She was just waiting for the day.

I was meant to stop that day from ever coming.

I had failed.

She had faced death without me. And I didn't think I could ever forgive myself for letting her go through what she did.

She had come into my life, abruptly, and she had left it the same way.

She took everything that made me me with her.

***

I hadn't touched drugs since Abby was taken. I also hadn't drunk. But I was doing both tonight. Because I sure as fuck wasn't going to sleep with tomorrow being what it was.

Her funeral.

I had to face her funeral in the morning.

I lit up another joint. I think I had smoked my weight in this stuff since I'd come to terms with the fact Abby was dead.

Kim had taken Tyson on full time.

She said I needed time to 'grieve.' That wasn't the case. I wasn't going to wake up one morning and be fucking smiling and happy. Abby was dead. My purpose, the reason I had been getting up in the morning, was gone.

Brad was running the club. He said I needed time. Everyone thought it was their place to tell me what I needed.

Even Roach had come around and told me that Abby wouldn't want me to be grieving for her like I was.

He had even said he was 'sorry for me.' I didn't believe it. The man was loving the fact he was right. He was right all along. He told me I would kill her. He was right.

So I wasn't going to argue with him over it.

The man was right.

I hadn't kept her safe. I hadn't looked after her. I had killed her.

I inhaled the joint, enjoying the fact I was getting slightly lightheaded. Maybe it would knock me out for the night and then I could face tomorrow still stoned and drunk. Because I didn't know how I was meant to get through tomorrow.

Or any day that would come after that. Because facing the world with no Abby, well, I didn't fucking want to do it.

My phone was ringing, doing what I had done all week. I ignored it. There was only one person I wanted to hear from and the dead couldn't make phone calls.

I was looking at her phone, rewatching videos when the private number called again.

Again, I ignored it.

A private number had basically been calling my phone all week but I didn't care who wanted me. Kim even rang me a few times when I needed air and went to a bar that wasn't at the clubhouse.

I still didn't remember how I got home that night. But I woke up there the next day. On my side of the bed. It hit me that morning. Her side of the bed was always going to be empty.

I pressed play on the video of her showing off her pregnancy in the mirror and telling me to be proud of it. I had watched that video I don't know how many times.

It was when her phone started ringing that the video stopped.

Abby was getting a phone call. I thought she had this phone for me and me alone. There were no contacts in it. I didn't even realize it had a SIM card in it. But it was ringing.

Did I answer it?

Whoever it was would want Abby, not me.

Who would she have given this number to? Kim said Abby used this phone as a spare. So no one should have this number.

I pressed answer and, for the first time this week, I answered a phone.

"Hello?"

"ALL WEEK, REAPER! ALL FUCKING WEEK I'VE BEEN CALLING YOU AND YOU HAVEN'T ANSWERED!"

"ABBY?"

"Do you have any idea what I have to do to get him out of the house? I can't just use the phone whenever I want!"

"You aren't dead."

"No. Which you would know if you had picked up your phone once this week!"

Abby was yelling at me. Abby was still breathing! "You're alive," I repeated myself. "You aren't dead."

"I'm not, Reaper. But I'm going to be gone in a matter of days. You're running out of time."

I was alert now. Not even the drugs stopped me from picking up on Abby's tone. She was serious.

"Where is he taking you?"

"Overseas. He isn't going to kill me. He did that so you would stop searching for me. He is, well, I think he is in love with me. He said something about how he couldn't lose the second love of his life. Actually, he is calling me the love of his life."

"You're mine."

"Kade, it doesn't matter whose I am. In a matter of days, I'll be gone. You have to find me now."

"I don't know where to look! I've pulled every connection I know, Abby. I can't find you!"

"That's the other reason I'm calling. There are two other people besides Jake who know where I am. You won't get shit out of Andrew but you might be able to get something from Billy."

"Who is Billy?"

"Shit, I've got to hurry up. He's back. Dad knows Billy. I don't know where he lives. But Dad knows him. He used to be his VP. He has a daughter named Shelly and a grandson named Charlie. They live in the suburbs with her husband, Daniel, who is an accountant. I don't know any more. But he knows where I am. I have to go."

"Don't, Abby. I just went through a whole week of thinking you were dead. Don't leave me again."

"Reaper, in a matter of days, you might as well consider me dead. Because as soon as I get on the plane, he won't be letting me go again. So find Billy. But if you don't get to me in time, I stand by my video."

"I'll find you. I promise you, Abby, I'll get you back."

"I hope so." She said those three words in so much pain. Like she couldn't face what would happen to her if I didn't.

"I'm coming. Hear me when I say that, Abby. I'll find this Billy and I'll make him tell me where you are."

She sighed. "You've never let me down."

And I wasn't starting now. I was already up opening my bedroom door. Roach, I needed Roach.

"Bye, Kade."

I didn't want her to hang up. And, as if she knew I was going to plead with her not to, she hung up, not giving me a chance.

She said I never let her down. Well, I had when I believed she was dead. I knew I would have felt something if she was dead. I was sure, though, I had felt it when the facts wouldn't leave me alone.

I banged on Roach's door.

He answered, looking how I felt before Abby called.

"Why the fuck are you grinning?" he barked at me.

"Abby isn't dead."

He grunted. "Back to denial, are we?"

"Who's Billy? Abby said he was your VP."

Roach frowned. "How would you know about Billy?"

"Abby said he knows where she is and you are going to tell me where he lives." And I was going to find Abby and I was going to get her back.

I had just gone a week thinking she was dead. I was meant to be going to her funeral tomorrow. She wasn't dead. I hadn't lost her. But I was going to, if I didn't find this Billy. There was only one way he was going to tell me where Abby was. That meant we were taking a trip to the suburbs to collect his daughter and grandson.

I really wasn't above threatening them or killing Billy's daughter to get the information I wanted.

I was desperate. And I would do anything if it meant I didn't have to face a world without Abby.

Chapter 22

Reaper

It took a day to track him down. But he came home. Came home to us waiting for him.

I punched him again, my knuckles bleeding, my fists aching. He still wasn't speaking. He made a point of telling Roach he would die before Roach saw his daughter again.

I had threatened him. I had beaten him close to knocking him out completely. I had even shot him in the leg. Still he wasn't speaking.

So I nodded for Brad to bring them in.

His good eye went wide when he saw his daughter and grandson with their mouths duct-taped. They were strangers. They meant nothing to me or Abby, as far as I knew. Which meant I would use them to get what I wanted.

"So this is what we are going to do next, Billy. You tell me where my wife is and I won't put a bullet in your daughter's head." I flexed my knuckles. My hands were going to be swollen tomorrow.

"Let them go," he gritted out.

"I'm planning on killing one of them. You can pick if you want." I wasn't above it. I would kill them if it meant I got Abby back. I was more Reaper now than Kade. I didn't care what I had to do to get her back.

I wasn't letting Jake fly off with her.

I wasn't willing to face a world without her.

So yeah, I would kill his grandson if he didn't start speaking. He must have realized I was serious because his facial expression changed.

"Even you are above killing a kid," he spat out, blood running from his mouth. I was sure he had internal bleeding.

"No, I'm not." I really wasn't. "So, you pick. The boy or her?"

"If I tell you where Abby is, will you leave them alone?"

"Maybe."

"Let them go and I'll tell you."

"The three of you won't be left unguarded till I have Abby back." I pulled out my gun. "Now, which one?"

"14 Clove Street. Two-story house. Gate code, four seven eight. He has cameras but no security."

Had I finally got an address? "You lying?"

"Why would I lie when you have a gun pointed at my daughter's head? I know you, Reaper. You aren't lying when you say you aren't above killing a kid for information. So there, I told you. Now leave us alone!"

I looked at Brad and then at Roach. "Do you think he is telling the truth?"

Roach stepped forward, taking the cigarette from his mouth. Nodding his head, he said, "Yeah, I think he is. Took him long enough."

The address repeated in my head. "Brad, get the boys ready. Leave a bunch here. They aren't free till I have Abby." I looked back at Billy. "If I don't get her, I'll come back and kill him first, then her, and I'll leave you breathing."

"You might be too late anyway. They are flying out tonight or tomorrow. So if they aren't there, it isn't my fault."

"It is. 'Cause you could have told me at the start. You made me nearly beat you to death. And gave him longer with her."

Billy spat out a mouthful of blood. "Well, nothing is stopping you now."

He was right. Nothing was stopping me. I had an address. "I'll be back if she isn't there." I turned and walked out. Brad was on the phone calling for the boys to meet us there. I was going into this guns blazing with as many men behind me as possible. I wasn't letting Jake slip from my grasp again.

"Roach, if we get there and she is there, you are in charge of getting her out." I mounted my bike.

"That man took my daughter. No way I'm walking out without letting him have it." Roach stomped on his cigarette, looking like the demon he was known to be.

"Trust me. He will get a slow death." And I didn't want Abby there to see that side of me. Because what I was planning on doing to him would scare anyone away.

Chapter 23

Abby

Pure, red panic filled me. This couldn't be happening. I looked at Jake, not believing him when he said we were leaving tomorrow.

Time, I needed more time.

"What's the rush?" I staggered out, my hands shaking as I gripped the knife. "Surely we don't have to leave right away."

"We're leaving tomorrow, Abby. You can't talk me out of it."

"And what has you thinking I won't bolt as soon as you open that door?"

He gave me a challenging smirk, stepping into the kitchen. "Because I'm knocking you out. It's called a private plane, sweetheart. No one will care if you are passed out for the whole trip. Then once we are settled into the new place and you're locked up again, I'll let you come to."

"You're a monster!" I gripped the knife tighter, my hands no longer shaking. I was consumed with anger, and I realized right then nothing was stopping me from doing what I wanted. Hell, I might be stuck here if I killed him. But the only other option I was being offered was a long, slow life with him. So I lunged for him.

But he must have been expecting it because he caught my hand before I could stab him in the chest.

"Come on, darling, I thought we were past this." He laughed mockingly. "You don't want your new husband dead, do you?"

"Reaper is my husband." I pulled my hand away, out of his grip, the knife falling to the floor. "And always will be." No matter what he said. No matter how many times he forced himself on me.

I was still Reaper's. His name was tattooed on my shoulder and he was the man I thought about every night.

Nothing Jake did or said could stop me from loving Reaper.

Jake opened his mouth to speak, but something on the security cameras caught his eye. He frowned, walking around me to the screen.

"I'm not expecting anyone," he muttered. I really didn't care if it was Billy or Andrew or both of them. Most likely a night game of poker was in order.

It was only when I noticed Jake's eyes widen and saw terror slowly creep across his face that I looked at the cameras.

It couldn't be. Could it be?

My hope skyrocketed as the gates opened and I saw the flashes of motorbikes. Kade. It was Kade. He'd found me.

Jake darted around me. No way was I letting him run. I quickly followed him, hearing the roaring of the motorbikes up the driveway. He wouldn't make it out the front door. So I was quick to block the back sliding doors.

I had attempted to get out of these doors so many times that I knew if you entered the wrong number three times, they would automatically lock for ten minutes. So I was typing in number after number. Just as Jake pushed me out of the way, it started flashing red.

"Fuck!" Jake was trying to override it.

But I knew his locking system well. No way he could override that without a key. It was when he reached into his pocket that I started to panic.

Just when I thought I'd have to get creative, the security light came on outside. Never in my life had I been so happy to see bikers. They were surrounding the house.

Reaper hadn't come here alone. Thank fuck for that. That meant there was a higher chance of me getting out of here alive.

"Looks like you are out of luck, Jake." I took a shaky breath in, not believing it was happening.

Jake cursed and then started to run to the garage but the front door busted open. And there he was. My purpose. My reason. Looking more furious than I had ever seen him, his shirt and vest covered in blood. It was like all the horrible moments that led to this one made this moment even sweeter. I didn't think it through. I didn't even care that his focus would be on Jake. I ran straight to him.

He caught me with ease. Was it possible he had put on even more muscle? He was bigger. My arms wrapped around his neck. It felt like home and I was suffocated immediately by a scent that I had sworn I would never get a hint of again.

"Abby, you alright?" He held me up with one arm while his hand cupped my face. The concern in his eyes told me he really wanted to know. But he was looking at me like he couldn't believe his luck.

Brad, Dad, Cameron and other members I didn't know but who all wore president patches had Jake surrounded.

I took a steady breath in. "I am now." I still couldn't believe it was happening. Moments ago, I was panicking about spending the rest of my life with Jake and now, now Kade was holding me. How had he gotten here just in time? "I didn't think you were going to make it." My fear surfaced. "I thought I was going to be with him for the rest of my life."

"I wouldn't have let that happen." He looked me in the eyes. And as they locked with mine, I knew every promise he had ever made about finding me and never giving up on me was true. "I'm here now." Reaper eased me down, looking torn as he put me back on the ground. "Now you have to go." He cupped my face, looking like he was half a second away from kissing me. "Your old man is taking you home and I'll be there as soon as I finish."

I gulped. Right. Of course, he didn't want me here for this bit. Hell, I didn't want to be here for this bit.

Dad put a hand on my back. "Come on, little one."

Reaper was walking toward Jake when my hand shot out and gripped his.

"Make it slow, Reaper." I didn't feel one bit guilty making this request. All those times Jake had beaten me. But I would still take being beaten over the rapes. But I wasn't about to tell Reaper Jake had raped me.

Reaper held my eyes for a few moments before nodding his head. That was all I needed to know. I didn't need to know the details of what was about to happen to Jake. I didn't care. And to be honest, it would be nothing compared to what he had put me through.

I just hoped that it came close to the pain I'd felt, the pain of being ripped from your family. To be raped. To be beaten. To be told you will never see the ones you love again. Yeah, I hoped Jake suffered.

Dad guided me outside and the fresh air smacked me hard and fast in the face. How long had it been since I was in fresh air? I inhaled it deeply and followed Dad to his bike.

***

"You alright, sweetheart?" Dad gripped my hand. "You are shaking."

"I'm just cold," I lied. I think I was in shock. Yep. Shock. It had to be that. My heart pumped so fast I felt like I'd just gotten off a roller coaster. I was too scared to close my eyes longer than half a second because if this was a dream, I didn't want to wake up.

It felt real. It had to be real, right? Maybe Jake had killed me and this was simply what my heaven was like. Because coming to terms with the fact Reaper had found me, got me out and saved my life, well, that was much harder to believe.

I followed Dad, wide-eyed, still in what I was assuming was shock, into the clubhouse. The familiar smell was welcoming as soon as the door opened. It smelt like home.

"Did it work? Was it the right place?" Kim started spraying questions at Dad.

A faint smile traced my lips hearing her. She was as demanding as ever. God, I had missed my twin. Even her annoying traits I had missed, like her lack of boundaries. How many times had she just walked into the bathroom when I was taking a shower? She always made a point of borrowing my clothes but never returning them. Or if she did, they would be dirty. I swear she was allergic to the washing machine.

I had missed the way she always kept me on my toes. She was the one person who, no matter what happened, could read me. I couldn't keep a secret from her and even when I tried, I usually failed. Which is why I would have to put on a harder front when she brought up the subject of Jake. 'Cause I knew she was going to. She didn't avoid subjects. Hell, she never avoided anything. She just faced things. So I knew as soon as she could, she would be peppering me with questions. And there was no way I would ever tell her or Reaper or any other living, breathing soul that Jake raped me.

I thought Dad was going to answer but before he had time to, I stepped out of his shadow.

"ABBY!" She was across the room and wrapping her arms around me within a second. Her familiar perfume was welcoming. Another thing we always shared, and she would steal, was perfume. I wonder if anyone picked up on the fact Kim and I shared perfume?

"Hey, Kim." My voice cracked but I hadn't gone through everything I had gone through to cry now. I hugged her back. It felt so weird to be touched after someone having forced himself on me. But at the same time, I had really missed her and I wanted her to hug me.

Maybe just for a second I could pretend like I was OK, just having her here, hugging me now. It gave me a dose of courage to put up a front.

Kim pulled back, tears running down her cheeks. I might have been putting on a front, but her emotions were clear on her face. "I never thought I'd see you again." She pulled me back in, hugging me tighter. "You have no idea how much I've missed you." She pulled back, tears running freely down her face.

I started wiping her tears away. I think the last time I saw her crying like this was when Mom died. Yeah. It was. And seeing her teared-up face was bringing back memories I really didn't have the courage to face. No matter how much courage her touch was giving me.

I kept wiping her tears away. "Stop crying."

"Why aren't you?" She looked at me, shaking her head. Her hair was dark and shorter. I had never seen Kim go dark before, unless you count the time I dyed her hair red. But still, then it wasn't dark. It was bright. "Seriously, why aren't you a mess right now?" Her questions started while she wiped away more tears.

"I think I'm dreaming." I was honest and she read my expression. I was serious. And when she realized I was, she was automatically pissed off. "OUCH!" I snapped at her. She just pinched me!

She looked at me mockingly. "Still think you are dreaming?"

"Yes, because that is something only you would do!"

One of Dad's hands fell on my shoulder and his other on Kim's. "Finally, my girls back together." He pulled us to him. "Never thought I'd miss you two fighting, but I have." He sounded like he genuinely had. I couldn't count how many times he yelled at us for fighting and now he was standing here saying he had missed it. A faint smile appeared on my lips.

"You're going soft in your old age, Dad," I said and didn't pull away from him.

"Kim, get us some beers. I think Abby needs something to drink and she needs to see her son." Dad let go of Kim. My heart started beating faster as soon as Dad said 'she needs to see her son.'

I had dreamed about seeing Tyson again. Maybe I was dreaming?

"Come on, Abby." Dad pulled me along.

But I wasn't ready. So I stopped. "I don't think I can." I was frozen. I had only had a few short days with him. He wouldn't remember me. I would be some stranger. And if I had to see that, that he felt completely uncomfortable around me, that would break the tough front I was putting up. Not crying would be impossible. I would flood this place with tears.

"Don't be scared, little one. He is your son." Dad stopped in front of me, lifting my head up, which dragged my eyes off the floor. He made me look him in the eye. "He has missed you."

I wanted to laugh at that. Not in a funny way, but because it was a lie, a complete lie.

"He doesn't know me." I pulled my head from Dad's grasp. About now the dream should end. I've realized the facts. Tyson doesn't know me. I had missed the two most important months of his life. Nothing was going to give me back time. But who was I kidding? Jake was going to make sure I never saw Tyson again anyway.

This dream was becoming a nightmare very quickly.

"She still thinks she dreaming." Kim appeared with beers, shoving one in my hand and handing one to Dad. "What do I have to say for you to believe me?"

"No way would it have been that simple. Jake would have seen that coming." I was speaking more to myself than to them. "But he looked scared. Normally in my dreams he doesn't look scared."

"It's 'cause you aren't dreaming, Abby. That was real fear on that man's face tonight." Dad made a point of taking the cap off my beer. "Here, drink something. Maybe then you'll realize you aren't dreaming."

"Also, you two aren't normally in my dreams." I looked between them, confused. Dad was looking at me with an understanding yet sad smile and Kim was frowning, like she was about to start crying again.

"He has really fucked you up, hasn't he?" she said, looking at me as if I was someone else. Someone she didn't know. Someone whose perfume she didn't steal and whose clothes she didn't borrow. Hell, she was looking at me like we had nothing in common at all.

What did it matter? This was just a dream. I was going to wake up lying beside Jake and possibly flying overseas. I pinched my eyes shut.

Just wake up, Abby.

This was worse than a nightmare because it felt real but, at the same time, so far from possible.

Wake up!

I opened my eyes. "I'm so confused. Did Jake give me those sleeping pills again? 'Cause that would explain this dream." Again, I was speaking to myself.

"Maybe when Reaper gets here, she will start making sense," Kim said to Dad. And I saw a tear slide down her cheek that she was quick to wipe away. "Must have killed you to leave, Dad." Kim smiled grimly at Dad.

"Losing your mother and leaving that man breathing are the two hardest things I have ever faced." Dad took a gulp from his beer. Why was he looking so upset?

I opened my mouth to say something, but a cry stopped me. It wasn't an unhappy cry. It was a 'you've forgotten about me' cry. How did I know the difference? I had never been around a baby before. How could I tell the difference?

I must have imagined it because neither Kim nor Dad moved.

Then I heard it again.

"OK, what is that noise?" I said to them.

They both looked at me, half-shocked. Was it a stupid question? Maybe this was the part of the dream where I was imagining sounds or something?

"It's your son." Kim smiled at me. "Still think you are dreaming?"

Suddenly, my fear of seeing him was gone. I had to see him. Because it was like he held the key. He would be just like I imagined him, small and so fucking perfect.

I put my beer on the table and walked past the pool tables and down the few stairs to one of the living rooms. There was a crib in front one of the couches, right in front of the television. The television was playing some children's show I didn't know.

Guess when it did come to children's television shows I wasn't an expert. I didn't have much knowledge.

I kneeled in front of the crib.

He was smiling at me. I looked at him, completely stunned. His eyes were the same, but he was longer, his face more full, his hair darker. It was identical to Kade's.

My fingers went through the gap in the crib and I touched his face. My mouth dropped open. Was he real? No way could I imagine the softness of his skin. Could I? It wasn't possible for my mind to come up with what he looked like now.

He was kicking his legs. I put my finger in his outstretched hand. When his hand wrapped around my finger, I swear it took all my willpower not to cry.

***

Reaper

I had come in the back entrance. I didn't want Abby seeing me covered in his blood. I had showered and changed. I was ready, ready to see her. Fuck. It had killed me to let her go. But it had to be done.

I jogged down the stairs. I was finally going to be able to hold her again, finally getting to touch her. I was so nervous about seeing her that my hands were shaking. It was stupid. I knew that. But it didn't stop my body from going into a fit about seeing her.

"Where is she?" I asked Kim when I got down the stairs. She was smoking at one of the tables. I didn't know it was possible to be this anxious about seeing someone. But this wasn't just anyone. This was my wife. The love of my life. The mother to my child. The woman who had been ripped away from my life for months.

"In the living room. She hasn't moved from the crib in, I'd say, over four hours. She's not talking, either." Kim took a sip from her beer. "Don't be surprised if she ignores you. It's like she is in her own world. She swore she was dreaming till she laid eyes on Tyson."

I nodded my head. I expected her to be in shock. Hell, I could handle her being in shock. What I couldn't handle was her gone.

I nervously walked through the clubhouse till I was at the stairs going down to the living room. And there she was, sitting on the floor, her legs tucked under her. I suddenly forgot how to move.

Be a man, Kade.

As I got closer, I noticed Tyson had his hand wrapped around her finger and he was asleep.

"Abby?"

She didn't move. She didn't turn her head. She didn't even acknowledge me. I stood behind her. Kim had said that Abby wasn't talking.

What did I do?

I didn't know exactly how to handle someone in shock. But this was Abby. I knew her. I knew her right down to the small details. So maybe her not talking was her being overwhelmed. She had just gone from being one-on-one with someone to seeing everyone she knew.

I had purposely made sure the clubhouse was empty in case we found her. And I had kicked out every member for the night and it would stay empty till she felt comfortable about being around people again.

I knew Abby. So what did she need right now? I remembered the time her dad had his heart attack. I didn't know what to do and I ended up calling Drake. But we had come so far from then. I knew her. And right now, I knew Abby would just need to know I was here.

I sat behind her, trapping her between my legs. She didn't move. She didn't even seem to notice I had joined her.

I tucked her hair behind her ear. It had been blocking my side view of her. I couldn't stop myself from kissing the side of her face. She was really here. I had got her back. It was like my kiss broke whatever spell was over her. She suddenly starting blinking quickly, frowning, and turned her face to look at me. Like she hadn't realized I was here till now.

Her expression changed to one of amazement. And she was looking at me like I wasn't real. Kim said something about Abby thinking she was dreaming. Maybe that explained the look she was giving me.

She turned her body and moved between my legs but she didn't pull her finger from Tyson. But her other hand went to my face, like she was testing to see if *I* was real.

I closed my eyes briefly, loving the feeling of her touch. To think this time two days ago, I was positive my heart was dead along with hers. I had given up on her. It was as if she knew it too, because she knew exactly when to reach out for me. If she hadn't called and I hadn't got her tonight… she'd be gone.

And that thought made my body go into a quick panic and made me wrap an arm around her. I had her. She was here.

I took a calming breath in. She was right here. I had her. But a part of me was telling me she wasn't here with me. The look in her eyes; that was all I needed to see. She wasn't with me.

Her hand ran down my neck, stopping on my shoulder. Then she did something I wasn't expecting. She fell into my arms, putting her head onto my chest.

"I don't want to wake up," she whispered into my chest.

I wrapped both my arms around her, holding onto her. "You aren't sleeping, sweetheart." God, she was smaller than I remembered.

Maybe after she did sleep and woke up here, she would realize it. Till then I just had to accept she wasn't with me right now. It didn't stop me from enjoying the moment, though. I had her back.

***

I woke up on the floor. When the hell did I go to sleep? I remembered lying down when Abby did. Tyson had still had her by the finger. I remembered trying to convince her to go to bed. But she wouldn't budge from the crib. She wouldn't sleep either. I had settled for her lying on my arm. But she wasn't there now.

Tyson was still asleep. It had to be early and I had searched the whole clubhouse looking for her. She wasn't in my room. She wasn't in her room. I had tried Kim. She wasn't there. And she wasn't with her dad, or in any other room in this fucking building.

WHERE THE FUCK WAS SHE?

The last thing I remember was that look in her eye, like she was with me but wasn't. Fuck, it was like she was drugged or something and I had left her unsupervised! While she was on this other planet!

Where would she go? I had to think.

Why the fuck did I leave her unsupervised?

I got her back only to lose her again. Where would she go?

I pushed open the clubhouse door, heading for my bike. I was so focused on going searching for her that I only just caught a bit of movement out of the corner of my eye.

She was lying on one of the picnic tables.

She was still here.

I stormed over to her. What was she thinking just disappearing like that? She should have woken me! She couldn't just disappear!

She must have heard me coming because she turned her head.

"I'm not used to it," she said.

"What?" I snapped. I was pissed off because I thought I had lost her again. I was furious at myself for having spent half an hour looking for her and she was out-fucking-side. Why didn't I look out here? Then again, why the hell would she be out here? It was fucking freezing and she was barely wearing anything. She hadn't answered me. Maybe because I had snapped at her. I forced myself to take a deep breath and asked her again, this time nicer. "What aren't you used to?" That came out better, less aggressive.

She sat up. Seeing all her skin, that dress barely covering her, I pulled my vest off and put it next to her. Then I took off my sweatshirt. "Arms up," I said to her. She did as I asked, and I put the sweatshirt on over her head. She pulled her hair out of the sweatshirt.

I stepped closer to her, my hands running down her. "What aren't you used to?" I had no idea what Jake had made her do. I had no idea what she was talking about. What wasn't she used to? Being home? Did that mean she finally had come to the conclusion she was here and not dreaming it?

"Fresh air."

And hearing that hit me in the chest. Hearing it was like taking a punch you weren't expecting that winded you. I just stared at her. Not knowing what to say. She had been locked up for months because of me. She nearly died. She was nearly flown to a new country. All because of me.

How the hell was I going to make it up to her?

I swallowed sharply. I guess starting with the basics. "I'm so sorry, Abby." My hands cupped her face. "You have no idea how incredibly sorry I am." That didn't even cover it. Didn't come close to how I felt about this situation. It was all because of me.

Roach had been right when he said she would pay for my mistakes. Because she just did two hard months of paying for them and if I hadn't found her, she would have been paying for them for the rest of her life.

"It's not your fault. You didn't lock me up, Kade." Her hands covered mine. "Stop looking at me like that."

"Like what?"

"Like you are regretting every decision you ever made that led me to you." She could always read me too easily. When my expression didn't change, she sighed. "Well, at least we got Tyson. Even if we don't make it."

We would always have Tyson. Wait a sec. I narrowed my eyes at her. "What do you mean 'if we don't make it?'"

"I'm being realistic."

"Only a couple of hours ago you weren't even on this fucking planet. You thought I was a dream! And now you are being *realistic*? What the fuck do you mean by that?" I didn't mean to grip her tighter but I did and she was quick to pull my hands off her.

"You're looking at me with such regret, Reaper. You are looking at me like I'm your weakness. How can you expect to stay in a relationship with me when you see me as your one weakness? You're looking at me now with this pained, regretful look and it's hurting me!" She was getting upset and it was the last thing I wanted. I had wanted her back. I didn't want her upset.

She started to get up but I gripped her by the hips and forced her back down in front of me.

"You're wrong. I have two weaknesses. You and Tyson."

She rolled her eyes. "Then cut us off if you don't want us! God, it's not like it is uncommon for a biker to do that! Because I won't let you look at me as a weakness when I look at you as a strength!"

"Abby, calm down!" She started to stand up again, and again I forced her back down. Like normal, when things got hard, she wanted to run. Some things never changed. "Abby, listen to me."

"No."

"Abby." I attempted to be calm with her. She hadn't slept. She looked like she had stopped eating altogether. And she had been tortured for two months. She wasn't in the right frame of mind to be making any decisions. And if she really thought I was going to cut her and Tyson off, she really was on another fucking planet.

She shoved me hard in the chest but it didn't budge me. "Reaper, let me go."

"Do you really think I would let you leave me? After everything we have been through? Do you think now, I will suddenly realize how much I put your life and my son's life in jeopardy and push you away?"

"Yes."

This time much more gently, I cupped her face. "I'm way too much of a greedy man for that, Abby. I know sense and history tell me to let you and Tyson go. But it's not going to happen." I was never letting her out of my sight again. "I'm never letting you go. You hear that part? Not even if it is the right thing to do."

"What if it is what I want?" She looked at me challengingly, arching her eyebrows, looking at me like it was possible.

I smiled, and she frowned at that. "I know what you want better than I know what I want." I took a step closer to her, hearing her take a sharp breath in. "You still want me as badly as you did when you were sixteen."

She didn't agree or disagree. She remained quiet. It was her breathing giving her away.

"I'm right, aren't I?" I dipped my head, looking her in the eye. She always struggled to lie to me when she was looking me in the eye.

She bit her bottom lip and started nervously shaking her leg. It was when I placed my hand over her knee that she stopped.

She was looking me in the eye when she nodded her head. "Yes," the word slipped from her mouth.

One word. I hadn't realized I was so tense till I heard it. I dropped my head to hers. "Thank fuck for that." I was never good at gambling and I had been praying she still had that unconditional love for me, even after everything I put her through.

It wasn't me reaching out for her this time. She was reaching out for me, her hands going to my face.

"But…"

I wanted to curse. Maybe I had counted my win too soon?

I nodded for her to keep going.

"But you are going to have to come to terms with what happened and forgive yourself as well as me." Her words were soft, barely a whisper. I almost missed the part when she said 'as well as me.'

"What would I have to forgive you for, Abby? You haven't done anything wrong."

A dim smile graced her lips and it was the type of smile you would see just before someone bursts out crying. It was the type of smile she gave when she was struggling with something.

"I did." She inhaled sharply. "I did something wrong."

"What?"

She looked me dead in the eye. "Some things you are better off not knowing."

"Nah, don't play that card. We don't do secrets." I was always honest with her when I could be. She had always been the same when she wasn't off killing people and keeping me in the dark. "Last time you kept a secret it nearly pulled us apart."

She traced my jaw and that dim smile was back on her face. "This one will only tear me apart. And I'd really like it if we never mention this again."

"It's something he did, isn't it?" I didn't know what he had done to her. He clearly as fuck didn't feed her. I knew she didn't want me to press her for details but knowing she was keeping something from me, well, that gave me an itch I couldn't scratch.

"Kade, stop." Her hand froze on my cheek. "Like I said, I don't want to mention it again."

"Was it the beating? 'Cause I know about that. Fuck, I made him pay for that. Is it the Russian roulette? 'Cause he paid for that too. Was it not feeding you? 'Cause I can clearly fucking see that. And not any of those things are your fault."

"Stop." She looked like she was in physical pain. "Please stop." She pinched her eyes shut. "I don't want to talk about it. Any of it. Ever."

"We have to talk about it."

"Why?" Her eyes sprung open, and they were on fire. "Because you want to know every single detail of what happened to me?"

"Yes." Wasn't that obvious?

"Not happening." Her eyes sliced through mine. "Ever. There is only one other person that knows the details and I'm assuming he's dead. So that leaves me. And I'm keeping my mouth shut."

Frustrating. So incredibly frustrating. Wouldn't she want to get it off her chest? Have someone to talk to about it? Instead, she was going to bottle it up and that wasn't healthy. I was going to point that out to her when she shivered.

And only then did I notice the mist of rain in between us.

"Come on. It's raining." I went to take her hand.

She suddenly looked uneasy. "Um, it's OK. I'll stay out here."

"Abby, did you hear me say the bit where it's raining?" I wasn't leaving her out here. More importantly, why did she want to be outside in the rain? I looked at her, trying to guess what she was thinking and I had it within a second. I knew the reason she wasn't getting up. "You can't avoid inside altogether, Abby. I'm not locking you in. You can come back out as soon as it stops raining."

Her eyes widened. I had hit the nail on the head. She was avoiding inside.

I pushed the sleeve of my sweatshirt up, taking her hand. "Come on, come inside with me?"

Her eyes darted from me to the clubhouse door. She still wasn't moving.

"Tyson will be awake soon. I'm sure he wants to see you." I kissed the back of her hand.

"Not you too," she groaned.

"What?"

"This delusion that Tyson knows who I am. Dad and Kim said the same thing. He has no idea who I am. I am a complete stranger and, frankly, his morning would be better if I didn't interrupt it." She was so harsh and cruel. She actually believed Tyson couldn't possibly know who his mother was.

I wanted to yell at her. Heck, it was the first thing I wanted to do after hearing that. Tyson didn't just go to anyone. He sure as fuck wouldn't hold onto someone's finger all night if he didn't know them.

"Start taking it back, Abby." I gave her a chance. She didn't know how wrong she was. It was her sweatshirt he slept with every night. It was her he kept looking for. Now she was sitting here like that didn't matter.

"No. I'm not playing the game that you and Dad and Kim want to play. He doesn't know me."

I gritted my teeth. How had I forgotten how stubborn she was? I let go of her hand.

"If you are so sure of that, then you should be fucking moving quicker."

"What?"

"He is your son. And if you think he doesn't know you, you should be the one making the first move. You should be fixing that. Not just washing your hands of him!"

I was expecting her to spray me for accusing her of washing her hands of him. But she remained quiet and dropped her eyes from mine. Whenever she wouldn't look me in the eye, I could guarantee I wouldn't like what she was thinking.

I stepped back, putting my hand out for her to take. "You coming or not?"

Seconds passed. Soon, minutes passed and I was still waiting. What was I going to have to say for her to realize Tyson needed his mother? I sighed. I needed to come up with something and fast, before that multifunctioning brain of hers did some serious damage.

It was when I felt her hand slip into mine that my mind stopped racing. I opened my eyes and watched her get up.

It was instinct to help her down.

God, she was thin.

Breakfast, that was the first thing we were doing.

"You've gotten bigger," she said, not fighting me when I pulled her to my side.

"And you're fucking smaller."

"Always yin and yang, aren't we?" She smiled, not caring that she basically weighed nothing at all. I noticed it wasn't one of her real smiles. She was faking it, forcing it. Fair enough. She had had a rough twelve hours. Hell, she had had a rough few months. Did it really matter if she couldn't smile naturally at me yet?

Yeah, it did.

I still had that picture of her standing at the car out in front of the hospital, that real full-blown smile of hers. Somehow I had to get her back to that.

I held the clubhouse door open for her. She didn't rush in.

"Do you want me to leave the door open?" I asked her when she didn't move.

"No. It's freezing out here." She took a deep breath and walked through the door. I knew that was hard for her to do. I felt pride immediately. She was always braver than I gave her credit for. She looked over at her shoulder, frowning at me. "What are you waiting for?"

Right. I was holding things up.

I closed the door and was quick to wrap my arms around her. I would never get enough of touching her.

"So what's your morning routine?" she asked, not pushing me away. Thank fuck for that.

Did I tell her the truth? Because the truth was I was usually gone most of the day looking for her. Kim looked after Tyson. I took over at night.

"Seeing as you are home, we need a new one."

"I'm sure the one you have is fine."

"Trust me, your boys have been struggling without you." I kissed the back of her head.

She turned in my arms, her arms going around my neck. "My boys, hey?" She smirked up at me.

I nodded my head. My eyes flashed to her lips. As much as I wanted to kiss her, I didn't want to rush it. She was letting me touch her which had to be big. Because she wouldn't be used to it. Hell, I wasn't used to it. But when it came to Abby, I found old habits came back quick.

Like right now, as she bit her bottom lip, it was killing me to not pull it from her teeth. Fuck it. I'd just do it. My thumb gently pulled her lip from her grasp. She realized what she was doing and didn't go back to doing it.

I didn't pull my thumb away. I had forgotten how soft she was. If I had forgotten that, was it possible I had forgotten what she tasted like? My memory hadn't done her justice at all. So I was guessing my memories of kissing her weren't living up to the real thing. She was more beautiful in person. The pictures and videos of her hadn't done her justice.

How the hell did I get so lucky?

My hand spread across her cheek. I didn't even realize I was pulling her in till she was so fucking close. My self-control was wavering. She wouldn't be ready. I knew that. So why the hell was I teasing myself by bringing her so close?

Then, just when I was about to withdraw, her lips brushed mine, making me freeze.

Had I forgotten how to kiss? Her lips met mine once more and I automatically switched gears. My hands going to her hips and lifting her up, I kissed her back. She was sweeter than I remembered. So fucking perfect.

I had lost my self-control and was kissing her desperately. I was frantic, unable to get enough. I sat her on a pool table and my hand was quick to go to the back of her neck, not wanting her to pull away. Needing to explore every inch of her mouth with my tongue.

"I see you two are back at it."

Abby froze as soon as she heard those words, pulling away from me. I groaned. I was nowhere near done with her.

I looked over my shoulder to see Kim standing there, smiling at us. "You picked a fucking great moment to show up." Couldn't she have slept in or something?

I wasn't ready to share Abby with anyone, not even her sister or father.

"I've been busy cooking breakfast." Kim walked into the room. "Abby looks too thin. She is back with us today, right?" She looked around me. "Not still dreaming, Abby?"

Kim wasn't teasing her. She was being serious. She wanted to know if her sister was back to being her sister. I had news for Kim. Abby might be back from her momentary flight from reality, but she was nowhere near back to who she was before she was taken.

I looked back at Abby.

Her blue eyes stared directly at me.

"You hungry?" My hands went around her and I lifted her off the pool table.

"No."

"Abby, you clearly haven't been fucking eating. So don't start this, 'no, I'm not eating' crap." Kim was down her throat before I could even say anything.

"I'm not hungry." Abby stood by her statement.

"You're eating," I said, ending her protest. "Don't bother arguing about it."

"Since when did you and Kim start agreeing on things?" Abby arched her eyebrows at me.

"Since it came to you," I answered her. Kim and I were closer. Being without Abby had brought us closer. So had looking after Tyson.

Speaking of Tyson, he was moving in the crib.

"I think someone's awake." Kim had noticed him moving as well.

Abby all of a sudden looked completely freaked out. I could tell by one look in her eyes that she wanted to bolt.

She opened her mouth. I was sure she was going to come out with a golden line to get away from facing Tyson. But I wasn't giving her a chance.

"Come on, Abby." I pulled on her hand. "Stop looking so frightened. He isn't going to hurt you."

"I'm more frightened of me hurting him." She pulled her hand from my grasp. "I think I'm going to have a shower."

I shook my head. "Don't even try and get away from us."

"Reaper, I really think it's for the best if I keep my distance when it comes to Tyson. He knows you and Kim. He feels safe with you two. I see no point in disturbing that."

"How's you having a relationship with him going to disturb anything?"

She was freaking out. It was clear on her face. She was a second from bolting and a second from deciding if she had to really give me any reason why she was doing it.

She shook her head. "Please don't make me."

She was that terrified of Tyson? He wasn't going to hurt her. Or maybe that's what she was scared of. Him not knowing her. Yeah, I bet that was what had her wanting to run. She didn't want him to not know her.

He knew who his mother was, and he knew she had been missing.

"He knows you, Abby. The first memories he has are all of you." I took her hand again and walked her to the crib. "Have some faith in him, Abby."

I let go of her hands and picked Tyson up. He yawned and, like normal, was smiling. She was stiff. I arched my eyebrows when she didn't put her arms out. Tyson caught sight of her and started kicking his legs and cooing.

"Still think he doesn't know who you are?" I said to her as our son basically had a fit trying to get to her. He was all smiles, looking directly at her.

She was watching his reaction. He was the one who got her to open her arms for him.

As soon as he was in her arms, she smiled, he giggled. And just like that my world snapped back into place. I had my wife back.

Chapter 24

Kim

I was tapping my fingers on my laptop, thinking. Well, more worrying.

"OK, you going to tell me what's wrong?"

My head snapped to look at Trigger. He was giving me a look that said he knew something was wrong with me and he was sick of watching me deal with it.

"It's Abby," I sighed.

"What about her?"

"Something's wrong with her." I couldn't explain it. I just knew. I knew she went through something huge and was coming back to us, slowly and as best as she could. But there was something else, something she wasn't telling us.

"Well, you can't expect her to be back to herself. Hell, look at what she went through."

"That's just it." I turned on the bed. "She isn't telling me something."

"I'm sure Reaper knows everything. So stop stressing."

I shook my head. "Nope, she hasn't told him either. Otherwise I would know."

Trigger hand ran down my leg. "Ever thought maybe you are expecting too much from her?"

"Nope. She is keeping something from me. We know she was beaten. She didn't eat but there is something else."

"He was going to kill her, Kim. Every day he would have reminded her of that. Physical torture is nothing compared to that shit, knowing her life was going to end at his hands." He took my hand. "I don't know how Reaper can live with himself after everything he put her through."

"He didn't do it on purpose. And he did get Abby in the end. And he killed Jake."

"Yeah, but still," Trigger shook his head, "knowing you've put your woman through months of torture and put her life at risk like that. Hell, I'm surprised he hasn't left the club altogether."

"Abby and Reaper breathe the club. As if that was ever a possibility."

"I'd give it up if it meant you were safe." He shrugged like it wasn't a big deal. "I don't make calls anymore. I made sure I'm answering to someone. Reaper should have learned his lesson and stepped away, not taken on the mother charter."

"Just because he left a loose end, he should, what, walk away from the only life he knows?"

"I'm just saying, Kim. When we start a family, I'll be making sure I'm not calling any shots. I never want something I've done to impact you."

"Is it my fault that you've basically washed your hands of the club then?" I'd finally put a finger on what had changed with him. "You and this club are the same. I don't want you out of it and I don't want you ever considering I'd want that. Sure, you don't have as many enemies as Reaper but you are always going to have someone on your bad side. Fuck. That's why you are called Trigger!"

"Like I said, I'd walk from the club if it meant it guaranteed your safety. And you wouldn't get dragged down by my shit."

Not believing what I was hearing, I pushed my laptop off my lap and threw my leg over him, straddling him. His hands gripped my hips. But the expression on his face told me he had really thought about this. He had already made the decision without even speaking to me.

"Don't ever pull away from the club. Don't second-guess yourself. You don't know how happy you make me wearing this vest." I ran my hands over his vest. My hand paused over his heart. "It feels like home to me. Don't ever take that from me."

He might think he was saving me when really, he'd really be cutting me off from the only life I had ever known. I saw his expression change.

"You're incredibly loyal, you know that, Kim?" His hand went to my face. "You're more loyal to this club than me."

"It's in my veins." I lowered my forehead to his. "And so are you." My two weaknesses. Family and Trigger. I'd break easily for either if anyone applied pressure to them.

Chapter 25

Abby

I felt his arm go around me, pulling me back to his chest and my eyes went wide. Oh my god, not again. I waited for his hands to go lower. I knew what followed this. I knew what happened when he touched me. Fear swallowed me completely. I could get through this one more time. I could do that.

I was so stiff from fear that I was barely breathing. I wished he would just go back to hitting me. I would take anything over being raped.

"Abby, you alright?"

Kade's voice was concerned. It was Kade. It wasn't Jake. It came back to me quickly. I was in Kade's bed. I was with Kade. He wouldn't hurt me. I closed my eyes, taking a much-needed breath in.

"Abby?"

"Um, yeah, I'm fine. I thought…" I stopped talking. I hadn't told Kade that Jake had raped me and I had never told him that we shared a bed. So I couldn't just say to him right now, *hey, I was freaking out thinking you were Jake about to rape me*.

"You thought?"

"Nothing," I lied and my hand went to his. Suddenly I needed him to hold me tighter. I rolled over, needing to see his face. It was Kade. How the hell could I forget I was in his bed? I ran my fingers over his jaw. "You didn't come to bed till late." I remembered going to sleep by myself.

He kissed my forehead. "Sorry. Trust me, I wanted to be with you."

He didn't have to be sorry. I knew he was busy. He had barely taken his eyes off me since I got back. So I knew his duties as mother charter president were adding up.

"You should focus on the club today," I said, knowing that he should have been doing that from the start. "I'll be fine with Tyson."

"Nah, I'm spending the day with you."

"Kade, you can't ignore your duties." I quickly kissed his lips. "Focus on the club. I'm not planning on going anywhere today. So I'll be around." Suddenly I was feeling sick.

"Do you want to talk about it?"

"What?"

"Whatever has you getting out of bed and leaving me?" I heard him say, but I was already running for the bathroom.

I just made it to the toilet and emptied the contents of my stomach. Why the hell was I being sick? I hadn't eaten anything that would upset my stomach. Actually, come to think of it, I'd had nausea the last couple of days.

My eyes widened. I couldn't be, could I? I thought I was going to be sick again and this time it wasn't because of nausea. It was because I could be pregnant.

"Abby, you alright?"

He was standing behind me and I felt him pull my hair back. My luck couldn't seriously be that bad, could it? I couldn't be pregnant.

"Abby?"

"Um, yeah, I'm fine. Just not used to eating," I lied, and stood up. Why was it that all I did was lie to him? Since I got back, I swore all I did was lie. I lied that I was fine. I lied that nothing was on my mind. I lied about what happened to me. And when I was lying, I was scared stiff.

I rinsed out my mouth and looked in the mirror and saw Kade's reflection. The anger in his eyes was scorching. But it wasn't directed at me. It was directed at a dead man.

"Um, so, about today. I actually do have to go out for something, but apart from that I'll be around." I turned around. "My car can be driven now, right?"

Kade looked up. "Yeah, it's back on the road. Don't know how I feel about you going anywhere by yourself, though."

"Well, it has to happen one day, doesn't it?"

"Doesn't have to be today, though. I can come with you." He took a step closer and reached out for me.

It had to be today. I had to know if I was pregnant or not. And I couldn't just buy a test and do it in front of him, now, could I?

"I'll be fine. I'll even carry a gun. You have to focus on the club." I kissed his cheek. "Seriously, I just need to pop into a store. I'll be less than half an hour and then I'll be back to being a couch blob with Tyson."

"Let me send someone with you."

"I'm more skilled with a gun than half your men."

"I don't like the idea of you going anywhere," Kade looked me in the eye, "especially without me. In fact, I was counting on you spending the rest of your life at the club under my eye."

I laughed. "That won't be happening."

"Why not?" He was serious right now. Like I had to be cut off from the world because he was that scared he would lose me again.

"No one is going to touch me and this time I won't be defenseless. Now I'm getting dressed and heading out. The sooner I leave, the sooner I am back. Anyway, you should be focusing on the club, not me."

"I couldn't give a fuck about the club right now."

I walked around him. "Don't say that shit." I wouldn't let him downplay the way he loved this club. "You're the mother charter president now. You can't say you don't care. All the clubs depend on you doing your job."

I pulled my shirt off and I was about to take my shorts off till I remembered what was on my leg. How long could I put off him seeing it?

I walked into the wardrobe and was looking for a dress that was long. Why did I own so many short dresses? All he had to do was run his hand up my thigh. He wouldn't just feel my scars and wounds, he would see them too in these dresses.

I finally found a long dress. It was black and still had tags on it. I would take a guess and say Kim had bought it and it somehow ended up in my closet.

"I'd rather spend the day with you."

"Kade, you have spent so much time with me. You must be sick of seeing me." I threaded my arms through the dress and pulled it down. As soon as it was down, I pulled down my shorts and stepped out of them.

I grabbed the knife that I used to have strapped to my leg. I put the strap on, securing it in place. I was wearing a long dress. It wasn't like anyone could see it.

I didn't know how much longer I could put off Kade seeing my thigh but I knew as soon as he did, he would have questions. The look that I knew would cover his face, well, it made me feel sick just picturing it.

His arms wrapped around me. "I could never get sick of you." He lowered his forehead to mine, looking me in the eye. "Not after what happened. I don't want you out of my sight."

I brushed my lips against his. "You won't ever be without me again." As if my son knew I needed to get moving, I heard him cry. "Tyson and I'll be gone half an hour. You can even time me and if I'm a second longer you can put me on lockdown when I get back."

"I like the idea of you being on lockdown."

I pulled away from him. "Where are my car keys?"

"In the garage. You sure you're alright to drive?"

"Of course," I threw over my shoulder and headed for Tyson. He was looking at me with wide eyes and a smile. "Hey, gorgeous boy." I swear I would never get enough of him. I never thought I could love someone as much as I loved Kade, but Tyson was right up there.

"I've never seen you in a long dress before."

I had just picked up Tyson and was about to turn around but didn't. My eyes went wide as he said that. Had he noticed yet that he hadn't seen me without bottoms on? My thigh was always covered.

"Um, just a change." I turned around with a large fake smile on my face. "I swear, your son is getting cuter every day."

"Yeah, he takes after his mother." Kade crossed his arms, looking at me with so much love, like Tyson and I were his whole world.

I wished I deserved him loving me like that. But after everything I had been through, I didn't deserve the love in his eyes.

"We're going." I picked up the diaper bag and my handbag. I kissed Kade on the cheek. "Seriously, I'm telling you, half an hour. If I'm longer, you can give me the longest lecture."

His hand wrapped around my waist. "You might think I won't notice if you're longer. But you are wrong. I'll be watching the clock. Half an hour. Any longer and I'll personally be coming out looking for you."

I smiled at Kade being so controlling. Now to get a pregnancy test and be back in half an hour.

***

I was normally a great driver, maybe a bit slow sometimes. But normally I was fine. Well, it seemed Reaper was right. I shouldn't have been back behind the wheel. I had made it into town, but now I was frozen at an intersection.

The light was red and everything that happened last time I was in this car came flooding back to me hard and fast. I could barely breathe. My hands were shaking. The van slamming into the side of my car. The sound of crashing metal. The noise of the bullets. The feeling of the glass shattering across my body.

The fear I felt as I was ripped from the car.

The cars behind started beeping. Right. The light was green. I had to drive.

The cars were beeping again and everything was too much. My whole body was shaking at this point. I had to get off the road. My foot hit the accelerator. As soon as I was out of the intersection, I pulled the car over.

Cars passed me, still honking their horns.

I was in town.

I had made it. I looked at the dashboard. I had twenty minutes. I couldn't waste time. How the hell was I going to explain me not driving back? I knew a little about cars after spending so much time with Brad. So maybe I could fake something?

I could say it just stopped going. But that wouldn't hold up long when Brad looked it over and found nothing wrong with it. No, I had to fake something.

I lifted my dress up and grabbed my knife. I could cut the wires to the electrical system. That would cause a malfunction, one that would come up when I was driving. I could easily lie and say it had.

Again, I was finding myself lying to the people that loved me.

I popped the hood and got out of the car. I couldn't just slice it. That would be obvious. It had to look like it had been missed.

I leaned over the engine and looked at the different wires. God, this car was fancier than anything I had ever owned. And here I was, about to make sure it would let me down.

I found the wire and shaved it with the knife. That should do it.

I put the hood down and went back inside the car, starting it up. Just like I hoped, the system light was on and it was saying 'error'. And the engine light was on.

Good.

Now, where the hell was I?

Middle of town, outside a drugstore and Target.

Perfect.

I glanced at the clock. Fifteen minutes.

"OK, little one, let's make this quick," I said to Tyson. I got out of the car and walked to his side.

Get him out and into the stroller. Buy a test. Take the test. Simple. I hoped to god I was wrong and I wasn't pregnant.

***

I stared at the two lines. Positive. I gulped. It was official. I was pregnant and it wasn't Kade's. I wanted to cry. Then I wanted to laugh at my luck. Then I wanted to run. Then I didn't want to face it. How the hell did I explain this to Kade? I couldn't bring myself to tell him I was raped. I just couldn't do it.

I knew then.

I couldn't tell him.

I lit up my phone. Ten minutes and I had to be back.

I picked up my phone and dialed Kim's number.

Could I tell her the truth?

"Hey, Abby." She sounded honestly happy to hear from me.

"Hey, Kim."

"Where are you? I just checked your room. I want a cuddle with my nephew."

"That's actually why I called you. My car has broken down in town. Can you come get us? We are in Target."

"Your car broke down?"

"Um, yeah. Lights were flashing on the dash. Some error or something."

"OK. I'm on way."

"And can you tell Reaper you're on your way? Saves me a phone call." And saved me telling him another lie.

"Sure. I'll see you in ten."

I hung up and looked at the pregnancy test. I opened the bin that was in the family bathroom and dropped it in.

I didn't know how to go about organizing an abortion. But I would somehow have to figure it out and make an appointment and, for fuck's sake, how was I going to explain a whole day away from the club?

Reaper wasn't joking when he said he wanted me on lockdown. But I couldn't just tell him the truth. I wouldn't tell him the truth.

Because my biggest fear was that he wouldn't want me once he realized something of his was violated.

I dropped to my knees and looked at Tyson. "What am I going to do, Tyson?" I sighed. I wished right now I had someone, anyone, to talk to. Right now I needed my mom. For the first time in my adult life, I needed my mother.

Pity she was dead, along with any chance of my life getting better.

***

Kim's

"Hey, Reaper." I walked into the bar, catching him just before he disappeared into the boardroom. "I'm going to pick up Abby."

He frowned. "Why would you be picking her up?"

"Her car broke down. Something about lights flashing."

Reaper looked at Brad. "You said it was running."

"It was!" Brad looked honestly surprised to hear the car had any type of problem. "I went over it personally. Nothing was wrong with it."

"Well, it's not like Abby would lie. I have to go now." I started walking away.

"Did she say where she went?" Reaper said.

"All I know is she is waiting for me at Target."

He nodded his head, but by the expression on his face, I knew something else was playing in his mind. I didn't have time to question him about it though. He was busy and Abby was waiting. So I quickly walked away.

Abby wasn't her normal self. She was acting like everything was fine. But I saw the fake smiles. I saw something else playing in her eyes. I didn't know if Reaper had realized yet that his wife was keeping secrets from us. But I had a feeling he was starting to see what I saw.

Something had happened that she wasn't telling us about. What had Jake done to her for her to want to lie to us? We knew about the beatings, the games with the gun. But there was something else. I was about to have some one-on-one time with her away from the club, away from Reaper.

I was going to do my best to get it out of her.

***

"I told Reaper I'd be half an hour. He will be having a fit," Abby gritted out, looking at me as if I was making all her problems worse. "Did he ask how long we would be?"

"You worry too much about what he thinks. Seriously. He was heading to the boardroom. I doubt he will be out of there for the rest of the day. Now, look at the menu."

Her eyes darted down to the menu. "I might call him and tell him I'm with you."

"He knows you are with me."

"Still, he will be worried."

"More like you are worried. Seriously, can you not be apart from him or something?"

"I just don't want him worrying about me." She looked me in the eye. "And I don't want to be put on house arrest because my dickhead of a sister decided she was hungry and had to eat now!"

"I'll call him." I pulled out my phone and dialed his number. Why did she look so relieved that I was calling him and not her?

"What?" Reaper answered.

"Abby and I are having lunch. For some reason, she thinks it is highly important you know her every move. So, can we stay for lunch or do we have to head back?"

"Is she alright?" Was he asking if she was showing signs of withdrawal, like something else was on her mind, that she was keeping something from us?

"Yeah, she's fine. I think she has forgotten about the importance of food, though," I lied. Abby was not fine. Something was on her mind. Something had her tapping her finger on the menu and only half listening to the conversation I was having with her husband.

"Fine. Be back by two. Also, tell her she is on lockdown. Her half an hour turned into hours." Reaper wasn't joking. OK, maybe Abby had been serious about not wanting to be put on lockdown.

"He said you're on lockdown," I told her. She rolled her eyes and ran a hand nervously through her hair. "She looks just so thrilled to hear that," I said to Reaper.

"She knew the conditions."

"You can't just lock her up in the club. She does have a life."

"Not anymore."

"You are very controlling. More than normal." I picked up on it.

"Just be back before two."

"Why? What is happening at two?"

"I want my wife and kid back by then. Understand, Kim?"

I sighed. "Fine. We will be back by then." I hung up. "Well, he is more controlling than normal," I muttered. "What's with that?"

"I've just got back from being kidnapped, Kim. He is just being overprotective," Abby shrugged it off. I had had enough of her not-caring attitude and the fact that she was nervously shaking her leg under the table.

Something was wrong. And now I was going to get it out of her.

"So, you going to lie to me as well? Or are you going to tell me the truth?" I said to her.

"About?"

"Something's wrong with you. And if I can pick up on it, so can Reaper."

"He hasn't said anything." Abby looked at me nervously. "God, have I been that obvious?"

I smiled. "Maybe just to me."

The waiter came and took our order and left again.

"So, Abby, tell me. What's going on? You lie every time you say you are fine. In fact, you've been lying a lot." I frowned. A hell of a lot. About little things. Big things. Everything. The only real smile she had had on her face was when she looked at Tyson.

She closed her eyes. At first, I thought she was doing it so I couldn't read her expression. Then I saw the tear run from the corner of her eye and down her cheek.

"OK, Abby, just tell me what the hell is going on." I reached out, taking the hand she was shaking nervously on the table. "Come on. It's me."

"You won't tell Reaper?" She opened her eyes. Her look hit me hard and fast in the chest. I had never seen her so upset.

"Promise."

She exhaled slowly. "I'm pregnant."

My face lit up and I couldn't stop grinning. "You have to be kidding! Already! Abby, that's nothing to be nervous or upset about! Why wouldn't you tell Reaper? God, he will be over the moon. I swear that man has a habit of knocking you up. Is it because it is so soon after Tyson? Is that why you are cagey about it?"

She looked at me blankly. "It's not his."

"What do you mean, it's not Reaper's?" I laughed. "Of course it is his! Hell, since you got back, you haven't been out of his sight."

She pulled her hand from mine. "It's not Kade's."

I frowned, not understanding. And then it clicked, slowly. My expression dropped. "It's Jake's, isn't it?"

She nodded her head and wiped the tears off her cheeks.

"He raped you."

She scoffed.

"How many times? Please tell me it was only once?" I knew she was keeping something from me, but I hadn't thought it was something like this. Something so heart-shaking. My heart broke for her. I didn't know what to say or do. I just… I was speechless. Why the hell hadn't she said something? Reaper could have made Jake's death even more painful if he'd known.

"He wanted a kid and decided he was having that kid with me. I lost count how many times. I just blocked it out every time it happened. He stopped beating me when it started. He said I was his now."

"How the hell did you cope?" I wouldn't have been strong enough for that. How the hell wasn't she a crumpled mess who couldn't get out of bed?

"Self harm."

My mouth dropped open. "Please tell me you didn't go there."

She shrugged her shoulders. "Jake introduced me to it. To cope. And it became a habit. Every time I thought about it. Afterward, too, I just would cut."

I reached across the table, grabbing her arms and flipping them over. They were clean. "Where?" I said.

"Thigh."

"How did you explain that one to Reaper?"

"He hasn't seen the cuts. And once he does, he is going to know how truly fucked up I am." She ran her hands down the side of her face. "What the hell am I going to do, Kim? I can't tell him I'm pregnant!"

"Why?"

Her expression went to anger in a second. "Because Reaper will see something that was his as violated. And do you really think he will want me after he knows I've been abused and raped?"

My face softened. "He will still love you." God, that man only loved two things and those were Abby and Tyson. He didn't even love the club nearly as much as he should, considering he was dedicating his life to it.

"I don't want him to know, ever," she said determinedly. "He won't cope. It's better if I handle it on my own. But how the hell am I supposed to have an abortion when I'm on lockdown?"

"Well, I can help with that."

"I don't even know how to organize an abortion!"

"I can help with that too. The clinic that did mine, well, they were fantastic. I can make an appointment for you with them this week."

"And how do I get away from Reaper for a full day?"

I pulled my phone out. "Like I said, I can help with that too."

***

"You can put the face on now," I said, unbuckling.

"What face?" Abby looked at me.

"The face you've been pulling since you got back. The 'I'm fine' face. The 'I'm happy' face. You know, the expression you had on your face when I picked you up."

Abby looked like doomsday had happened. She looked shell-shocked. All her worries were painted across her face. She had to pull herself together if she wanted to stick to the plan of not telling Reaper.

She put a fake smile on her face.

"Now, that's the face." I whacked her arm. "Maybe one day soon you will be smiling because you want to and aren't being forced."

"I doubt that."

I got out of the car. And, as if he had been waiting the whole day, Reaper was storming from the garage toward us. The look on his face told me he was pissed off. What? I had her back before two!

Abby was getting Tyson out of the car seat.

"Where the fuck have you been?" Reaper roared as soon as he was within hearing distance.

"You said two and it's like ten minutes to two! So I'm back in time."

He scoffed. "Where's Abby?"

As if on cue, she walked around the car. I had to admit she was looking smokingly sexy today. Her blonde hair was up in a free bun and she had her glasses on. But she pulled off wearing a long, black strapless dress really well. I wonder where she had gotten that from?

"Hey, babe, sorry we are late." Abby was on autopilot. She could at least act like she was human. I knew she was dealing with a lot of stress right now. But if she didn't want her husband to know, she would have to put on a better act than that.

"You alright?" He went to her, pushing her sunglasses up, looking her in the eye. "I swear, Brad told me the car was working fine."

"It's not a big deal."

"The boys are looking at it now."

"What, you've already had it towed here?"

"Yeah, Brad drove it home. Some faulty electronics or something." He cupped her face. "What's wrong?"

It was painted in her eyes. She was dealing with demons. She was firm about not telling him. So I guessed this was my cue to step in.

"She was kidnapped and locked up in a house for months, Reaper. How do you expect her to be?" I snapped, like I was pissed off at him for even asking. But I knew why he was really concerned. He had a right to be. I was worried and I knew. "Abby and I booked a spa treatment for this Thursday. It's an all-day thing. Before you rant about her being on lockdown, remember that being locked up in one place is part of the problem."

He looked at me, and then at her. "That's fine."

Thank Christ for that because I didn't know how I was going to fight him on that.

"Really?" Abby said, not believing he would just give in like that.

He nodded his head. "But after that, you don't leave this place without me. No more lunch dates or spa dates."

"Fine," I snapped on Abby's behalf. "Just means you will have two more useless bodies around the club."

"I didn't say you were on lockdown." Reaper looked at me, annoyed.

I grinned. "Like I am leaving my sister. Anyway, why did we have to be back by two?" I was interested in why he had been so set on it.

"Nothing to do with you, Kim," he said, taking Abby's hand. "Come on. I've got someone I want you meet."

"Oh, can I meet them too?"

"No."

"But that's not fair! We're twins! You can't just introduce her to someone and not me." I followed them, enjoying annoying Reaper. Abby knew what I was doing. I was taking the attention off her.

"Get lost, Kim." He looked over his shoulder. "Go annoy Trigger or something."

"Why would I go annoy him when I could annoy you?"

He scoffed.

"Where are we going?" Abby said when we didn't head inside.

Who would they be meeting in the garage? Was it about her car?

"Kim, fuck off," Reaper said, stopping. "Now."

"Can I have Tyson at least?" I said, opening my arms for him, seeing as they were off to meet someone. Who they could be meeting in the garage I had no idea.

Abby turned and gave him to me. "I swear I won't be long."

"Take your time. I've got my number one man." I kissed Tyson's cheek. "I'll see you when you are done with your secret meeting."

Abby laughed and nodded her head, taking Reaper's hand. "OK, Kim's leaving and I'm all yours. Who are we meeting?"

Chapter 26

Abby

I didn't understand where we were going. I had lived here my whole life and I had never been down this dirt path that led along the side of the garage. As far as I knew, it went to paddocks.

"OK, Reaper, what are we doing?" I said to his back as he pulled me along.

Finally, the dirt path opened up and I frowned, seeing construction workers. The paddock that I knew was here used to be covered in trees, but they were all gone. It was empty, and concrete trucks were in the middle. I frowned, seeing the dirt driveway that now led to the paddock.

We were at the back of the club. All this land just was vacant. Well, apart from trees, but they had been cleared in the middle.

"Abby, this is Tim," Reaper said, walking us up to an older man who was standing, watching the trucks and talking to a few other guys.

These guys weren't members. So why would they be on club land?

"Abby, lovely to meet you." Tim extended a hand.

"Um, hi." I smiled and then looked at Reaper. What the fuck was going on? I gave him a look that said he'd better start explaining.

"I've hired Tim and his crew," Reaper said, like I was supposed to know it what it was Tim did. I looked at him. Maybe a construction worker as well? I didn't know shit when it came to trades.

"And what is it that Tim does?" I asked the most obvious question, looking between them.

"I'm a builder," Tim answered my question.

"Oh." I looked at Reaper. "You extending the clubhouse or something?" It was club land. I guess it made sense to extend the clubhouse. I'm sure Dad had had plans for this land back in the day. But he just let the trees have it after he built the clubhouse and garage.

Reaper pulled on my hand and walked me to a table. There were plans laid out on it. I could see that from here. I wasn't that stupid; I knew what a plan looked like from afar.

He stopped me at the table and went to stand behind me while I ran my eyes over the plans. I frowned. This didn't look like a clubhouse. It didn't have enough rooms, bedrooms or living rooms. There was no bar.

"OK, Kade, I'm confused."

He wrapped his arms around me and pulled me back to his chest. "What do you see?"

"Plans. But they look like…" There weren't enough rooms for it be a clubhouse but there were enough rooms to make it one fucking large house. It was a two-story by the plans.

"It looks like what, Abby?" I could hear the smile in his voice.

"A house?"

He mouth went to my ear. "Your house."

I turned the side of my face to look at him, seeing the smirk on his face. "Wait a sec. Are you saying...?" No, he had to be joking with me. He wasn't seriously building me... a house… was he?

He kissed the side of my head. "I told you I wasn't letting you leave the club."

"So you're building me a house?" I looked at the plans and then spun around to look at him. "Here?"

He nodded his head. "I'll be living here because I'm needed and I don't want my family living in a clubhouse. And I'm too selfish not to have you and Tyson here."

"So you're building us a house!" I threw my arms around his neck, grinning. And I wasn't forcing the grin. I was seriously happy. "You know I would have settled for living at the clubhouse."

"You've lived in a clubhouse all your life. I want you to have a house, one that everyone knows to stay the fuck away from. And I want Tyson to have a somewhat normal life."

"You're amazing, you know that, Kade?" I went to kiss his lips but he spun me around.

"Now, is there anything you want to change?" He redirected my attention to the plans.

"Nope, it's amazing."

"Abby, at least look."

"OK, fine. But I'm not changing anything. Who designed it anyway?"

"I did."

I looked over my shoulder and up at him. "And you expect me to change things?"

"Yes. Start looking."

I rolled my eyes and looked back at the plans. "How many kids are you expecting to have?" I had counted five bedrooms now.

"As many as I can get."

I scoffed. "And what if I said Tyson was going to be an only child?" I kept looking over the plans.

"I'm pretty sure I could knock you up if I wanted to."

I laughed. He was right. Even though I was pregnant right now, I didn't let that ruin the gift Kade was giving me. I was dealing with that on Thursday. Till then, I was just going to pretend like it wasn't happening. My eyes froze on the word 'studio.' It was right next to the study.

"Is that a studio as in art studio?" I asked, looking closer, my fingers running over the plans.

He nodded his head. "It will have a plumbed-in sink right here." He pointed. And sure enough, it was on the plan.

"You've thought of everything," I muttered and looked at the master room. I smiled. "I see we have two wardrobes."

"His and hers. Because you own more fucking clothes than anything else."

"So I can take over yours then?" I smirked and snuck a glance over my shoulder, seeing him roll his eyes.

"Whatever you want, babe." He kissed my shoulder. "Now, anything you want to change?"

"Isn't that a bit late? Aren't they about to pour the slab?" I snuck a glance around Kade. Sure enough, men were waiting. But they hadn't started.

"Nothing starts till you approve it."

I twisted in his arms, looking up at him. "How do you always think of everything?"

"So you like it?"

"I love it and I love that Tyson and I'll never be far from you. But…"

"But?" he prompted me to keep going.

"But with all these kids you plan on having, you haven't left a room for Kim," I smirked.

He rolled his eyes. "Here I thought it was something serious."

"It is. You and she have gotten close. I swear, she only annoys people she loves. And she loves to annoy you."

"She just kept me sane while you were gone." Reaper shrugged it off, like their friendship wasn't a big deal. "Apart from the no room for Kim, you happy?"

"Very."

"So I can give the go ahead for the slab?"

"Yes!" My eyes lit up and I grinned. "How long till I can move in?"

"It won't be finished for months."

"Did you ever think, just once, maybe you didn't want me living right here? Because normally a guy goes to the club to get away from his family." I knew that's why Dad lived here when I was little.

"Babe, I never want to be away from you ever again. I know being mother charter president means I'll be busy, but when I'm not, I'll be right here for you. Plus having a permanent president old lady on club land means the girls will stay in line."

"So you did it just to keep the girls in line, huh?" I was only joking. "Well, I've always thought of this place as home."

Chapter 27

Abby

Thursday was hands down one of the worst day of my life. But I got through it, thanks to Kim. I got through it. Reaper didn't even pick up on the fact that something had been wrong. I hid it that well.

The days passed with ease after it. I was sore, but fine and no longer pregnant.

Thank Christ for that.

Tyson was having a checkup today, which was the only reason Reaper was letting me leave. I assumed I was going by myself till he appeared, taking Tyson from me and putting him in the car seat.

"Um, what you doing?" I asked.

"Coming with you." Reaper closed the door. "I told you, you aren't leaving here without me."

"But you're busy."

"Club comes second. Now get in the car, Abby."

I walked around the car and got in.

"Do you have a cigarette? I'm out," Reaper said, patting himself down.

"Yep." I handed him my handbag.

I was putting my chapstick on when I noticed Reaper frowning. I looked at him. And then my stomach dropped, twisted and then turned so sharply it made me feel physically sick.

"What's this?" Reaper was holding my hospital tag from Thursday. I had forgotten I put that in there. "It's a hospital tag, but you weren't in the hospital this week, were you?"

Oh god, this couldn't be happening. I had avoided it and avoided it. And now I was being forced to see it, to see the look on his face when he heard the truth.

"I was," I staggered out.

He looked at the date, frowning. "What? Last Thursday?"

I nodded my head, waiting for the look he was going to give me. Could I tell him the truth?

"Why?" He looked at me.

I clenched my eyes shut. I hadn't cried yet. But this, admitting to Reaper that Jake had raped me, well, that had me nearly crying. I just wanted to run and my hand went to the door handle. He knew what I was going to do because he quickly locked the doors.

Fuck.

"Abby, why were you in the hospital?"

"Because I was..." I couldn't say it. I literally could not form the words. My body was shutting down. I did not want to have this conversation with him.

"Abby, tell me what's going on. Now."

I looked back at him. I was half-prepared for his reaction.

"I was pregnant," I stuttered the words out.

He frowned. "But we haven't had sex."

God, he was going to make me say it. "It wasn't yours."

The realization slowly appeared on his face. The shock. He was putting it together. I watched his face as he clicked the pieces together. "You had sex with Jake?"

"He raped me. But yes." There, I had said it out loud. The anger that was on his face scared me. He twisted, looking at me.

"How many times?"

"Does it matter?"

"HOW MANY TIMES?"

I cringed. He wanted details. Fine. "All the time, once he decided he wanted to have a family with me. That's why we were heading overseas. He wanted me to have his children. He was planning on us starting a family."

He was clenching the steering wheel and then he let go of it like it had burned him. I saw the disgust on his face. And it hit me hard right in the chest, right in the heart. That's what that look on his face did to me. It made my heart ache. Because it was exactly what I had been afraid of.

He got out of the car and slammed the door, storming off.

And that was the reaction I had been expecting, the disgust on his face. Yeah, I was expecting that. I got out of the car, walked around it and got in the driver's seat. He could be as disgusted as he wanted. I couldn't turn back time and change what had happened.

I hadn't cried through this whole experience.

Not once had I cried. Not once when Jake raped me. Not once when he had beaten me. Not once when I got back home. Not even when I saw Tyson for the first time.

But as I pulled out of the lot, I was crying. Because I had just lost him. Whether he realized it or not, I had lost him. I saw the disgust on his face. There was no way that those eyes would look at me with love again.

It just wasn't possible.

Chapter 28

Reaper

I picked a fight at a bar, took out three men and it still didn't take the edge off my rage. I had sped to get back to the clubhouse. And now I was here. I needed to see her. My reaction hadn't been the best. But if I had stayed a second longer, she would have seen another side to me.

"Where's Abby?" I demanded of Kim, who was at the bar with Trigger.

Abby and Tyson weren't in our room. I didn't know where she was. But I knew I had to talk to her. I had known she was keeping something from me. Now I knew what it was. I knew what she had been keeping from me. I understood why she didn't tell me. But if she had told me before I killed him, I could have made him suffer more.

"I thought she was with you? Didn't Tyson have his checkup?" Kim frowned.

"So she hasn't been here all day?" Surely she hadn't done what I was thinking she had done, had she?

"No. I haven't seen her since this morning. Which is odd because it's after nine and Tyson should be in bed." Kim looked at me harder. "What did you do?"

"Nothing."

"Don't give me that shit." She looked at my bloody knuckles and sighed. "She told you."

"YOU KNEW!"

"Yes! God, who do you think organized the abortion? You didn't react like I think you did, did you?"

"How was I meant to react?" Wanting to kill everyone that was within arm's reach? Was that an acceptable reaction? Because that's how I reacted!

"She ran," Kim said, shaking her head at me. "You are a real dickhead, Reaper! Look at what you've done! You've made her run!"

Run? She wouldn't seriously run from me, would she? It dawned on me. She might think I didn't want her anymore. "Where would she go?" I asked Kim, suddenly feeling panic. "Where would she go if she wanted to run?"

"Anywhere away from you!" Kim pushed me hard on the shoulder and walked over to Brad. "Brad, track Abby's phone. If it is dead, then she has run."

Brad pulled up his phone.

"She wouldn't run," I said. But when things got hard, she did tend to run. I was always stopping her. If she thought I didn't want her anymore, she would run. My eyes widened. God, I was such an idiot.

"Phone's dead," Brad said, confirming what Kim thought.

She turned to look at me with such anger. "She knew you were going to react like this. She knew you would push her away. And what do you do? YOU DID IT!"

"I wasn't thinking!" God, the rage I felt. It just happened! "I just needed time." I ran a hand through my hair. "I didn't want her to run."

"Well, she has." Kim crossed her arms. "And she isn't going to call me. And I can't call her because she has gone off the grid."

"Track Tyson's stroller," I said to Brad. "And my credit cards. Check them." If she was running, she would need money.

I was thankful Brad had put trackers on everything possible when it came to Tyson and Abby.

Brad frowned. "Tyson's signal is dead. I'm guessing she found it. And there's no activity on your cards or your bank account. She hasn't touched any of your money."

"FUCK!" Now what was I supposed to do? I couldn't track her down.

"I'm guessing she is in another state by now." Kim whacked me hard on the shoulder. "I've lost her again. Thanks to you. Again!"

Roach got up to leave. "Where are you going?" I said. If he knew where she was, he'd better fucking tell me.

Roach looked at me hard. "Your mess, your problem. Abby was always more than capable of looking after herself. When she was by herself, that is."

"You're lying to me."

"Maybe. Maybe not."

"You are lying, Dad. Just tell Reaper the truth," Kim snapped. "Has she reached out to you?"

Roach looked from me to Kim and then sighed. "Only one place she would go if she really thought about running. Before she had decided where to go, I would know where she'd be."

"That being?" I asked him, feeling impatience.

"Home."

"What, here? She isn't here. I've looked!"

"No." Roach rolled his eyes. "To her mom. She would go home to her mom."

Kim's eyes widened in understanding. "Makes sense she would go there."

"To the graveyard? How does that make sense? It's after nine at night and Tyson should be in bed!

Kim turned to me with a grim smile on her face. "She's not in a graveyard. She's at our home in Spencer Street. Dad never sold it cause she's buried there."

"Abby never told me that." Not once had she told me where her mother was. I just assumed she was in a graveyard.

"Abby doesn't like to talk about it. She used to live there when she was younger. Then she met you and stopped going." Kim crossed her arms and looked at Roach. "Well, which one of us is going to speak to her before she runs?" Her eyes glanced at me. "She won't want to see you."

"I'll see her," Roach said.

"No. I did the damage. I'll fix it." I pulled out my bike keys. "She is running from me to begin with."

I shouldn't have reacted like I did. It was my fault that she wanted nothing to do with me. Hell, I knew how her brain worked. She would be thinking I didn't want her.

But what had my heart beating that bit faster with panic was this: what if she decided she didn't want me after seeing my reaction?

Chapter 29

Abby

Tyson was in my arms and we were sitting out back with Mom. I told her everything, every little detail. I told her. For once, I had someone to share my experience with. I wasn't just saying I was fine. I wasn't just shrugging it off. I was speaking the truth.

Tyson and I were on a blanket. He should have been asleep, but he wouldn't sleep in the crib I had put together. It was funny being back here. Everything was exactly the same. Dad had kept the place clean. I assumed there was a cleaner who came and wiped the dust away, keeping the house frozen in time.

I looked at Mom's headstone. "OK, Mom. Now you know. What do I do next?"

"Forgive him."

I turned, looking over my shoulder. My eyes widened. How the hell did he know to come here? I had picked here because he wouldn't know about it.

"How the hell did you find me?" The anger I felt about him being here crept into my voice. I had never once told him where Mom was. Never once had I ever mentioned my home to him.

I could see the guilt creep across his face as he stood under the porch light.

"Your dad might have given me a tip-off."

Curse Dad for knowing me too well. I turned back to the headstone. He could fuck off, as far as I was concerned. I was asking Mom what to do. I wasn't asking him.

"I'm sorry, Abby."

I ignored him. I was raped. Me. I had to deal with that every day. I had to deal with the pregnancy. And when I told him, he was mad at me? Yeah, he really had a right to be pissed off. I realized all this as soon as I got here.

Reaper reacted the only way he knew how, with anger. And he wanted me to just take it, to accept it. Fuck him.

"Abby, I'm really sorry."

He was getting closer, his shadow covering me. It didn't matter anymore. He reacted like I had expected him to react.

And now. Now I had to move on. I had to put Jake behind me and everything that happened. I had to move on. And one day, when someone asks if I'm OK, I might be able to say I really am fine.

I got up, holding Tyson, turning to face him and then walked past him.

I was done.

But just because I was done didn't mean he was. I was surprised when he followed me inside.

"You should go, Reaper. Tyson is fine." I walked through the living room and paused in the hallway. I turned to look at him. "Go. I'm done."

I didn't have any more to give. I couldn't live with him, knowing how disgusted he was. Who knew the one to destroy us would be Jake? I had been sure we would make it.

"And you? You aren't fine, Abby." He walked toward me. "I know you."

He was right. I wasn't fine. "One day I will be." I couldn't handle being touched by him so I headed down the hallway to my room. I had set up the crib there. Funny thing was, it was actually mine and Kim's. Dad had kept it.

Reaper always said I ran when I didn't want to face something. I guess right now I was doing just that. Running.

But I couldn't face the truth. Not when it hurt so much.

"Abby, I'm not leaving."

He followed me. I clenched my eyes shut. Why couldn't he just let me go?

"I wasn't angry with you. You have to believe me when I say that."

I scoffed. "Sure, you weren't."

"Were you ever going to tell me?"

His reaction had been exactly what I expected. I put Tyson in his crib and then turned and looked at him.

"What do you think?"

He glared down at the carpet. "I'm sorry." He looked up. The expression on his face told me he genuinely was. "I'm sorry that you couldn't come to me."

I had never felt more alone than I did right now. Even when I was with Jake, I still had this invisible connection to Reaper. But now I felt like someone, no, not someone, him, had cut that connection.

"I can't be with you anymore." For once I was going to fight the pull toward him. I had always been the one chasing him or waiting for him to take me back. I had always turned to him and, by doing that, I think I had written our ending. Because how could I be with him when everything in my body was telling me to run and run as far as I could?

Away from my need to be near him.

Away from the love I had for him.

Run from it.

That look in his eyes when he found out, that would never go away.

"You can't say that." He stepped closer to me and my arm shot out. I couldn't handle being touched by him. I saw the panic in his face, heard the panic in his words. "You said you love me unconditionally."

My face softened. "I will always love you. But I can't be with you anymore." I shook my head. "I just can't do it anymore, Reaper."

"Because of what happened? What I put you through?" He was switching gears now. He knew I was serious.

"No, because I saw the look on your face when I told you. The disgust. You won't ever come to terms with that. And I can't be with you while you struggle with it." I took a staggered breath in. The hand I had on his chest to keep him away from me was burning. Unable to take it anymore, I pulled my hand away from him and hoped he got the hint that I didn't want him touching me.

He shook his head. "I wasn't angry with you. I was disgusted in myself for putting you through that. Me, Abby, I was disgusted with myself, not with you."

"I still can't be with you." Run. That was what I needed to do. Run from my feelings for him. Run from a future with him. Run from the need to always be with him.

"Abby, don't." He looked like he was physical pain. "Stop saying that."

I didn't know what to do to ease his pain. The truth was, I had reached a fork in the road and facing a life with him scared me. Because I knew I would do anything for him, be anything for him. And knowing you loved someone that much, well, it was frightening.

"I'm sorry, Kade." And I was. I really was. But running meant I didn't have to face my feelings for him. "I will always love you and I'll never keep Tyson from you."

Those two things I could promise. But I couldn't stay with him.

He ignored the fact I didn't want him touching me and cupped my face. "If you love me, hold on to me. Don't push me away." His words were panicked. He was scared. He didn't need to be. He would be fine without me.

"You'll be OK, Kade, without me. You'll be OK." I felt like I needed to reassure him.

"NO. I WON'T BE!" Tears welled in his eyes. "My life revolves around you. Don't you get that? When I don't have you, I'm nothing. I don't give a fuck if I'm breathing or not. I need you. If you love me, don't let go."

I remained quiet. But it was a natural reaction to wipe the tears off his cheeks. I didn't want him crying. I didn't think I'd ever seen him cry before. He was panicking. He was scared. He would be fine.

"Abby, please don't let go of me. I need you to hold on to me. I need you. Please."

He was pleading with me, begging. Hoping I would change my mind.

"I'll never bring the rapes up again. I promise you that. I'll do anything. Just don't give up on me. Not now."

I had come to the fork in the road: leave him or stay with him. A future with him meant my life wouldn't be crystal clear. If I left him, I could bet my life would be less complicated. But a life without him, well, that scared me nearly as much as how much I loved him.

"Just tell me what you need to hear from me for you not to leave me? Just tell me, Abby. Because I'll do fucking anything."

Was there anything he could promise that would help me make a decision? Maybe there wasn't anything he could promise me. But there was something I could do to make him see the girl he'd loved died in Jake's house.

I pushed his hands off me and took a step back, gripping the bottom of my dress and lifting it up. He frowned at first, and then he saw them. Some still bleeding, some just healing, some faded.

"The girl you loved died in that house, Kade. You mightn't realize it but you lost me a long time ago."

His eyes were glued to them. I saw the flash of anger. But, as if he knew he couldn't be angry right now, he reined it in.

His fingers went to them, barely touching them, but checking to see if that were real. They were real and they would be on my body for the rest of my life.

"Do you still do it?" he said. His eyes came back to mine. "Self harm, do you still do it?"

"Every time I think about what Jake did to me. Yes."

He nodded his head. "We will find another way for you to cope. Counseling or something. But I'll personally be making sure there isn't a razor in the clubhouse. You won't ever get your hands on another one."

I clenched my eyes shut. Did he miss the part where I said the girl he loved had died?

"It doesn't matter anymore." I opened my eyes and lowered my dress. "I'll handle it somehow. It's not your problem."

His hands took mine, as gently as if I were made of glass.

"If it affects you, it affects me. Your problem is my problem. You should have told me you were doing that to cope."

Wasn't this what every girl dreamed of? To have a man who would stand by her in the toughest times? To take on her problems and make sure she didn't have to face them alone?

I guess that was all I ever wanted, just to have Kade. That was all I'd ever wanted.

"I'll help you get through this, Abby. It's my fault you went through it to begin with."

"I don't need pity," I wanted to snap at him, but stopped myself. "And I don't need you blaming yourself more."

He already felt bad enough for what happened to me. That guilt he felt was what was pushing me away, what had me wanting to run. Because how could he ever look at me with love and not guilt? Maybe I should just tell him that was the problem.

I wanted to run as soon as I saw more guilt in his eyes. He didn't realize that was the problem.

"The guilt, Kade, that you keep looking at me with. That's what's making me want to run. So if you want me to change my mind, you need to stop it," I blew out, running a hand through my hair. I couldn't handle the look in his eyes. "Please leave if you are going to keep looking at me like that. I can't take it, Reaper. Go!"

His expression changed immediately. It was blank at first and then changed to a look he had given me numerous times. It used to be painted on his face when he looked at me. Love. It was the same look he gave Tyson every time he looked at him.

"You know we never got a honeymoon." His hands linked with mine.

I frowned. "So?"

"So, maybe we should have one now."

"Kade, did you not hear me when I said I was ending us?"

Hurt covered his face immediately. And then it was wiped away and he was looking at me with love again.

"I think we should take one." He pulled me to him. "Somewhere hot."

"You don't take vacations."

"I'll make an exception. You need to get away from here and I want to take you."

"A vacation isn't going to make me go back to normal." I knew even leaving here, leaving him, wouldn't bring me back to myself. If anything, leaving him would put me further away from myself because I always found myself when I was with him.

Things just came naturally when I was with him.

I didn't overthink it. When I was away from him, when I was keeping secrets from him, it was hard, so terribly hard to do.

He cupped my face, bringing it to his. "It's a start."

"What about Tyson? What about your commitments to the club? The mother charter president doesn't get a break."

"We can take Tyson with us. Or we can leave him with Kim. As for the club, I told you once before, it comes second."

I was chewing my bottom lip. I had been planning on running from him, not having a honeymoon with him.

He pulled my lip from my grasp. "A break will do you good. And if you still want to leave me afterward, I'll let you go."

I knew what he was playing at. I knew it as soon as those words left his lips.

I rolled my eyes. "Don't lie to me. You are never planning on letting me go even if it is something I want." I knew him too well. I saw the determination in his eyes. I saw the passion. I saw that his heart was on the line and he wasn't about to let me slip past him. Even if I begged him to let me go, I doubted he would.

But still, I had to make a decision.

Stay or go. Flight or fight.

"You're right." He smiled for the first time tonight. "You are my world, Abby, and if you think I'm letting you leave me, you're wrong."

"But I can't keep seeing that look in your eyes." I clenched my eyes shut, the look he had been giving me crystal fucking clear in my mind. "That guilt that is eating you up, I can't take it. I just can't." I went to push his hands off me but he just gripped me tighter.

"I didn't even realize I was doing it."

"Well, you have been all the time. And now that you know about the rapes, I'm doubting you will ever be able to look at me the same way."

He shook his head. "I'll stop, Abby. I promise. I only see one thing when I look at you and that is my world. I'm sorry if I've been looking at you like you aren't that. Because you are my world, Abby."

"Cut, raped, abused and neglected, and you still want me." I shook my head. "You must be crazy."

"In love, yes."

I let go of his hand and ran my finger across his jaw. He wanted me to hold on to him. I guess when it came down to it, I never wanted to let him go to begin with.

"I love you too, Kade." And it was the honest truth.

"But?" He arched his eyebrows, expecting me to have something else to say.

I shook my head. "No buts."

"So you'll come home with me?"

I nodded my head.

"You aren't leaving me?" There was panic in his voice as he said it. As if there was still a chance he was going to have to perform a miracle.

"I'm not leaving you." I knew it then. That there wasn't a chance in hell I could ever leave him because he had the other half of my heart. He had since I was sixteen and he would always have it. I knew wherever I was, he would be right there beside me.

Epilogue

Five years later - Reaper

I lit up a cigarette and watched Tyson. Any minute, Abby was going to be out here screaming. I knew that but I couldn't break the kid's heart by not letting him on.

"REAPER!"

She must have heard it.

The porch door burst open and out walked my furious blonde. It wasn't a surprise to find her shadows following her. Our two daughters. Twins. Eve and Hannah. They were too fucking perfect for their own good.

I knocked her up on our honeymoon. While I was happy for one baby, I was over the moon that we got two. They were identical, and double trouble. They were only four and already had me on my toes trying to keep up with them.

"I told you over and over, he is not allowed on it!" She stormed down the porch. "He is too young to be on a motorbike!"

"It's a dirt bike, Abby. It doesn't even have gears."

"I told you and him no!"

"I'm watching him and he is fine." I reached out for her, pulling her onto my lap. "You worry too much."

She had an angry pout on her face as she searched the backyard for him. "Did you and him make that track?" she asked, still sounding furious, while watching Tyson whiz around the track we had made this morning. "You even did fucking jumps!" She looked me in the eye. "Is it your mission and his to give me a heart attack?"

"Calm down, sweetheart." I kissed her arm. "He is fine."

"If he falls off, I swear to god, Kade, you will have a slow death." She meant it too.

"He is a natural."

"I always knew he would take after you." She crossed her arms. "You and fucking motorbikes."

I smirked. When Tyson wasn't testing Abby's patience, he was in the garage pulling something apart or helping Brad. He would be five this weekend and Abby was hating him getting older.

I didn't know how she was going to cope when he actually did grow up. People always mistook him for being older than he was because he was so tall and switched on.

Still, he was closer to Abby than ever. So were the girls. The four of them made it their mission to get paint everywhere whenever they used the art studio. How many times had I told them paint stays in the art studio? Still I would find it on walls, on the carpet, in my study. Just this morning, the cash flow chart, which had been safe in my study, had gotten a handprint on it.

Eve or Hannah, by the looks of it, had gotten to it.

But I wouldn't have had it any other way.

"Don't you have a board meeting to get to?" Abby said, her eyes on the girls, who were jumping on the trampoline. Abby saw the trampoline as a death trap. She hated it. It didn't help that the girls were always seeing how high they could jump.

"Brad can handle it. I'm staying here."

She looked at me. "Since when do you blow off board meetings?"

"Since I would rather spend time with my family. I've been busy with the club lately. Brad can handle a meeting." I moved her on my lap. "Plus I told Tyson I would show him how to pull the motor out of his bike as soon as he is finished riding it."

She groaned. "Great, more grease stains!"

I laughed. "Come on, babe. You wouldn't have it any other way."

She looked me in the eye and smiled. "You're right. I wouldn't. I might see if Kim and Trigger will come over, then. She is panicking, coming up to labor."

"She'll be fine."

"I told her that. Still, can you imagine Trigger and Kim as parents?" She smiled. "It's going to be one eventful summer."

"You're just excited to be an aunt."

"Yep." She linked her hands around my neck. "But not nearly as excited as I was to become a mom."

I smiled at that. Then I kissed her and, like always, it sent a rush of excitement and lust through my blood. I never thought I would get a wife and family. I always thought I would be by myself for the rest of my life.

Then I met her.

And I didn't know what I was missing till I got her. Now she had given me three perfect children and I still loved her more than humanly possible.

The End.

Made in the USA
Middletown, DE
09 July 2019